This is Maaneborg, the "Castle of the Moon"—where a young bride enters a nightmare world of treachery and deception unequaled since Daphne Du Maurier took Rebecca to Manderley.

She had already been scarred once by love, and the vital, resplendent Dane needed all his charm to win her. But why did he insist that they hide their marriage from his family—and why, when she lost her child, did he deny the marriage had ever taken place?

THE SHADOW WIFE

By Dorothy Eden

A FAWCETT CREST BOOK

Fawcett Publications, Inc., Greenwich, Connecticut

THE SHADOW
WIFE

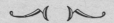

Chapter One

WHILE waiting in the old house in Copenhagen, Det Gamle Huus, as the Danes would call it, with a fire crackling on the wide hearth and a gale sweeping up the Sound so that flying spume clouded the windows, I decided to write my autobiography.

It was the only way to make what had happened to me believable.

I searched for a beginning, knowing that something in my own character was more than half to blame for my strange predicament. So I had better start by being completely honest.

Vulnerability was my trouble. I was both emotionally and financially insecure, and those two things were a dangerous combination.

I will explain at once that this is not an autobiography in the conventional sense, because it covers such a short period of my life. Yet it is in the true sense, since this past year was the one in which I began to live. None of those childhood anecdotes and total recall for me. This was the year I, me, began. The other person, the child, the adolescent, the dreamer, the only sister of five brothers, had become a ghost.

My brothers called me Lou or Lulu. I was the youngest, and they had kept me a baby. So had my parents. I hadn't realized the loving, claustrophobic atmosphere I had lived in until suddenly it all vanished and I was thrust out into the chilly, hard world.

Five years ago my parents had died within six months of each other. Soon after that two of my brothers emigrated to Australia, one joined the army and was sent overseas, and the remaining two had jobs in Scotland and the north of England, respectively. I had decided to live in London and pursue my chosen but terribly difficult career as a writer.

I won't dwell on the intervening five years, except to mention briefly a disastrous love affair that inevitably shaped subsequent events. It appeared that from the beginning the man had never intended to marry me, and had eventually become bored by my too intense devotion. After that moment of truth, badly scarred but still alive, I had avoided any serious relationships and devoted myself to my career. My

7

looks had gone off, kind friends said, but my career was developing.

I had a flair for writing amusing, lighthearted and original pieces about foreign places. When the editor of the newspaper for which I worked discovered this, he asked me if I would like to do regular travel articles, and if so, it would mean I would have to spend most of the year traveling.

I didn't hesitate. I shut up my flat (which was too full of memories of Ivor, although it was more than a year since we had parted) and began my new life of living out of suitcases. I spent the summer in Austria, Yugoslavia and Hungary, the autumn in Italy and Spain, the winter in Morocco and Sardinia, and now, the spring, in Majorca and Minorca.

It was in Majorca that I met Otto Winther. And began calling myself Luise, instead of Louise, a subtle difference.

We met, of all places, in the dark green shadowy garden belonging to Chopin's house at Valldemossa. We had both just made the discovery that the house was not open on Sundays.

We stood in the small mossy garden with its palm trees, privet borders, hyacinths and auriculas, looking at each other.

"You, too, are frustrated," said this large, smiling foreigner.

At first I thought he was being remarkably familiar. Surely my almost constant loneliness didn't show that much.

Then I realized he was talking about the house being closed.

"Yes, isn't it disappointing? I did want to touch that piano—forbidden or not."

"Then you must be a romantic. The old yellowed keys speaking again? Conjuring up a ghost?"

Was I a romantic? That was almost a word of derision nowadays. But if loving scenes like this—the old peach-colored monastery with the austere little house tucked against it, and the leafless chestnuts casting scribbles of shadow over the cobblestones—made me one, then I wouldn't argue about the term.

"Europe is full of houses like this, with small dark bedrooms where famous consumptives have coughed away their lives."

"Surely that's an exaggeration. There was Keats ..." I stopped, unable to think of anyone else.

"You forget your famous Brontës?"

"Of course. Am I so unmistakably English?"

"Unmistakably. Even without opening your mouth." He

stood there, blocking my path, smiling a genial smile, his blue eyes teasing kindly. He looked like a Scandinavian. He was about forty, I thought. Perhaps a little older. And at least six feet three inches, with broad shoulders and a large head with thick fair hair. He was a most impressive specimen. I wondered if his wife were waiting for him in his car.

I couldn't pass him on the narrow path without stepping into the garden border. He seemed to be enjoying the encounter. The great pianist's house was closed, but I, the unmistakably English woman, was there instead.

"It was meant to be a compliment," he said. "We Danes like the English."

"Well, thank you."

"I noticed a café just outside. I intend to have some coffee. Since I am deprived of the morbid pleasure of looking inside a dead man's house, will you join me? It's chilly here, anyway. The Ice Maiden can't be far away."

"Who is she?"

"She came for Herre Chopin, didn't she? In Danish mythology the Ice Maiden is death."

Copenhagen, I was thinking. I remembered a picture of a green spire twisted like a peppermint stick. And the Tivoli Gardens, with balloons and colored fountains and luxury restaurants. And storks, and Hans Andersen, and moated castles and wild, windy beechwoods. Denmark. A country that, to me, belonged entirely to fairy tales.

He was right when he accused me of being a romantic.

"You're here alone?" I asked.

"Alas. And you?"

I shrugged. "I usually am. I have a job that requires a lot of traveling."

"Then you must arrange that it bring you to Denmark sometime. You could visit me on my farm. But coffee first, yes?"

He stood aside to let me go ahead of him. The air, crisp and cool from the mountains, that couldn't cure poor Frédéric Chopin of his tuberculosis, made me feel absolutely bursting with life. My middle-aged pickup might later require a little handling, but I could do that, too.

"My name," he said, "is Otto Winther."

"I'm Louise Amberley."

"Miss?"

I held my ringless fingers together. "Yes."

"Remarkable," he said.

"Why?"

He gave his genial laugh. His blue eyes twinkled. He was one of the most pleasant-looking men I had ever met.

"I pay compliments better over coffee. Come."

"Or perhaps," he said, when we had gotten our coffee served at a table on the pavement outside the café, "you are younger than you look."

My agony over that finished love affair had produced a premature gray lock across my temples. It made me look like one of those freak blackbirds with white feathers. But I hadn't done anything about disguising it because I frankly hadn't cared.

"We've only just met, Mr. Winther. My age can't interest you." I took out a cigarette, smoking mostly because it was something to do with my fingers. As he lit it for me, I added, "I'm twenty-six."

He surveyed me with the most embarrassing frankness.

"You are twenty-six, have black hair and green eyes, and are unmarried. It is remarkable. There's a reason, of course."

"Of course."

He stretched and relaxed his big frame in the rather rickety chair. The sun fell on our faces, warming the crisp air. It was extremely pleasant here. It would be even more hauntingly lovely and melancholy in the autumn, when the chestnut trees had begun to drop brown leaves and prickly husks on the cobblestones.

"This is a place for autumn," I said.

"Yes?"

"I wasted three years of my life," I suddenly said.

"Only three? Oh, dear, Miss Amberley! I wasted seventeen."

"You? How? Over a woman? You're not married either?" How did we get to be so intimate so quickly? But I had noticed that that happened abroad, as if one shed inhibitions and privacies. One used strangers as mirrors, looking at oneself frankly for a little while, indulging in confessions, knowing one would never see the accommodating stranger again.

"Not now."

"You've left your wife?"

"No, she left me. She died, not so long ago."

"I'm sorry."

He looked at me with his smiling eyes. "Who for? Me or her?"

"Her, I suppose. She must have been young to die."

"She had a blood condition. It had gone on for some time."

"Of course, I'm sorry for you, too"—I stubbed out my half-smoked cigarette, again for something to do with my hands—"if your marriage was unhappy. Have you any children?"

"A son and a daughter." His voice had scarcely changed, yet I knew that the children had sympathized with the mother. There was a moment of chill, or hurt, or some other emotion in the sunny eyes. "My son Niels is grown up, now. I'm getting to be an old man. I'm forty-six this year. So now you know all about me, Miss Amberley. How did you come up here? In a car?"

"No, by bus. There's one back at five o'clock."

"In two hours? What will you do for two hours?"

"I'll sit here drinking coffee and writing my piece."

"You keep a travel diary that takes two hours to write?"

"No, no, I write articles for one of the London newspapers."

"About what hotels to stay at, what food to eat, where not to be cheated?"

"That sort of thing."

"And what will you say about Valldemossa? Not to come on a Sunday? Or to come on a Sunday and drink coffee instead of playing Chopin's piano?"

"I'll say that the sky is blue and that the monastery looks as old as the pyramids, and there are small pointed cypress trees in the garden. And that at nights there must surely be echoes of ballades and sonatas coming out of that dark house."

Otto Winther didn't speak for a moment. He regarded me with half-closed eyes through which the sunny blue just showed. Then he said, "I was more right than I realized. You are most certainly a romantic. My car is over there. Now I propose wandering in the garden and listening for the ballades and sonatas, while you write your inspired prose. Then you will allow me to drive you back to Palma?"

It would have been ungracious to refuse. I didn't want to refuse. Anyway, the car was an Aston Martin with the top down, and that was quite a vehicle to compare with the bumpy bus.

My Dane must be rich.

Not that that mattered. I would have driven back with him if he had been in an ancient van. I had decided he was not completely trustworthy. What man is with a reasonably attractive, unmarried, not so young woman, and how would the woman like it if he were? But beneath his poise—of which he had a remarkable amount for a farmer, a tiller of the soil and a herder of cows, unless this was how Danish farmers were—there was a simplicity and sincerity which I liked immensely.

I wondered how long it was since his wife had died.

There were some other people getting out of a car and wandering off toward the monastery. Two small boys chased a tennis ball across the cobblestones, yelling in shrill Spanish. A cool wind moved the scribbled shadows back and forth on the peach-colored walls. The waiter stood at the door of his dark café, watching me with large mournful Spanish eyes as I held my pencil poised over my ever-present notebook. I realized that I hadn't written a word.

I would do it back at the hotel this evening. Emotions remembered in tranquillity. What emotion had I so far but curiosity, and a fairly certain intuition that the lonely widower would want something more than a companion on the comparatively short drive back to Palma?

I closed my notebook, put away my pencil, and took out my compact. The little mirror showed me my all too familiar face. I imagined I was looking at it with a stranger's eyes. What would a man see in this quite pleasant arrangement of eyes, nose, mouth, cheeks, forehead? Sensuality? Generosity? Gaiety? Intelligence? Vitality? I didn't know. I supposed I would have liked to look all those things.

But I merely saw a healthy face with a too-long nose, slightly bent in the middle, a wide mouth that turned either up or down according to my mood, and the first fine wrinkles in a square forehead. As well as that feather of white hair. And an anxious look in eyes that were green only when I wore something green. They could be blue, too. Or turquoise. Just in my own skin they were a nondescript gray. And still anxious.

Ivor had done that to me. He had printed himself forever on my body and in my eyes. I suppose a woman's first lover always does that.

So I wore this anxious look and a streak of white in black hair, and waited for Herre Otto Winther to return from his contemplation of the mossy, cool green garden behind the monastery.

He was coming across the courtyard toward the monastery gates. He gave me a little wave, and before he had crossed the road he called, "Am I too soon? Have you finished?"

12

I didn't tell him I hadn't written a word. I nodded briskly, and stood up.

"I'm ready to go if you are."

"Yes, yes. It will be cold here soon. It's warmer on the coast. Besides, we mustn't miss the evening light over Palma."

I was pleased that he had noticed that daily miracle that turned the old city into a dream of rose and pearl as the setting sun flushed over it. One had to observe it at a distance, however, and from the right direction.

"You must be staying at a hotel outside of the town."

"The Mediterraneo. Very rococo. With a palm court orchestra, although the pianist is not Chopin. And you?"

"Not as grand as that. I'm a working girl. I'm in a guesthouse near the cathedral. I don't mind the noise, or the bells."

"Then you certainly must come to Copenhagen. There we have carillons to wake you."

I laughed at the way he tucked his length into the low car. He asked me what I was laughing at, and looked pleased when I told him. He was a little vain of his looks, obviously. Probably he imagined himself a real Viking.

In accord with this vanity, I thought he might have shown me what a good, fast driver he was. But on the contrary, he drove slowly, as if wanting to make the drive last as long as possible. We talked about general things—travel, styles of living, hotels, theaters, economics. Nothing personal at all.

But when the Aston Martin had nosed its way through the crowded streets of Palma, and up the twisting, narrow alley that led to my modest guesthouse, he said without any preamble:

"I'll pick you up at eight. That will give you two hours to rest and change. Enough?"

I detested coyness so much that I was inclined to be overly honest.

"And what are you proposing to do with my rejuvenated person?"

He threw back his large blond head and gave a burst of hearty laughter.

"I merely propose to feed and nourish it. We can eat at my hotel, or anywhere else you prefer."

"Thank you, Herre Winther, but—"

"If you call me Herre Winther, I must call you Froken Amberley, and that is not so friendly. I am Otto and you are Louise."

The way he said "Louise" made it sound different, although, of course, it wasn't.

"And I won't hear any excuses. You will eat tonight with a lonely widower, age forty-six. For now," he lifted a large, square hand, *"adios."*

The slim car roared away before I could tell him that I wasn't going to refuse his invitation to dinner, that I was merely going to say that I never traveled with jewelry or very good clothes. I had done that on my first trip and found it made the inexpensive guesthouses where I stayed seem more than ordinarily lonely. So now I packed skirts and sweaters, and one uncrushable silk jersey dress that had to see me through any cocktail party or whatever.

I expected it would be good enough for the Mediterraneo out of season.

About an hour later, while I was still writing my article that come hell, high weather or an ardent Dane, I had to finish and mail that evening, there was a knock at my door. When I said "Come in," the proprietress herself, a large melancholy-eyed Spaniard who constantly bemoaned the lost glories of her home town, Seville, appeared. For once she was looking animated. She held a florist's box.

"For you, señorita," she said, and then lapsed into excited Spanish. I had clearly gone up enormously in her estimation now that I was receiving flowers.

I wasn't unmoved myself, for my heart suddenly bumped uncomfortably. Was Herre Winther becoming serious so quickly?

I was flattered, but also slightly alarmed. Payment would undoubtedly be expected for expensive flowers and expensive dinners. I didn't like being in debt, and it seemed very likely that I was going to be. For this little game was not going to be played the gallant Herre Winther's way. I had made up my mind to that before I had swallowed the first mouthful of the first drink he had bought for me, the deplorable coffee served in the street-side café in Valldemossa.

I had already wasted three of the most valuable years of my life. Hadn't I told him?

Well, in view of the beaming Señora Caterina, I had to accept the box of flowers and untie the ribbon and lift the lid.

Red roses. Half a gardenful. That farm in Denmark must be considered profitable. We must be eating a great deal of Herre Winther's butter and cheese in England.

Fat old Caterina was saying that she would bring a bowl

of water. The card attached to the floral tribute was addressed to Miss Luise Amberley. I stared at it, feeling a faint, strange tingle beneath my skin. That was how he spelled my name. It was foreign. Different. I can't say why it made me feel much more interesting and even a little beautiful. I was going to think of myself as that in future. Luise.

So with the roses scenting the room, I bathed and dressed for dinner. It was a pity about my one and only and much worn and traveled silk jersey dress. Still, it lived up to its reputation for being uncrushable and undateable, and I did have a good figure. an essential for that sort of dress. Sheer stockings, high-heeled black suede shoes, impeccable gloves, my hair done rather more festively than I wore it in the daytime. I supposed I wouldn't shame the man. Not that I was dressing up for him, but rather for my own ego. I liked, as much as any woman, the admiring glance, the deferential bow of waiters.

Luise Amberley.

There's no point in relating the evening in detail. We had a very good dinner. and later sat in the red plush and gilt lounge of the Hotel Mediterraneo and listened to the gay little orchestra play old-fashioned, sentimental tunes, which I liked much better than the brassy, bossy ones that were so popular nowadays. The lights of Palma shone across the bay, and anchored pleasure cruise ships strung out lines of illumination that quivered in the black water. The Mediterraneo was full of aged ladies covered in jewels, the washed-up treasure from Edwardian days, wrinkling and atrophying in the Majorcan sun.

It's a pity one has to go on and on being so intensely oneself. I would like. sometimes, to let pleasant events wash over me like a soothing. beneficent sun, getting relaxation and calm from them. Good food, pleasant company, music. And yet I couldn't relax one bit. The tingle beneath my skin that had begun when I had seen my name written in Otto's handwriting had remained with me. One would think I had never had dinner with a stranger before. I had, all the time, a vague but unreasonable apprehension. There was this look beneath Herre Winther's pleasant, smiling gaze. a vague shadow of another person. A thoughtful, considering and calculating person.

Well. what was odd about that? Because. beneath my own animation. I was doing quite a bit of calculation myself.

I suppose most women play a little game of wondering how the man who pays them attentions would be as a husband, I used to do that with other men even when I was still in love with Ivor. Now there was no Ivor, and my heart was free for Otto Winther if I felt like bestowing it on him.

I had the certain feeling, even at this early stage in our relationship, that he was going to want it. Or my body, anyway, although that went without saying.

He had asked me too many questions about myself, my family and my background. He had done it very cleverly, never seeming to be inquisitive, and I had fallen into the trap of responding to a sympathetic listener. I told him about my childhood, my brothers, my parents, who had both died too young, my mother perhaps from childbearing and hard work, and my father from the strain of educating decently and conventionally five sons.

They had all gone to Charterhouse and Oxford. I, being the only girl, could not be skimped, so I had gone to Heathfield. Poor Father and poor Mother, with their determination to conform.

Herre Winther knew the schools I mentioned. He made the comment that my school friends possibly included princesses. So he was a snob. Well, of course he was, with his fashionable car and his good clothes. But more than my education, he seemed to be interested in the large family I came from. Were six children unusual in Denmark, I asked?

"Nowadays, yes. It's a pity. We have to suddenly be a new kind of people, thinking more of producing cars and television sets than babies. It's quite unnatural. Perhaps we'll find a way that a woman can give birth to a washing machine instead of a child."

"Are you fond of children? Are you disappointed you have only one son?"

There was that sudden shadow in his eyes, a cloud over the sun.

"My wife was not strong, unfortunately."

"Then perhaps your son will marry soon and make you a grandfather several times over."

He didn't like my flippancy. Perhaps he thought he was too young to be a grandfather. But in a moment he had gotten over his offense, and was saying with the greatest good humor:

"I think you underestimate me, Luise. What is wrong with my being a father several times over? Why should I sit back and wait to be a grandfather?" He gave his great merry roar of laughter. "I'm a very fit man. My grandfather had a child when he was seventy-three. And I'm a mere forty-six. My dear Luise, you should apologize for that remark."

"I do, I do," I said, laughing with him.

But I was thinking that there was always a reserved note in his voice when he spoke about the son he already had. Like a lot of men, he probably loved his virility more than the children it produced. Or was it more likely that he wanted to prove his virility now that his delicate wife was dead? How many girls like me had he already made rapid acquaintance with? And how long had his wife been dead, anyway? That was a question I had too much sensitivity to ask. I became rather silent, and let him talk.

This he did in snatches between long companionable silences, when he pulled on his cigar and sipped the very excellent brandy he had ordered with our coffee. I had observed that there wasn't too much of the rustic about him when it came to a knowledge of food and wine.

He talked about Denmark, the three big islands Zealand, Fyn and Jutland, and the many small islands with their isolated farms and castles, and always the beechwoods. The Great Belt and the Little Belt, and the Sound that separated Denmark from Sweden, the ice floes in the winter and the sudden sparkling gaiety of spring, the bird sanctuaries, the gales that blew straight from Siberia, the Viking graves.

"Was the war a terrible time?" I asked, surely unnecessarily, for we all knew how the Danes had stoically opposed the German occupation, to their own great hardship and peril.

"*Ja,*" he said briefly, the other person looking out of frozen blue eyes. The light turned on and off inside his skull. This large, smiling man was intriguingly not all on the surface.

"I was too young to remember it."

"Lucky for you." He stood up and held out his hand to me, smiling again. "Come. I'll drive you home—the long way around."

That, I discovered, meant a drive into the hills up a curving road bordered with moon-silvered olive trees, the headlights of the car throwing their branches into startling shapes, like heraldic beasts. At a spot where the hills opened, giving a view over the twinkling bay, Otto stopped the car.

So now there would be the expected pass. Well, I had asked for it, more or less, by consenting to spend the evening with him, and to come on this drive. I wasn't so sure now that I could cope, because that tingle was under my skin again, and I realized that I was quite amenable to being kissed.

But that was all. Definitely.

He laid his soft, large hand over mine.

"Well, Luise. I think we might see more of each other, yes? How long are you staying here?"

"Two more days."

"Send your office a telegram saying you must have at least another week."

"Why?"

"So that we get to know each other better."

"It's countries I'm supposed to learn about, not men."

"You're clever, too." He said that reflectively, as if he had been adding up my assets. Then said softly, *"Mine kaer."*

"What does that mean?"

"My dear. My love. Whatever you like, but something nice. We could move over to the hotel at Formentor."

"That costs the earth!"

"Why not? I have some money."

I turned to face him. I couldn't see his face very clearly in the dark, but I knew he was still smiling.

"Look, Otto, if you're proposing an affair, that's out."

"There is a cynical note in your voice?"

"There is."

"I wouldn't do anything to make you cynical."

"No?"

"Luise, I like you. From the moment I saw you standing in that dark, sad garden this afternoon, looking quite lost, and lonely—sadder even than Herre Chopin dying of lung disease because he at least had his bossy mistress."

"What nonsense—"

His fingers closed my lips. "No, listen to me. We have met by fate, but that's all fate does for us. The progression from there is up to us. And don't you agree it would be a pity to have such a brief friendship when we both like each other so much? Well, I must speak only for myself, but I've watched your eyes, your smile, and I think you have been liking me. Wouldn't it be a pity to say *farvel* at this stage?"

I hadn't realized I had looked so lonely. I hadn't known I was. His perception hurt. I didn't want to be lonely any more than he did and as he said, it didn't have to be one's fate. A little constructive action would be timely. I needed to look ahead, not backward at those three lost years.

"Farvel? Is that farewell? It sounds sadder in your language."

"Then it must be a word we never use."

"Are you proposing to pay all my expenses?"

"Only for one week—as friends."

"That's a promise? As friends?"

"My dear Luise, what are you so afraid of?"

I was irritated.

"Now you say that as if you're talking to a nervous virgin. That's not the aspect I'm thinking of." My lip trembled as I thought of all the terrible insecurity and lack of confidence that had been Ivor's legacy to me. I had made a desperate vow never to allow myself to be placed in such a vulnerable position again.

"Otto, look!"

"Yes. I am looking. It's too dark to see what is in your eyes."

"If I agree to do this, if we find we fall in love, it is to be marriage only. Nothing less. So if you're thinking of a short and delightful love affair in a luxury hotel in the sun, you had better drive me home and we'll say goodbye. *Farvel.*"

"A business proposition," he murmured, and I wasn't sure whether there was amusement in his voice or not.

"*No!* I said, *if* we fall in love."

"You have a strong mind, Luise."

"I have learned to have that."

He was silent then, for so long that I thought he had changed his own mind. My proposition was as little to his liking as his had been to mine. I was unreasonably disappointed. For the last quarter of an hour I had been, if not glowing with happiness, at least stimulated and excited. I hated the thought of Señora Caterina's gloomy guesthouse, and my room filled with the seductive scent of red roses. And a late London spring with squalls and iron-gray skies in two days' time. I had even, so quickly and at such a tangent does the female mind work, been trying to think of the Danish word for housewife. *Husmoder*, I believed.

"We will fall in love," said Otto then, stirring me out of my momentary depression and immediately plunging me into a more perilous gloom. For there had been such a curious fatalistic note in his voice.

Chapter Two

IN the early hours of the morning I had a period of panic and incredulity. Whatever mental aberration had I suffered to think I could do this extraordinary thing? I knew nothing whatever about Otto Winther except that he was a widower with two children and was rich, or comparatively so. Unless he was spending his life's savings on this trip abroad to have a love affair in private, or—less likely—to find another wife.

Before I had gone to bed I had written my letter to my editor, Tim MacFarlane, saying that if he didn't want any more Majorcan stuff, I intended taking a week's holiday. He might say that my job was one long holiday, but of course it wasn't. I was working even when I sat at street cafés or in airplanes. I needed a rest. The strain of constant traveling, et cetera. I said it all very convincingly, because I was also convincing myself.

I believed Otto's promise about friendship if our relationship didn't develop. So what was wrong with this week of luxury?

It was only in the early hours that the nagging thoughts came. Why was Otto doing this? I couldn't believe it was because he had already fallen madly in love with me.

He found me congenial, as I found him. But was this enough to justify this invitation? Was it enough to justify my acceptance? Were we both as lonely as that? Well, I was. So he must be, too. I had better leave it at that.

I slept at last, and woke with the most vivid feeling of excitement and anticipation. The morning was lovely, crisp but glowing. I decided to rush out and buy some new clothes, a swimsuit and a good dress, and some lingerie (which I would have needed, even if I had not been sharing a room with my large handsome Dane). I couldn't arrive at the Hotel Formentor looking like a typist on holiday.

I even had time to get my hair shampooed. When Otto arrived just before midday I had my luggage downstairs, and was wearing the pants and Pucci silk shirt I had extravagantly added to my purchases. I might as well look the part, I had decided. I really did want to do Otto credit. I believe that I wanted a happy outcome to this experiment more than I would admit.

A happy outcome out of all their afflictions . . . The ancient prayer echoed in my head. How was I to know that my afflictions had scarcely begun?

All the same, that was a wonderful week. We had separate rooms. We didn't meet until eleven in the mornings, and parted again at approximately midnight, after a day spent swimming, sunbathing, driving up into the hills, eating at small restaurants we discovered, dancing after dinner, or simply strolling in the moonlight. And we talked. One would have thought a week would have been long enough to get to know somebody in whose company one was constantly, but the strange thing was that although I heard a great deal about life in Denmark, and even learned a little Danish, I learned almost nothing about Otto's personal life.

He evaded my questions. He appeared to answer them without doing so. Yes, he had a family: the son, Niels, who had recently come of age, a brother, Erik, who was ten years younger than himself, his mother, who had lived with them during his wife's illness, and had continued to do so after poor Cristina had died. He did not get on so well with his mother, he said, but his eyes twinkled as if the differences were not serious. She spoiled Niels, he said.

Werc there servants on the farm, I persisted? I still couldn't reconcile Otto's expensive tastes and his obvious culture with his being a simple farmer.

But of course he was not a simple farmer. He must be a type of country squire, for I found that he had a farm manager and a groom, and cowboys, and a housekeeper and maids. The house was large, he admitted. How large? He waved his arms vaguely. There was a moat, he said. It was a very old house. It was called Maaneborg.

So that explained the luxury hotel and all the other extravagances. If not rich, Otto was at least decidedly comfortable. Not that I cared, for by then I was more or less falling in love.

More or less. We had begun to kiss goodnight, and I must say I was beginning to enjoy that. I must have been wound up tight ever since Ivor and I had parted, and only now was I beginning to unwind. Slowly and peacefully and sensuously. Sun, wine, Otto's lips which I didn't try to imagine were Ivor's, and that was a small victory in itself.

Tim, my editor, had written, "Time you had a lucky

break. Good luck, whoever he is. But don't let your work go off. That's the only thing I won't forgive."

I hadn't written to any of my brothers. In the past they had behaved like watchdogs, and their growlings and snarlings over the Ivor affair had taught me to be secretive about my life.

Sunday, Monday, Tuesday, Wednesday. I suppose I was lucky to have gotten that far before Otto made the inevitable proposition.

I didn't blame him. I had begun to want him rather badly, and it showed in my kisses. This didn't mean I was in love, though who could make distinctions at this stage? I only knew that my body clamored while my mind coolly held back.

You're being a calculating bitch, Luise Amberley. (But you see that even in my thoughts I was now spelling my name Luise.)

Well, I was being calculating, because I was absolutely determined not to have another affair that didn't lead to marriage. It was the woman who got hurt in these things, the woman who was totally committed once she had slept with a man. Or a woman of my kind, anyway. A man seemed to be able to walk away, uncommitted and unscathed.

I don't think I was in love, but I would be once we had gone to bed together. Or if the emotion I would then feel wasn't love, it would be an extraordinarily belonging, possessive feeling that was really the same thing.

So I refused Otto's request.

He was awfully nice about it.

"Perhaps tomorrow night?" he said. "It seems such a pity. You alone in your room and I in mine."

"Yes. But it's what we agreed, isn't it?"

"That business proposition you talked about?"

"Otto, it was never business! You know that very well."

He kissed me. He had a way of moving his lips gently against mine that made me feel—oh hell! I pulled away from him sharply, and he laughed, though not with any malice.

"You see, *mine kaer*. You feel just as I do. And bless you for that."

"I knew I couldn't trust you," I said furiously.

"But you can, unfortunately for me." His voice seemed sad. I tried to keep my anger, which I knew very well was my only defense. "Am I too old?"

"Don't be absurd."

"Then you have some English puritan feeling."

"I don't see why such a feeling should be English. And I haven't got it, anyway. Please stop cross-examining me. You have broken your promise and I'm angry about it. That's all."

We were walking on the terrace of the hotel. There was no one about, and we were in shadow. The air was balmy, the moon shining, and some flower I hadn't identified scented the air. It was a perfect setting which Otto had chosen for his seduction, the brute.

"We'll stay another week," he said abruptly.

"Oh, no, we won't. I have to be back in London. And if you think time will break me down, you're wrong. I'm not being coy, I'm being realistic. If I let you make love to me, you'll go off home feeling you haven't wasted your holiday, and I'll be left high and dry"—my voice quivered unintentionally—"remembering your arms round me."

"You would do that?" he said. He was obviously moved. His voice was amazed and gentle.

"What do you think?" I said irritably. "I don't live for the moment, as you seem to."

"The moment can be worth living for." He stroked my arm, and I hadn't the self-discipline to move away. "Perhaps you're afraid of getting pregnant. But put that fear out of your mind. I promise you most faithfully, even if you don't believe in my promises, that in that case I would marry you at once."

I laughed with some scorn. "Good heavens, Otto, we're not in the dark ages. There are ways." If I had wanted to play that trick, I would have played it long ago, on Ivor, and lived the rest of my life with a resentful husband.

"I suppose so," he said vaguely. "Myself, I don't care for—" He didn't finish what he had begun to say, but began to walk up and down the terrace, leaving me standing rather foolishly, watching him. He was big, handsome, virile, charming. He had gentleness and humor and a good mind. During this week he hadn't once shown a glimpse of the stranger I had suspected, or imagined, behind his smiling face. I really believed that I could marry him—if he asked me.

But it was a pity that I had to wrest the proposal out of him.

Suddenly he said, with all his old good humor, "Come, let's go to bed, Luise. In our separate rooms. Tomorrow we'll start early and drive up into the mountains. What do you say?"

So it was the first round to me, I supposed.

But the knowledge didn't make me sleep. Indeed, it made my brain overactive, and my half-drowsing thoughts became distorted. I was remembering the odd, intense way in which Otto had spoken of wanting to have not grandchildren but children of his own. Cristina, his delicate wife, had only given him two. So now he wanted a wife who could bear several healthy children. I, one of a big family, seemed a fairly safe bet. But he was taking no chances. He wanted to prove my fertility before he married me. Otherwise, I would have to be put aside regretfully, even though he loved me. As I believed he did.

Now why should he so passionately want children?

This I would never know—unless I won the next round, and the next and the next, and at last he married me.

But supposing, then, I could not conceive . . .

Maaneborg, the moated farmhouse. Perhaps it had dungeons. Perhaps the moat was unfathomably deep.

My unclear thoughts, partly nightmare, went on. But I woke in the morning to the certainty that my first intuition was correct. Otto wanted me pregnant.

And I was having none of that until there was a wedding ring on my finger.

There's an old saying: Be careful what you want in case you get it. I was being careful, so much so that at the end of the week at Formentor, Otto proposed flying to London with me.

I wouldn't allow this. I said that a little distance between us for a few weeks was a much better idea. Then if we found we missed each other very much, and longed to be together, well, what was wrong with getting married? We could write in the interval, I went on, not much caring for the thoughtfulness in his face. Letters were very revealing. Some people fell in love simply because of how they learned to love one another through letters. This was a much safer and more cautious way than being deceived by the aphrodisiacs of sun and wine and moonlight.

"My God, why must you be so cautious?" Otto burst out. "I suppose if I said, marry me now, you would still have these arguments."

"Certainly I would," I said coolly. "I want to be sure of my husband. I should loathe a divorce court."

"Then marry me now," said Otto, calling my bluff.

So I had to stick to my cautious line, in spite of the sudden, violently impulsive feeling I had. Yes, I will marry you and go to Maaneborg and find out all your secrets, I wanted to say. But I wasn't quite so reckless. And I was certain he wasn't as deeply in love with me as all that. Although he did care for me. He couldn't have pretended that tenderness and passion. Dear Otto. I, at least, was almost in love with him. I might even lose him by insisting on this parting. I would have to risk that. For if there was a good reason for his urgency, then I ought to find it out before we were irrevocably tied to one another. It was just possible he might be more forthcoming in letters. Especially if he missed me.

He had had his week at Formentor. Now I would have my session at my writing desk.

And I did, and so did he, for we both discovered we missed each other a great deal.

I loathed London, with spring going through its usual prolonged labor pains, involving much rain and clouds, and even a foolish snowstorm. In retrospect, those balmy days in Majorca seemed idyllic, and all the Englishmen I knew were undersized, narrow-minded, and ink-stained.

I don't know what Otto was thinking about Danish women, but I do know he had quite a talent for writing love letters. They had a direct simplicity that was impossible to disbelieve. He said he had never written love letters before, and now could only do so because they were addressed to me. "I think of your lovely serious eyes bent on them," he wrote. And, "Today, wonderful news came from England because you said that you missed me." And again, "I think your black hair has got into my eyes because I can't see anyone else, although Erik tells me women can be good-looking in Denmark, also. But I am strangely uninterested."

So he must have told his brother about me. Surely that indicated his sincerity.

He didn't mention any comment his son Niels might have made.

Then, four weeks after I had come back to London, his ultimatum arrived.

"Luise, this separation makes no sense. I think of you all the time. You must come to Denmark. Our laws require that you live here for six weeks before we can marry. Isn't that time enough for you to make up your cautious mind? I will meet you at Kastrup Airport on the first of May, not a day later, and then have the pleasure of showing you my country for those six weeks, so long as I have you with me. It is very silly of an old man of forty-six, but I am in love."

Tim, my editor, had been losing patience with me. I couldn't do my job sitting in my small flat in south Kensington. I had had long enough to rest from my last trip. What had I in mind for the summer?

"Scandinavia," I said.

"Good idea. Where will you start?"

"Copenhagen."

"That's a foregone conclusion. Don't leave out Fyn and Jutland, and perhaps even Samso, where the cheese comes from."

"Tim, I might not come back."

Tim was one of the undersized Englishmen who had worried me of late. But his intelligence made up for his lack of size. He turned his sharp honest eyes on me, and I realized how much I liked and respected him. The thought came to me that I might need him as a much closer friend than he was already. So far, he was the only person in England who knew about my probable intention of abandoning my country.

His knowledge was as of this minute only, for he exclaimed in surprise:

"Is he a Viking? I've been wondering who you had on your mind. I thought he must be some Spaniard you had met in Majorca."

"You see too much," I grumbled. "Does it really show?"

"You've been distrait. Of course it shows. To people who are fond of you, anyway. Is he a good chap? Does he deserve you?"

"I think it might be the other way round. Do I deserve him? He's a widower and he has a farm, and an old manor house with a moat. He's big and blond and very charming. I'll have a grown-up stepson. I don't know, Tim. I think I'm in love, and then I have moments of being completely uncertain. But I do want to go to Copenhagen. It's the only thing to do."

Tim, the newspaperman, said, "What's his name?"

"Otto Winther."

Tim frowned. "Rings a bell. Or does it? Something to do with the war, I think. I'll try to remember. Well, you're a big girl now, Louise. You must make up your own mind."

"Yes, I know. I'd like to fly over next week, if that's all right."

"Sure. Will you be too lovesick to send us an article or two? Let me know if you are, so I can find a replacement."

I wanted to kiss Tim for his unemotional understanding.

He was giving me a way out, if I needed it, and his blessing as well. I found that I infinitely preferred him to know of my problem rather than my brothers, who continued to see me as their baby sister, slightly tarnished but still in need of protection.

I wrote to Otto and told him I would be a little late. I would arrive at Kastrup Airport on the second, not the first of May. Tim and his wife, Barbara, gave me a farewell dinner, for which they had bought a bottle of aquavit and some Carlsberg beer to make me familiar with the customs of the country to which I was going. Tim said he still couldn't remember why the name Otto Winther rang a bell, a very small, dim bell, in his mind. But no matter, he was sure it was not for any Doctor Crippen or Pierre Landru tendencies. All the same, he knew I would have the sense to take a long cool look at the man in his own background.

Before I left England, I made a sentimental journey to my old home in a small Buckinghamshire village. But that was a mistake. It was occupied by strangers, and I didn't like their curtains or the way they had trimmed and formalized the lovely wild garden. They had cut down the old pear tree, damn their souls. I walked up and down the road outside, occupied with overemotional feelings that not only this ugly beloved Victorian house but my country itself was casting me out. I still avoided confiding in any of my brothers, who were occupied with their own marriages. I had neglected my friends during my long, obsessional affair with Ivor, and now I had no really close ones. Self-pityingly, I realized I was even more alone than I had thought. I needed Otto badly. I might even be mistaking need for love.

But my first glimpse of him at Kastrup Airport would surely define my feelings.

It did, too. When I saw his tall blond head above the crowd and caught his smiling welcoming gaze, I was suddenly happy and excited. Perhaps I wasn't deeply in love with him, but this happy warm feeling was fine. It would wear better than passion.

As soon as I had my baggage and was through customs, he whisked me into his arms.

"*Mine kaer,*" he said.

All I could say, foolishly, was, "Today I intend to begin learning Danish."

"In the meantime, could you say something nice to me in English?"

"Oh, yes. I'm delighted to see you again."

He began laughing with pleasure, and we laughed all the way to Copenhagen, where we left my bags at the Hotel d'Angleterre. Separate rooms again, and not even on the same floor. Otto was being discreet in his own country. I scarcely had time to notice the elegant foyer with the surprising portrait of the young Queen Victoria by Winterhalter (I mean, surprising to be hanging there and not at Windsor Castle), before Otto carried me off to lunch in the Tivoli Gardens.

It was a beautiful spring day, and he didn't think I knew how entrancing Tivoli was. It was indeed, with the tulips, and the balloon sellers, and the fountains, and the budding trees. We lunched on the balcony of a luxury restaurant. It had pale pink tablecloths, silver and crystal, and was like the Caprice set down in the middle of Regents Park. Habit made me begin to write my piece for Tim in my head until Otto reminded me that he was there.

I couldn't forget that for long. He seemed so much bigger than life—he had put on a little weight, which I thought privately I would persuade him to lose, for his own good, when we were married—and it wasn't possible not to observe the waiters' deference.

"Do they know you here?" I asked.

"Perhaps. I expect I'm known in most places. I enjoy my food," he added with his jolly laugh, "and I'm not exactly a dwarf, you observe. People remember me."

In the distance a band was playing "Wonderful, Wonderful Copenhagen," and trite as that was, it made my head swim. I thought that I was going to love this city, with its green copper spires and old red brick towers and whimsical statues and blond boys and girls. And my big merry Otto . . .

"You do mean to marry me, don't you, Luise?"

"If you mean to marry me. Yes, I think so."

He gave a sigh, as if a difficult problem had been solved. Difficult? Had it been?

"Now, then,"—his hand was over mine, but his voice was less adoring than businesslike—"we have six weeks to wait. We'll leave Copenhagen tomorrow and do some traveling."

"So soon? But this is all so enchanting."

"There'll be plenty of time for it later."

"But your family? Aren't I to meet them?"

"They'll keep. Maaneborg is on the island of Samso. It is too long a journey."

This time I knew that I didn't imagine the undercurrent in his voice. Hostility? A dislike of his own son? Well, why not?

28

The accident of parenthood did not demand that one's off-spring be loved uncritically. I began to wonder about the young man, Niels. After all, I was to be his stepmother, which was a ridiculous enough situation, without my disliking him into the bargain.

"Luise, you're having secret thoughts. I don't like that."

"Well, so are you."

He laughed and beckoned the waiter. I was beginning to realize that Otto was quite good at evasions. My second qualm of uneasiness had to be forgotten as I listened to Otto asking the waiter to bring the wine list. He wanted to choose a champagne suitable to celebrate such a beautiful spring day.

The waiter, looking at me with his rheumy old eyes, had clearly guessed our secret. And I thought that my dear Otto was not going to be easy to understand, since he would tell a waiter what he would not tell his family.

All the same, it was a beautiful day. I looked at the purple tulips and the rhododendrons, at the balloon seller, with his great bouquet of ballons that threatened to waft him away, at the frivolous peacock fan of the open-air theater, at the towheaded children chattering in their strange language. I was in a fairy tale, that was for certain. And I really couldn't believe that Otto was the ogre, even if he were so secretive about his family.

Anyway, the champagne was going to my head, and I had a last sober thought that that also he had intended to happen.

We went to the ballet that night. The Royal Danish Ballet at Det Kongelige Teater (in English the Royal Theater, but if I was going to be Danish, I must learn the correct terms). And the ballet was that most comical gifted gem, *The Three Musketeers*, all flashing swords and whirling cloaks, with choreography by Flemming Flindt.

As we promenaded during the interval, several people greeted Otto and looked curiously at me. But Otto chose to introduce me to only one person, whose name I didn't quite catch. It was Svend something. And he introduced me as Miss Luise Amberley, in Copenhagen on a visit.

Svend something gave me a correct little bow and asked me if I intended to stay in Denmark long.

Otto answered for me. "Six weeks or so. Isn't that right, Luise?"

The two men then had a short conversation in Danish, for which Otto apologized afterward. "That was just a little business, Luise. It was rude of me when you couldn't understand."

There was a lot I couldn't understand. For instance, why did this friend have to be kept in the dark about our marriage?

"I thought you might have been telling him that you were getting married again," I said, with assumed innocence.

Otto laughed and squeezed my arm.

"Certainly not. That's our secret. Don't you enjoy having a secret, darling?"

"I simply see no particular reason for it. I had thought—"

I stopped as Otto gripped my arm tighter, not in affection but warning.

Then abruptly he wheeled me around, and took me back to our seats.

"Whatever was that for?" I asked, with some asperity. "Are you running away from the bailiff, or something?"

Otto's face, which had been so genial, was flushed and had a hard expression. Now I was getting fanciful, but there seemed to be a witch or an ogre or something in this fairy tale atmosphere.

Then abruptly he laughed.

"You are pondering over the mystery, darling. It was only that I just saw my brother, Erik. Imagine him being at the ballet on this night of all nights!"

"Your brother, and you run away!" I turned on him with indignation. "Are you *ashamed* of me?"

He patted my hand, still chuckling. "Good heavens, that would be the last thing. No, it's only that Erik and I aren't very good friends. We don't agree on most things, that's all. He's ten years younger than me. He's never really seemed like a brother at all. He's fond of Niels, and he was fond of Cristina, so he comes to Maaneborg a good deal. We have to make an appearance of friendship. But, sadly, that is all it is."

Smiling Otto with enemies. Hating his own brother. Not caring for his own son.

"He'll meet you soon enough," he said.

I didn't think I wanted to hear all this.

"Otto, you've never shown me a picture of Maaneborg," I said carefully.

"No, and I don't intend to. I want it to be quite new to you."

People were returning to their seats. There was a bustle and a lot of conversation, the curious throaty Danish, with an occasional carrying American or English voice indicating the presence of the usual flock of tourists.

Otto settled his big body into the seat, as if relieved the lights were going out.

"Why did you bring me here if you didn't want me to be seen?" I asked, still more perplexed than offended.

"Hush!" he said. And then, "Look. Fourth row from the front at the end. With the dark head. That's my brother."

In the next moment the lights dimmed, and I had caught only a glimpse of that surprisingly dark, curling hair. I had thought all Danes were fair.

I could no longer give the charming ballet more than vague attention. I looked hard, most of the time, at Erik Winther. He was with a fair-haired girl. He turned to murmur something to her once or twice. I thought that he had the same strong nose as Otto, but a much thinner face. I was trying to see in that face, in the dim light, the reason for hostility toward his older brother. I really couldn't imagine that the fault would be Otto's.

I longed to meet him. When the ballet ended and the lights went up, I even tried to maneuver an accidental encounter, hanging back in the pretense of looking for my gloves.

But Otto was not to be caught this way. He snatched up the glove I had deliberately dropped, and taking my arm, hustled me out in the most skillful way. Again, I caught only a glimpse of Erik, smiling at his companion in a gentle, affectionate manner.

Otto, when I asked him, informed me rather shortly that Erik was not married.

"He's a womanizer, and I don't intend to let him set eyes on you until we're married."

I wanted to believe that. I was irritated with myself for my suspicion that Otto was a little devious. He was wishing he hadn't taken me to the ballet to be seen by too many people. But for heaven's sake, why?

Chapter Three

ALL the same, I must admit I was a little intrigued by Otto's cloak-and-dagger behavior. At least, *dullness* was not a word I would have to use about our relationship.

Mind you, I would have been more practical if I had insisted on a more explicit explanation for all this secrecy. But by this time I was very tired, and it didn't seem as important as it might have been if my head had been clearer. So we had a brief goodnight kiss under the wide blue innocent eyes of the Winterhalter Queen Victoria in the foyer of the Angleterre, and I went off to bed.

In the morning we left for Jutland, sailing on one of the comfortable ferries across the Great Belt. We were going to Aarhus, Denmark's second largest city, Otto explained. I couldn't help being disappointed that we had left Zealand without going to Elsinore to see Hamlet's castle, Kronberg, but Otto said that it would be overrun by tourists at this time of year. There would be plenty of time later for it. That seemed a valid argument. After all, if he had really wanted to keep me out of sight of his friends, he wouldn't have risked taking me to the ballet last night.

After that, the time went by with the greatest pleasantness. Otto behaved impeccably, when really, had he tested me, he might have found I was not quite so adamant about waiting for a wedding ring to be put on my finger. At this point, I was willing to trust him. I was really growing very devoted to him.

But he waited, and I respected him for that. And after all, six weeks was not so long.

We came back to Zealand, though not to Copenhagen. We had had a day in Sweden, which was the easiest thing to do, not even passports being required, and crossed back from Malmo to a little fishing village on the tip of Amager, the island which was separated from Copenhagen by only a narrow bridge. Dragor was the name of the village, and it was near Kastrup Airport. It had a pleasant seafront and the village itself was enchanting, full of cozy houses with thatched roofs, walls painted saffron yellow or a warm red, and gardens full of petunias. The streets were narrow and cobbled. There was a very old inn called the Dragor Kro. Otto took me in to have a drink, and when he observed my pleasure in the cosy interior with its gay red wallpaper, the flowerpots on the windowsills, the grandfather clock painted white, the old potbellied stove in the corner, he suddenly said:

"Let's get married here. Why not?"

Not in Copenhagen? Not at Maaneborg, with his family as witnesses?

The thoughts flew through my head. Otto had been so patient. Why so impatient now that we must be married in haste in a small seaside village?

Where was my sense of romance? I asked myself. Had I lost it, or had I never had one? For the place was charming. The calm sea scattered with yachts and pleasure boats stretched outside the window. The sky was blue with little bits of white cloud, like the flocks of white geese wandering on the seashore. Seabirds cried. Fishermen sat mending their nets. Occasionally, airliners came floating in on a downward curve to land at the Kastrup Airport, and the small ferryboats for Sweden sent a trickle of people or cars down to the jetty.

Otto was demanding that I turn my gaze from that peaceful scene to him.

"Why do we wait any longer, Luise?" he was saying, with urgency. "Who do we want at our wedding but ourselves?"

My heart was beating too fast. I don't know why it was at that moment only that I chose to be frightened.

"But we won't even have witnesses."

"That can be easily arranged."

"You wouldn't want friends? Even your brother?"

"What does it matter? Anyone who can sign his name will do. Come!" He held out his hands, and I rose as if I were hypnotized. I certainly felt hypnotized; I can't imagine why. But Otto could have a surprising intensity in his blue eyes. Once, in Aalborg, when something had upset him, he had lost his temper, and for a moment he had looked very odd indeed. But that was the only time I had seen him lose his good humor.

We walked along the front to a hotel called the Kongelige Hotel. It was a modest enough place, though pleasant. Flocks of geese were picking at the grass outside the garden fence. There were elm trees, and tables set out in the garden, and a long balcony.

Otto went in, while I wandered in the garden. The sea

wind was sharp, and I shivered a little. I couldn't think why suddenly I had a feeling about this place, a lost and lonely sort of feeling. For the first time in six weeks, I felt homesick. I wanted to see Tim and Barbara, and would not have objected to the critical inspection of my brothers, either.

But Otto was coming out, looking triumphant.

"I've booked the best double room they have," he said. "It's not the Hotel d'Angleterre, but it has a wonderful view. Would you like to go up at once?"

I was twenty-six years old, and this nervous. It really was ridiculous.

"Not yet. I'll sit in the garden. What are you going to do?"

"Get our bags and find a *sognepraest*."

"A what?"

"A priest. A parson. To marry us, of course. I already have the license. I've had it in my pocket for a day or two, to tell the truth."

On an impulse, while Otto was gone, I went into the hotel and rang London. I was suddenly so nervous I had to speak to Tim.

Fortunately I caught him just before he was going to lunch.

I said, "Hullo, Tim. It's me, Luise, here."

"Good heavens, I thought you were in Denmark!" The well-remembered, dry, slightly ironic, voice was reassuring to hear.

"So I am. In a little place called Dragor, although that's not how the Danes pronounce it. Tim, I just wanted to tell you I'm marrying Otto today."

There was a brief silence. Then, quietly, Tim said, "Are you sure you want to?"

"Not entirely, but I can't imagine why I'm not sure. I'm getting a well-heeled Danish farmer, and he's getting a restless, not particularly happy spinster with no money, who can't even speak his native tongue. But I'm tired of being cautious. I'm ready for a bit of uncautiousness."

There was another short silence.

"Well, I suppose there is divorce in his native tongue, if necessary," said Tim.

"They say the divorce rate in Denmark—oh, hell, Tim, that's a fine thought on which to start a marriage. I really do care for Otto. We've had the happiest time."

"Well, if you ask me, you've made the right decision. The pieces you've been sending have been lousy. I'm sacking you.

But you might have let me know in time to send flowers, or something. How about the stepson?"

"I haven't met him yet."

"You haven't!"

"Otto has been showing me Denmark. We've been traveling all the time. We haven't been to Maaneborg yet. It is on Samso, rather a long way off."

"Well, darling, for a trusting nature where men are concerned—"

"What do you mean?"

"Nothing, love. I withdraw that remark. But Louise, because Ivor was a heel, don't go to the other extreme and marry for the sake of marrying."

"What do you take me for?" I asked, my voice cool.

"For a damned nice girl who deserves a bit of luck."

"Which now she has got. How's London looking?"

"The same pigeons making love on my windowsill. Do they have them in Dragor?"

"No. Geese, mostly." I thought a moment. "Perhaps I'm one of them. But from today on, you call me Frue Luise Winther, and don't forget it. Give my love to Barbara." For the life of me, I couldn't stop my voice quivering. "Goodbye, Tim. *Farvel*."

"Wait a minute," Tim said. "I still can't think why the name Winther rings a bell. But if I remember I'll write. Maaneborg find you?"

"Maaneborg, Samso."

"Well, invite me to the first christening," Tim said, and was gone. And with him, London and all my past life seemed to be gone, too. I wished I hadn't had the impulse to ring him.

I went upstairs to the double room that Otto was so pleased about, and tried to decide what to wear to my wedding. Something quiet. I believed that Otto would refuse to marry me if I came out in a too-noticeable hat or dress. He had never seemed to want people to look at me, from the night of the ballet until this day.

What was wrong with me?

Tim needn't have sounded so cautious, I thought resentfully. He was wasting his time, hinting that I was marrying my big Dane simply because I was still in a state of shock and trauma from the Ivor affair. I knew that already.

But if I waited to get out of that unhappy state, I would be twenty-seven, twenty-eight, nearly thirty. And eligible men were not so thick on the ground at that age.

Well, here I was, sitting in front of the mirror in the big

bedroom with the windows open to the cool sea wind, trying on my one and only hat, and looking scared.

Otto should have taken me to Maaneborg first, I kept muttering. I was crazy to get married without knowing the kind of life I would be expected to lead. What was there to be so secretive about at Maaneborg? Perhaps his first wife wasn't dead after all. Perhaps he was in the process of arranging to commit bigamy.

This hat was awful. I would go to the church without one. I would do my hair elaborately, as I did it for a party. And wear my black wool, which was sleeveless and very elegant.

Black for a wedding?

Otto's face appeared above mine in the mirror, and I jumped with surprise. He shouldn't come into my room without knocking. Then I remembered that this was not my room, but our room. With a very large double bed and one of those stuffed quilts called a *dyne* which I was reasonably certain he would hog, leaving me shivering on the outside.

He bent to kiss the top of my head. His fingers came round to smooth my forehead.

"Why the worry lines, my darling?"

I turned to look at him.

"What did you do? Did you find a parson and a church?"

"A parson, yes. Not a church at such short notice."

"A registry office in this little village?" I asked in surprise.

"No, a room. What would you call it in English? A parlor. The parson's parlor, I suppose, though I think that sounds very funny. Don't you?"

His blue eyes were twinkling, and he was laughing with such infectious happiness and amusement that before I knew it, I was joining in.

"That's better," he said approvingly. "The lines have gone. You look a little more like a bride."

I stopped laughing.

"Otto, I don't look remotely like a bride. I don't even feel like one."

"Well, I feel like a bridegroom, I can tell you. Now, let us see how we can improve your feelings. I would like you to wear the dress you wore to our first dinner together at the Hotel Mediterraneo, when we fell in love. If you haven't forgotten."

"Did we?"

"Of course. Where is the dress? I am going to put it on you. Dressing you instead of undressing you. You see how patient I can be."

"Our wedding today isn't being so patient. Shouldn't we have had it in Copenhagen, at least?"

"Why?"

"Well, your friends—your brother—"

"Luise, tell me, who am I marrying? You or my friends? And what is the matter with Dragor? You said yourself how delightful it was. This being timid at the last moment doesn't suit you. You may be having me change *my* mind."

He was right, of course. Timidity didn't suit me, and I didn't want to tell him that that wasn't entirely what I was suffering from. It was more apprehension and mystification. A strange foreknowledge of some kind of doom. Which was nonsensical. Besides, it would have been pretty dishonest to have strung him along for six weeks, and then run off. When we had lunched in the Tivoli Gardens that first day in Copenhagen, I had been so sure.

Well, he shouldn't have refused to let me meet his brother that night at the ballet. That was when my doubts had started.

"Otto, how did you register us at the desk?"

"As Herre and Frue Winther, of course."

Really, the superb confidence of him! But he had kept to his promise; he hadn't attempted to make love to me at any time during the six weeks we had been together. If I were to let him down now, I would be behaving as badly as Ivor had behaved to me. That was unthinkable.

So I must dress for my strange wedding in the front parlor of a *sognepraest's* house in a Danish fishing village.

My attack of premarital nerves had been mastered. I smiled at Otto, and he immediately swooped me into his arms and kissed me very completely. And then, of course, my body got treacherous, as he had known it would, and I would have been very prepared to delay the marriage ceremony for an hour or two. He hadn't kissed me like that since those moonlit nights in Majorca.

Now his patience was going to be rewarded. And mine, too.

So I was able to smile during the ceremony, though I must say this was remarkably offhanded, and almost totally lacking in reverence. Indeed, the priest seemed in a great hurry to get it over. He also seemed nervous, and dropped the ring onto the wooden floor of his little parlor. It ran away into a corner, and his wife, who was one of the witnesses, a fat jolly woman who gave a little gurgle of mirth, had to look for it on her hands and knees.

The other witness was a rather dissolute-looking man who wore a fisherman's jersey that was none too clean. He had a stubble of beard, and a thickened bluish nose that suggested the drinker. He looked like a lay-about who had been picked up by chance on the quay. He grinned broadly all the time.

The priest's house was a yellow one facing the sea on the Strandlinien. It had a thatched roof and a tiny window in the eaves. The door was dark brown. A large tabby cat was curled up in the window box of geraniums. The parlor itself was a simple room. I noticed a rocking chair, a rather revolting stuffed canary in a gilt cage on the mantelpiece, a shabby Bible on the table that served as an altar.

The priest was elderly, with blue eyes set close together and a fuzz of white hair around his scalp. He was neatly dressed in a dark suit and wore a clerical collar. Even if his manner was hasty, he looked solemn enough. I thought I must be imagining that I could smell schnapps on his breath.

I confess I heard little of the ceremony until I was asked, in English, if I, Luise Martha Amberley, would take Otto Frederick Gustav Winther to be my husband.

I said yes, and it was then that the ring foolishly rolled away. When it was at last safely on my finger, Otto bent to give me a smacking kiss and everyone laughed loudly.

Then the names were carefully entered on a certificate, and we all signed. The fat woman's name was Anna Hansen, and the fisherman's Jens Larsen. The priest was Peter Hansen. I noticed that name particularly.

Otto must have paid the fee before the ceremony, because immediately it was over he refused a celebration drink of aquavit and said goodbye quite abruptly. I must say I didn't feel at all married, but Otto obviously did. Walking briskly down the front, his arm tucked in mine, he laughed happily, saying how sensible we had been, saving the fuss of a conventional wedding.

"I can tell you now, Luise, I was completely miserable during the whole of the ceremony with my first wife. I believe that that was the beginning of our unhappy marriage. There were so many guests and such a parade of fashion. Was it me or a big wedding my wife wanted?" He squeezed my arm. "With us it is going to be quite different."

"How many guests did you have?"

"Oh, about five hundred."

"Five hundred! Otto! What are you? You can't tell me a farmer could afford a wedding that size?"

"My wife had some money," he said carelessly. "I'm sorry,

mine kaer. That was tactless of me. It's you who are my wife. I promise not to speak any more about Cristina."

I looked at the gold band on my finger. I thought of the big, formal, fashionable ceremony compared with our hasty and furtive one. I supposed I was married. I supposed this gold ring did tell the truth.

"Of course, all that was before the war," Otto was saying. "Times were different then. Much more lavish. My parents were both alive. Now there is only my mother. I'm afraid you will have to put up with her at Maaneborg. But don't look so anxious. She will like you."

I had a premonition that she wouldn't, and asked if she must live there.

He nodded. "Yes. But the house is quite big. We can lose ourselves in it."

I still wasn't reassured, but I told myself that Otto had been right. We wanted to belong to each other, and now had achieved this with the smallest possible fuss. We were not marrying a house or a farm or any number of in-laws. We stood here, uncluttered and unprejudiced by any background. Even the unpretentious hotel was fine. We would lie tonight feeling the sea wind on our faces and listening to the waves.

I was already Luise Winther on a piece of paper signed by myself and Otto and laboriously by that strange trio in the saffron cottage.

After tonight my sense of unreality would leave me.

Chapter Four

TO my alarm, just after dinner, Otto had a dizzy spell. We had gotten up from the table and were about to leave the dining room when his hand came down heavily on my shoulder. He had to stand a minute leaning on me while he recovered himself. His face was suffused with a dark color. I got a bad fright. I thought he was about to have a stroke.

But in a moment he shook his head, and attempted to smile.

"It's nothing." His voice was a little thick, but otherwise normal. "Let's get some fresh air."

He was able to walk out of the room unaided. We paused for a minute or two in the hall, then Otto suggested going upstairs. The flush was dying out of his face. His eyes still looked a little strange, but he vigorously denied that he was ill when I asked him.

"One glass too many of champagne, that's all."

We had drunk champagne on other occasions without this result. Anyway, I had had as much as he, and I was no more than pleasantly glowing.

But perhaps Otto had drunk during the day, when I hadn't been with him. He had waited for me in the bar this evening, for instance.

I certainly wasn't going to cross-examine him about that, so I agreed that it had been a particularly good champagne, and I was feeling its effect, too. We went upstairs arm in arm. In our room, Otto sat in the armchair at the window for a little while. I believe he fell asleep, although he denied this twenty minutes later, when he opened his eyes and looked at me with his familiar warm look of love and excitement.

He was my husband, I thought with pride and pleasure. I was already possessive about him, and a little anxious about his blood pressure and that strange dizzy spell. Perhaps we should be careful tonight.

This tentative suggestion made him angry and unfairly suspicious.

"Are you going to be the sort of wife who makes excuses? Who has headaches and other ailments?"

"It's not me who has the ailment," I pointed out gently. "You did worry me a little, Otto. Have you had your blood pressure taken lately?"

He sprang up and reached out for me, pulling me toward him and beginning to unzip my dress.

"I'll show you how high my blood pressure is. If you want to know, it's very high at this minute, and only you can lower it."

I didn't know that I had secretly dreaded this night until it was over. There was only one bad moment when I had a vivid remembrance of Ivor's spare muscular body. But Otto mistook my uncontrollable sob for passion, and presently his big body blotted out all thought. High blood pressure or not, there was nothing wrong with his virility.

And in the morning I woke to realize that Ivor was forever washed out of my mind, and I was Frue Luise Winther, keenly alive, strangely new.

I lay watching dawn grow over the peaceful Baltic. Sea and sky slowly separated, light came into the room, and I was able to look at Otto sleeping quietly beside me. It was true that he had gotten most of the quilt, but the warmth from his body kept me warm. I pondered my feelings for him. Possessiveness, certainly. I knew I would have that. A desire to see his eyes open and look at me with their lazy smile. A still lingering anxiety about that strange turn he had had last night. An admiration for his good looks and a purely sensuous pleasure in that thick mane of rope-colored hair tousled on the pillow. Pleasure, too, in the warmth of his body against mine. Surely all that added up to love, although reflecting on it like this was vaguely chilling, like putting one's emotions through a computer.

I only wanted to assure myself that any difficulties ahead at Maaneborg would find us firmly united. Hostility from his son, for instance. Or his mother, or his brother, whom he had been so anxious to avoid that night at the theater.

Otto was stirring. "What are you thinking, Luise?" came his sleepy voice.

"About whether your brother would like me or not."

He frowned slightly, his eyes still closed.

"What Erik thinks isn't important. You won't be seeing much of him."

"Doesn't he live on the farm?"

"No, he has an apartment in Copenhagen. He's an architect. We're very different, I told you. He has brown hair, I have yellow. Do you like my yellow hair, *mine kaer?* Tell me."

Naturally, demonstrating my admiration for his looks led to vigorous response on Otto's part. Until suddenly he made a violent turn sideways as if to get out of bed, and instead fell out. He didn't crash to the floor. He slid quite quietly. He couldn't have hurt himself. But he didn't get up or say anything. I leaned over, laughing, then stopped abruptly as I saw that he was twitching in a peculiar way. His eyes were rolled up, and a slight dribble came from his mouth.

I was terrified. For a moment I could only stare stupidly, clutching at my thumping heart. Water! That was it. Getting back my senses, I sprang out of bed and rushed to the bathroom.

When I got back with a filled tumbler, Otto had stopped twitching and was lying quietly, with his eyes closed.

For one terrible moment I thought he was dead. I flung the water in his face, then knelt down to mop it off with a corner of my nightdress. And he opened his eyes. And smiled, heaven bless him!

"Sorry, Luise," he said, quite naturally. "I hoped I wouldn't scare you like that so soon."

"What do you mean?" I demanded. How dare he lie there, smiling when he had almost scared the life out of me!

He sat up slowly, shaking his damp head.

"You nearly drowned me. Give me a towel, for God's sake."

"Otto," I said, speaking quietly now, for my brain was beginning to function, "are you an epileptic?"

He buried his face in the towel I had given him and rubbed his head furiously.

"Not exactly," he said in a muffled voice. "At least, only in a very mild way. I have what the doctors call *petit mal.* It isn't serious. I rarely have an attack. But I suppose last night, the excitement, and so on—" He dropped the towel and looked up at me with a sadness that was quite alien to his usually merry face. "Forgive me for not telling you. I was afraid if I did you wouldn't marry me."

Would I have? I didn't want to face the implications of that question just now. I was still too shaken.

I got his dressing gown and put it around his shoulders.

"Get back into bed. I'll ring for some coffee."

"You talk as if life is going on normally."

"What else can it do?" He saw me twisting the ring on my

finger, and I had to add, because it was the thought that had instantly leaped into my mind, "I don't mind for myself. You're my husband, and if you're ill, of course I'll take care of you. But you have kept saying how much you want children. What about them?"

"This isn't hereditary," he said quickly. "It's due to a little brain damage I suffered at birth. Our child will be perfect. You'll see."

Our child . . . Already he was speaking as if one was on the way. Perhaps it was.

I felt a strange thrill in my body, and suddenly began to cry. I couldn't stop myself. At one moment a bride, and the next the wife of an epileptic. But his arms around me felt strong and comforting, and I could hardly believe it was only ten minutes since he had lain on the floor with his eyes turned up in that horrible way.

"You should have told me. It wasn't fair not to. It wasn't honest."

"Poor child. Do you hate me? Don't hate me."

"It will happen again—"

"Not if I take my pills. I forgot last night. I was too full of happiness. I promise not to forget again. You can remember for me."

"Does that make it all right?"

"Perfectly. It's only that I'm forgetful."

I remembered that once in Majorca he had had a bruise on his temple. He said he had bumped into a door.

"Does Erik have this—trouble?"

"No," he said sharply. "I told you it wasn't hereditary. Neither does Niels. Though of course—"

"Of course, what?"

"Of course, he wouldn't, any more than our son would."

I withdrew from his frostiness. What a time to be cross-examining him! My poor flawed Otto. I must be so kind. I must love him.

"It's your turn to forgive me, now. Crying like a baby. I'm not a crying woman, I promise. Let's get our breakfast. Then we can talk about what we'll do today. That's if you feel like doing anything."

"If you're referring to my health, my love," said Otto, smiling again, "I don't feel like going outside these four walls. All I need is here."

We couldn't stay forever in that rather indifferent hotel, although I loved the flat coastline, the green grass growing right down to the sea, and the fat waddling geese. I didn't urge Otto to leave at once because I thought he needed a rest. He was naturally an indolent type of man, and was quite content to let me go for long walks alone while he read, or wandered down to the harbor and gossiped with fishermen.

To tell the truth, I wanted time alone. I had a lot to think about. I was still deeply uneasy—*shocked* was a better word, though I didn't want to use it—about this *petit mal* from which he suffered. I suppose my shock was mostly because I was upset he hadn't told me. The attacks were not too distressing and he had assured me again that his form of the disease was not hereditary. This probably was true, since his son, Niels, and his brother were not afflicted with it. I could cope with the physical part of it, although I knew that until I adjusted myself to the knowledge it was going to inhibit our lovemaking.

But I did wish Otto had not been so secretive. It was this secretiveness in his nature, about everything, not only his illness, but also Maaneborg and his family, that held me back from loving him wholeheartedly. I could only hope that marriage would overcome that.

All the same, on those long walks I came to one conclusion. I regretted being persuaded into that impulsive and furtive marriage. For it had been furtive, there was no arguing that. I wished I had insisted on being taken to Maaneborg to meet his family first.

But there it was. Like a cautious Victorian heroine, I had held out for marriage, and then, in shame at my calculating attitude, had conceded the last point.

The wind blew in my face, the air was balmy, and I was too young for pessimism. Otto and I would make a success of our marriage. He was darling and sweet, and I must sympathize with his deep aversion for his physical flaw. This must be what had come between him and his first wife. I was determined not to let it come between us.

I did think that as soon as Otto felt completely fit again we would go to Samso, and Maaneborg.

Not a bit of it. To my astonishment he announced that now we would have our honeymoon trip. He had reserved a suite in one of the best hotels in Stockholm. We would also visit Oslo and perhaps even Helsinki. I couldn't possibly say I had seen Scandinavia until I had visited the capitals of Sweden and Norway. I could even send articles back to my newspaper, if I wished.

This last was thrown in as a sop, because he had seen my outraged face.

"Now what is it, Luise? Do you find the thought of a trip with me so distasteful? Are you afraid?"

"Of your illness?" I had to reassure him on that point. "No, it's simply that I begin to think your home and your family don't exist."

He laughed heartily. "You saw my brother at the theater."

"You said he was your brother. You didn't introduce me."

"Well, he was, and I wanted to keep you to myself. I still do." Although he still smiled, the cold flicker was in his eyes. "You will find soon enough that my family exists. Let us postpone that day."

"Why? Won't they like me?"

He looked at me coolly and thoughtfully.

"You? Yes. Your existence, no. If you understand what I mean."

There was only one thing he could mean. That for some reason his family would resent his having married again.

I wondered why that was, too, but it was obviously no use asking. This silly contretemps was my own fault, for having been persuaded into the secretive marriage.

But perhaps if I had waited until all was clear, I wouldn't have been able to marry Otto at all.

Now why that suspicion came to me, I don't know.

I simply had to be patient and try to enjoy our further travels.

This was easy enough, for they were done in luxury, and Otto could not have been a kinder or more attentive husband. He didn't have another attack, either. I was beginning to watch whether he took his pills. I would remind him occasionally, and he didn't mind that, either. I think he rather liked my fussing.

And he was a good lover. His big body was like a downy bed. It didn't surprise me at all that at the end of six weeks I was almost certain I was pregnant.

Unlike him, my nature couldn't be less secretive. I immediately wanted to share my suspicion with him. I was so sure, after his talk of wanting children, that he would be delighted.

He was, too. But not entirely in the way of a man longing for another son. Rather in a triumphant way as if he had won some kind of wager.

He seized me around the waist, and began kissing me all over my face.

"Luise, we'll go home! Now we have something to go home for."

He smothered me with his eager lips, so that I couldn't speak.

"Luise, my little love, I knew we could do it."

I drew away, not altogether sure I understood what he was getting at.

I said drily, "It isn't a particularly unusual feat."

"Our baby is. Oh, I assure you it is. It means more than just having a son. You'll find out."

"Otto, you say that in a way as if it's some kind of revenge."

He snatched me to him again, and for the first time I had a feeling of aversion for his big demanding hands.

"No, don't kiss me, Otto. Talk to me. Tell me things, for once."

He laughed tenderly and his hands were gentle. But there was no doubting the authority in his voice.

"You are my wife and you do as I wish. That's all it is, my dear." He kissed me on my brow. "Your old Otto loves you very much. And that is all the nicer. Not only to have a son, but to love his mother."

Even that was not the end of his strangeness. For that night in bed, when the light was out—perhaps he thought I would be more amenable in the dark with his arms around me—he said, "Luise, would you mind being married again, in a church?"

I was startled. I hadn't thought he was a particularly religious man. And I had thought he had wanted to avoid a big wedding.

When I pointed out this, he said quickly, "Just with my family there, of course."

My voice must have sounded too cool and cautious, for he held me more tightly and asked if I imagined he had been happy about that rather squalid ceremony at Dragor.

"It wasn't fair to you, my darling. And I thought the priest was very poor, although he charged a high enough fee. So let's pretend to my family that you are only my fiancée, and that we are going to have a proper wedding in the church at Maaneborg."

I drew away.

"I believe you intended this all the time."

He sighed. "You know me too well."

"I don't know you at all. I hadn't thought a wedding in church would be so important to you."

"It isn't. It's only for the feeling of my family. I'm afraid that even as my fiancée only you will have to overcome

46

their objections. I might as well tell you that my son and daughter adored their mother. So for future good relations in the house, it would be wise to make friends with them before you are my wife."

"But I *am* your wife."

Otto made an exasperated sound.

"You are not as stupid as you are pretending to be. A little private game isn't going to hurt us in the very least. It only means we won't share a bedroom for a week or two. Can't you understand that I am doing this for the sake of peace?"

"Then why didn't you take me to Maaneborg long ago and marry me there?" I asked sulkily.

He took me by the shoulders. His fingers hurt.

"Because I am a selfish old man and liked it this way," he shouted. "Let us say no more and go to sleep."

As if sleep were possible. I listened to his quiet breathing for ten minutes or more, then said cautiously,

"Otto, is it true that this would make things easier?"

He was awake instantly.

"Oh, infinitely. You can persuade Niels and Dinna to like you, and my mother won't be outraged, as she would be if she knew she had been kept in the dark."

"Then I suppose I must, as usual, let you have your own way."

His embrace was gentle and loving.

"We will have a small, quiet, beautiful wedding to make up for that other one." His voice took on a note of caution. "But once we have embarked on this course we must keep to it. You understand that?"

"I understand that I would look pretty silly exhibiting my wedding ring prematurely," I said drily.

"That's it. Wear it round your neck if you like. But keep it out of sight."

I was sick on the crossing from the little port of Kalunolborg in Zealand to Kolby Kaas on the tiny island of Samso. For one thing, the ferryboat was very small and the sea choppy. For another, I suppose it proved beyond doubt that I was in a delicate condition, because I wasn't habitually a bad sailor.

Otto viewed my green face sympathetically.

"You look terrible, *mine kaer,* but I still love you. Get a little color back before we arrive. I want to show you off."

I went to the little upper deck to let the wind blow on my face. The nausea was passing. I breathed deeply, feeling nothing at that moment but relief in the cessation of sickness.

This must have shown in my face, because a man came to stand beside me at the rail and said, sympathetically, "There is nothing worse than being a bad sailor, is there? At least, at the time."

"I'm not a bad sailor usually," I said, turning to look at him, trying to laugh. "You don't look as if you would even know the sensation."

He laughed, running his fingers through his dark windblown hair. It was true that he had a look of absolutely unassailable good health. His eyes shone with it.

"Oh, even I can be stricken when a gale comes up. Are you visiting friends on Samso?"

"Not exactly." I didn't want to be mysterious, but Otto, with his curious secretiveness, had made me nervous. Why didn't I say that I was going to Maaneborg?

Instead, I said, "And you? Are you visiting friends?"

"My family. I don't go home often enough, my mother tells me."

"You're Danish?"

"Couldn't you have guessed that?"

"Actually, no. Not by your accent or your looks. You speak English perfectly, and I thought most Danes were fair."

"How monotonous that would be." He had taken out a pipe, decided against trying to light it in the wind, and put it away again. "If you've come here to sightsee, you'll find only cows, and cheese factories, and wild birds. Perhaps," he added, giving me an assessing look, "you're a bird watcher?"

With a small stab of some dark emotion—pain? regret?— it frightened me to identify it—I realized how much I was enjoying this first spontaneous conversation with a native since I had come to Denmark. Otto's shadow had loomed very large over me all the time.

"I long to see storks nesting," I said. "I thought every chimney in Denmark had a pair. Where have they flown to?"

"Well, perhaps they don't like our central heating and our social security. You must make do with swans and geese."

The white geese waddling in clusters, like plump housemaids in white aprons on the beach at Dragor. Otto on the floor in his epileptic fit, and the geese honking outside, like the voice of a nightmare. The sun shining, and the clouds drifting, like white feathers behind lace curtains, and the priest who smelled of schnapps, saying, "Do you, Otto Frederick Gustav Winther, take this woman . . ."

"I always thought I liked geese more than I do," I said. He was looking at me with perhaps too much interest, and I added lamely, "I'm sure I'll like the swans."

"On the lake," he said.

"The lake? Where?"

"At Maaneborg." Seeing my startled look, which he took to be bewilderment, he explained, "My home. Look down there."

We were edging slowly into the wharf, and on it, I suddenly noticed, was a very large Rolls Royce. At least, it wasn't larger than ordinary, but it certainly seemed so on that pocket-sized jetty.

My seasick dizziness came back.

"Whose is it?" I was afraid I didn't need to ask. My Otto, the gentleman farmer, not too rich, just comfortable . . .

"The Greve's. As you would call him, the Count's. Count Otto Winther's." I don't think he noticed my returned pallor. He was smiling, a faint satirical smile. His eyes had a chill that was suddenly, startlingly familiar. "My dear brother's," he said.

Then he did notice my expression, and he asked, "What's that to you? I can see by your face that it means something. Do you know my brother?"

I burst out laughing. Not with amusement.

"I should say I do. He's my—fiancé." I had almost given the show away at the very beginning. Otto would have been furious.

The ferry had berthed with a slight bump, and people were beginning to disembark. In a moment Otto would be coming to look for me. And here I stood with his brother, the man I had seen in the theater and the shape of whose head I hadn't forgotten. I saw no resemblance in him to Otto—except that momentary chill in his dark eyes.

But otherwise, here was a serious face, not good-looking, almost plain, the nose too broad at the tip, the mouth a wide, straight line tending to severity. But with a quality of honesty, I thought. Or was I being fooled again? I had thought Otto honest.

"I don't think I believe you," he was saying, softly, with astonishment.

The shape of his head was pleasing, I thought abstractedly. A square brow, with that thick, springing dark hair. Yes, definitely pleasing. But his face was too serious. Frowning. Hostile?

"I hardly believe it myself, to tell the truth." I held out my hand to shake his. "Otto meant to surprise his family."

"But I talked to him at the bar not ten minutes ago."

"And he didn't mention me? Oh, how naughty he is! Has he always been secretive like this? He didn't tell me he was a count, either. He called himself just plain Herre."

"He doesn't use his title. Yes, he did mention you at the bar." The gray eyes watched me closely. "He said he was traveling with a friend and she was a bit under the weather."

Friend? Now why would he have said that?

"He must have been having a joke," I said. "I'd better go down. He'll be looking for me."

"He isn't a man to make jokes." Erik's voice came after me as I went down the companionway.

But he *was!* I told myself. He laughed so much. He loved fun.

Fun? Dismissing me like that, as if he were ashamed of me? And I seemed suddenly to have become a countess. He had kept that from me. How could he? Unless—the thought gripped me and I nearly fell—unless he were not only epileptic but also a little mad.

It appeared that he had been just about to come and look for me. He swaggered over to the companionway, really looking lordly, now that he had come back to his small kingdom.

"There you are, darling. Are you feeling better? I was just—" The smile left his eyes. He had seen Erik. "I see you two have met."

"Your brother," I said coldly, "is under the impression that he has been talking to an acquaintance of yours, not your fiancée."

Otto threw back his head and began to laugh merrily.

"That's it. I was stretching his leg. Isn't that how you say it in English? I wanted to surprise him. If it comes to that, he surprised me by being on this ferry."

"Otherwise our—engagement (I had nearly said marriage) would have gone on being a secret?" I wasn't mollified. I was remembering Otto's behavior on the night of the ballet, too. He went to such lengths to avoid his brother.

"No, my darling, don't be absurd." Otto tucked his arm comfortably in mine. "I only wanted to present you with more of a flourish, not when you're a little travel-worn and seasick. But now we make formal acquaintance. My brother Erik— Luise Amberley, my fiancée."

Erik gave a small stiff bow, and then we shook hands

again, since this seemed to be expected. The crew were bustling about, and looking at us sideways, expecting us to leave the boat.

"I am pleased to meet you, Luise. I hope you will be very happy. I can't say this is not a great surprise," he went on in a quiet, ironic voice, "though it scarcely needs to be, since Otto has been a widower for quite six months."

Only six months! But Otto had told me it was a year since his wife's death. So I had been sorry for him. I still was, but I was beginning to wonder uneasily what other small deceptions he had played.

"I imagine," Erik was saying, "that neither Mama nor Niels and Dinna know about Luise."

"No more than you do, old fellow," Otto said, his eyes twinkling.

"They're expecting you alone?"

"With a lady, I told them. Can you imagine their faces when they hear our news?"

"Perhaps I can," said Erik thoughtfully. "Well, at least I now get a ride. I was going to hire a taxi."

"Then let us get on our way," said Otto. "Come, Luise. I can read your face. Maaneborg at last, you are thinking."

My heart was beating with curious apprehension. It was not only the thought of meeting Otto's mother and children, and of acting the part of a countess, though that was bad enough. My brothers would be suitably surprised when they heard, and Tim, being opposed to the class system, would hoot with ironic laughter.

It was more than that. It was Maaneborg itself, the swans Erik had talked about, the moat . . .

"Otto, how could you not have told me about your title?" I murmured, out of Erik's hearing.

"Oh, that. It's nothing. I never use it. And don't think you are to be the Grevinde. You will be called Frue Winther, and nothing else. And also, don't imagine that we have flocks of servants. We haven't, as I have already told you. We aren't rich. The house is imposing enough, but we only live in half of it."

"Why, who lives in the other half?" I asked in surprise.

It was Erik, back at our side, who answered. The chauffeur, a square, short, elderly man with lumpy features, like a troll, had opened the door of the Rolls, and Otto was giving him a friendly greeting.

"The other half of Maaneborg is an old ladies' home,"

Erik was saying surprisingly. "Do you mean to say Otto hasn't even told you that?"

"I haven't because it doesn't need to concern Luise," Otto said. He patted my knee reassuringly as he sat beside me in the Rolls. "You need never encounter the old crows. We have our garden walled off from theirs. We've had to sacrifice the ballroom, unfortunately. It has been made into a hospital for them. But Cristina was ill for so many years, we never had balls. Now, of course—perhaps it's a pity. Perhaps I was too generous."

"It was you who donated the house?" I said, with relief. At last, out of this strange morning, something had come to my husband's credit.

Otto nodded, saying something about how in this socialistic age, one was ashamed to have too much property. This was spoiled by the curiously contemptuous look I caught Erik giving him.

But already it was clear Otto's dislike for Erik was returned in full measure.

"The old ladies are well-bred," he added, as if this would make their presence more acceptable to me. "They're all impoverished gentlefolk."

"And quite safe to speak to if Luise encounters them," Erik said drily.

"Luise will have no occasion to encounter them." Otto's voice held an undercurrent of distaste. I realized that although he had thought his philanthropy necessary, he didn't enjoy it at all. I was beginning to wonder, to my shame, why the gesture had been necessary. He must have gotten something important out of it. Erik must know what it was.

I felt a slight spasm of sickness and remembered my baby. Please let me go on loving his father, I was saying voicelessly.

Chapter Five

SO there it was, lying at the end of a long beech avenue. The ancient red brick castle with the high sloping eaves in the Scandinavian manner. It was built in two wings divided by a courtyard. There was a bridge, flanked on either side with an elaborate row of stone lions, over the moat, and then the stone archway into the courtyard. The water in the moat, flecked with patches of water lilies, was a dark, swooning green that must turn black when the sky was dark. Beyond the house I caught a glimpse of a wide lake bordered with reeds, the water turning alternately dark and silver as the wind stroked it.

The house had tall turrets on either side, with circular windows that must give wonderful views of the estate. I wondered if the old ladies were able to climb the winding turret stairs. Set in the walls at regular intervals there were stone faces, petrified and frowning. They looked as if they might have been the faces of enemies of the Winther family perpetuated in these unflattering guises. They grimaced sourly down on me as I got out of the car. I could hear crows cawing with a raucous sound.

It seemed an age ago that I had imagined I was being brought to a cozy, comfortable farmhouse. But I was realizing already that this Gothic edifice was the only possible background for Otto, who was so much larger than life himself. Where was my intelligence, that I hadn't guessed this from the beginning? I had been hypnotized from start to finish.

I shouldn't say finish, because I was still in my tranced state and we still had a lot of life to live. I had only to glance at Otto beside me, his big blond head not unlike those of the lions on the bridge, to understand why I weakly gave in to him most of the time. Whether it was the effect of the Rolls Royce and the chauffeur, and now this first sight of Maaneborg, I didn't know, but Otto seemed to have grown in impressiveness. Beside him, I felt small and ordinary. Erik, on my other side, was also an unalarming life-size. But Otto was every inch the lord of the manor, and must, I supposed, be forgiven his eccentric behavior.

Although I wasn't too overawed to intend to have the whole thing out with him as soon as we were alone.

An elderly man, stooped and white-whiskered, whom Otto called Jacob, let us in.

We crossed a hall with a black and white tiled floor, and an immense ceiling.

Jacob said something in answer to a question of Otto's. I heard a name: Frue Dorothea.

"My mother is in the drawing room," Otto explained to me.

"Frue Dorothea?"

"That is what she likes to be called. I told you we have no use for titles."

I looked back to see if Erik was coming, but he had stopped to speak to the chauffeur.

"Now remember," Otto whispered.

Why? I asked silently. Why? If his mother didn't approve of me, would I be cast out and divorced as secretly as I had been married?

The drawing room was too magnificent for my taste. I wondered if the old ladies, in the other half of the house, had a room as grand as this, with its painted ceiling, panoramic pictures of battles and pink frosty dawns over marshland, heavy ornate furniture and tapestries.

But some sun came through the tall embrasured windows at the west end of the room, where, on a yellow couch, sat a gray-haired woman. She looked up as we came in, then put down the book she had been reading, and rose, showing that she was a woman at least six feet tall, very thin, very straight, and completely composed.

She might have been expecting us. But if she showed no surprise, neither did she show pleasure. Here, I thought, was the Snow Queen herself, the thin icy face, the cold blue eyes. Otto went forward and greeted her, kissing her on the cheek and saying something in Danish.

Then he turned to me with his warm smile, and I loved him that minute, if only because of the contrast of his warmth with his mother's coldness.

"Mama, this is a friend of mine, Luise Amberley. She is English so we will all be able to practice our English!"

The narrow, cool, dry hand of Frue Dorothea touched mine.

"How do you do, Miss Amberley? It is Miss?"

I bent my head slightly. I couldn't answer. Otto was squeezing my other hand.

"You should have let us know you were coming, Otto. You are staying?"

"But of course. Luise is getting to know Denmark. She writes for a London newspaper. Perhaps we can persuade her to say something flattering about us. She's interested in our experiment with the impoverished ladies."

Frue Dorothea, who had a long nose and big teeth, was very plain and overwhelmingly patrician, the kind of woman who turned ugliness into an asset. She was obviously wondering furiously who I was and what I meant to Otto, but she wouldn't dream of asking. At least, not directly.

"Then I'll have a room prepared. Yours is ready, as you know it always is, Otto. It's a long time since you honored us with a visit."

"Do you blame me?" Otto muttered, and his mother said sympathetically, and with deliberation:

"Of course I don't, my dear boy. One knows what unhappy associations there are here for you. Perhaps he has told you, Miss Amberley? He has been mourning his wife."

I remembered Otto's gay laughter in Majorca, his whole air of having at last escaped from an unhappy marriage. What went on here? A morbid desire to keep him tied to his dead wife?

Otto quickly changed the subject by asking where Niels was. And his daughter, Dinna.

His mother gave a tolerant laugh.

"Oh, Niels has a new car and is trying it out."

"A new car? Is this your doing?"

Frue Dorothea was not in the least intimidated by Otto's scowling anger. I was beginning to think she was, and always had been, more than a match for him.

"It was his birthday. I didn't forget, even if you did."

"Mama, the boy is spoiled!"

"One must make up for his father's neglect," Frue Dorothea said smoothly. "But we're boring Miss Amberley. Which room do you wish her to have? The usual one?"

There was a look in her eyes that could hardly be described as a leer; she was much too patrician for that sort of thing. But it was certainly suggestive. Was there a room where Otto had girls while his sick wife lay dying? After all, Cristina had taken several years to die, or so he had told me, and he was a virile man. There was probably a back staircase to the room from his bedroom. There usually was in these old castles.

I didn't know whether my guess was right or wrong, but I

55

did know that I wasn't going to stay here to be insulted and patronized by this unpleasant woman.

I turned sharply on my heel.

Otto caught my arm. "Luise!"

I was livid. I could scarcely speak for anger. So much for all our pacts, and all my resolve to humor Otto's eccentricities.

"Leave me, Otto. I don't want to stay here. I intend going back to Copenhagen at once, unless you feel like telling your mother the truth."

"The truth?" said Frue Dorothea, delicately and coolly.

Otto became a big bumbling boy, intimidated by this exceptionally strong-minded woman. But I knew him pretty well by now. His embarrassment wasn't entirely sincere. While he smiled first at me, then at his mother, his eyes remained quite cold.

"I should have explained at once, Mama." I waited, biting my lip. Now he will say, This is my wife. Instead he said, as he had said to Erik, "Luise is my fiancée."

"So," said Frue Dorothea, on a long slow breath.

One would have thought from the look on her face that Otto had said, Luise is my executioner. What, for goodness sake, was it to do with her if he married again?

But now I was beginning to understand his reluctance to present his mother with a *fait accompli*. She certainly did need to be smoothed down and softened. If I *were* to live here happily we would have to come to some kind of a pact. I looked around the big impressive room with its cold grandeur, and was filled with panic at the thought of trying to live here at all. It was medieval. I could imagine keys rattling in locks, dungeons, instruments of torture. Look at those battle scenes decorating the walls! In a drawing room! This was a far cry from gay Copenhagen, and even from quiet Dragor, with its flocks of geese.

"Then I must greet you again, Miss Amberley," Frue Dorothea said, not intending to be caught lacking in manners. "This is a great surprise. I think you must know it's scarcely more than six months since Otto's wife died. I hope you aren't planning to marry too soon."

I found that I was being as hypnotized by her as I had been by Otto. I almost said that there was no hurry at all. Through the windows I saw a cloud passing over the lake, and the water rippling like black silk. A cool ripple passed over my skin, too, as I came back to reality and remembered the baby about which Otto and I had been so happy. Could I face this dragon of a woman with a premature birth?

I knew I couldn't, and answered quickly, before Otto could speak.

"Actually, we were. Weren't we, Otto? We thought very quietly, in a few days' time."

"At the Maaneborg Kirken, Mama," Otto said, holding my arm tightly.

I swear that Frue Dorothea had grown three inches in height. She looked down at me with those eyes of glittering blue ice, and said, "Where Cristina is buried?" in the most outrageous conversational tone, so that I felt as if I were driving my high heels into that poor woman's grave, standing on her body to get Otto.

"Oh, come, Mama," said Otto—and thank goodness he had got back his wheedling jovial voice!—"what is there to wait for? Life goes by too quickly. I haven't had a wife since Dinna's birth and you know it. Let people say what they like. Do you honestly admit that you have ever cared what people said?"

"No, but I care about Niels' and Dinna's happiness."

Otto nuzzled his lips against my neck.

"And can you honestly say Luise looks like a wicked stepmother? She's beautiful and happy and gay, and Maaneborg is going to stop being such a haunted miserable place when she lives here. So you must make up your mind to it, Mama. And I ask you not to prejudice Niels and Dinna."

As abruptly as I had done a few minutes ago, Frue Dorothea turned on her heel. But she was only going to pull the bell rope by the fireplace. A servant, a rosy-faced old woman in a white apron, answered the bell and Frue Dorothea said something in Danish. The woman bobbed and went off, and Frue Dorothea explained to me that Birgitte would prepare a room for me. If I would come she would show me the way.

It was awful being abandoned by Otto. What a coward I had become! But I followed Frue Dorothea's tall figure up a broad wooden staircase and along a long corridor to a room that was quite charming. Birgitte was bustling about, plumping up pillowcases and putting a linen cover on the down quilt on the carved four-poster bed.

Frue Dorothea drew back the curtains and showed me the view of beechwoods and lake. From this side of the house the other wing was invisible.

There was a walled garden beneath the window. Climbing

roses flourished over the old bricks. There was a sundial and a pretty little fountain with spouting dolphins.

"This is our garden," said Frue Dorothea. "The ladies have another one on the other side of the wall. You won't hear or see anything of them. We have given up half our house, but not our privacy."

Who gave it up? Otto? And you hated it, didn't you, you old patrician. Perhaps I can persuade Otto to move you over to the other side of the wall to be with your contemporaries. And I would, too, if I got half a chance.

"I'll leave you now. I'm sure you would like to rest after your journey."

It was an order. So she could pick Otto's brain, turn him to putty. Do everything, in fact, but persuade him not to marry me. For that last, although she didn't know it, was an impossibility.

I lifted my chin. I was feeling better now. The room, and the view, and Birgitte's cosy face, had reassured me.

"When will I meet Otto's children?"

"They're hardly children. Niels is twenty-one and Dinna seventeen. You'll meet them at dinner." Her face changed. She was looking past me, through the window. "Why, there's Erik."

"Yes, he crossed over with us."

"You mean he's in this plot, too?"

I found I could match her for coldness.

"Plot? I don't understand." We tried to outstare each other, but regrettably, my eyes fell first. "No, Erik knows nothing about it. We only met him by chance on the ferry. Anyway, why should he mind?"

Frue Dorothea looked at me a moment longer, then said, "We will talk more later," and swept out of the room. Old Birgitte was smiling at me in a welcoming way. And I, looking out of the window to see what Erik was doing, saw him in the garden below, talking to a girl.

That must be Dinna. She had fair, almost white hair falling around her face and to her waist. She wore a white dress and looked like the Snow Queen's daughter.

Snow Queen and Snow Queen's daughter—what was all this fairy-tale stuff I was letting myself get carried away with?

At least Erik looked comfortably ordinary, with his untidy dark head and spare body. He hadn't Otto's height or size. Actually, Otto was a little flabby, but then he was ten years older than Erik. I wondered why Erik wasn't married. He must be very eligible. I was glad that he hadn't shown the antagonism that his mother had toward Otto and me.

The thought came to me that one day I might need to turn to someone with honest eyes like Erik.

But not yet. I still had the Grevinde Dorothea to vanquish. I was myself, all unwittingly, a countess. The situation was highly intriguing. I was determined to enjoy it.

But when I had rested. For when the old servant, Birgitte, had left the room, I found that I was deadly tired. I lay down on the bed and pulled the soft white quilt over me and went instantly to sleep.

I woke a long time later to far-off cackling laughter.

Otto's mother, and she has gone mad, I thought, half asleep, half in a nightmare.

Then there was someone else laughing, also in the dry croaking way of the aged, and I realized that the sound must come from over the garden wall in the old ladies' garden. Though invisible, they were not inaudible.

Otto had made me take off my wedding ring. I had resented this perhaps most of all, but I had obeyed him. I kept it in my handbag. Waking up in this strange room, and to the sound of that eerie laughter, I felt intensely forlorn and in need of reassurance. My situation wasn't so enjoyably intriguing after all. The house was completely silent. No one had told me what time dinner was. I seemed to have been put in this room and forgotten.

Were they all talking about me downstairs?

The long northern summer days went on until nearly midnight. It was only six o'clock, and the sun still glittered on the lake, and shone warmly on the old faded red brick garden walls. I leaned out of the window and saw that a flight of steps led from a downstairs room into the garden. Perhaps I could get into it without being noticed. The air would refresh me, and give me courage to face the evening.

I could smell the roses. At the end of the lawn there was a glassy green gleam of water, which meant that the garden was bordered by the moat. This was picturesque, but had a slightly prisonlike effect. Perhaps it didn't seem so when one was in the garden.

It wasn't difficult to find the way down. On the ground floor there was a tiled passage leading to a kind of conservatory or solarium, which had tall glass doors leading into the garden.

It was wonderful being outdoors in the warmth of the

early evening sunshine. I strolled about, sniffing the roses, trailing my hand in the softly splashing fountain, not caring whether I was being watched from the windows or not. I walked to the edge of the moat, which had a cool, faintly slimy smell, and turned back to study the house, identifying my bedroom window and wondering whose were the other rooms.

I tried to realize that I was now the mistress of this mansion, with its ugly twin turrets and its high tiled roof. Instead, I sighed for the cosy farmhouse I had imagined. Erik said there were swans on the lake, but I wanted waddling geese and ducks and chickens. My heart was sinking again. The goose girl had become the princess, and she wasn't very happy about it.

There was a low murmur of voices coming from beyond the wall. It must be the old ladies gossiping as they sat in the evening sun. I wondered what they were saying? Had the news filtered through that Herre Winther. the so recent widower, had come home with a new bride? I wished I could hear what they were saying, but they would be speaking in Danish, of course.

I strolled restlessly. That was a pretty climbing rose, pure white and cascading like snowflakes. It was arched over a trellis. No, it wasn't a trellis, it was a little green door in the wall. I took hold of the big rusty key and it turned in my hand. The door creaked. It wasn't jammed with age. It was perfectly usable, and would open if I wanted it to.

I meant only to take an inquisitive peep into the old ladies' prison. But as I gently pulled the door open, a voice just on the other side said very clearly in English, "Since I speak her language I will take it upon myself to varn her."

Another voice, querulous and cynical, answered, "You are not the only one who has had an education, Emilie. Pray do not show yourself off so much. And if you are so clever, you would know the word is *warn,* not *varn.*"

"That is what I said. The girl should be varned. She is marrying a villain."

"A villain who gives us all this? Emilie, how can you be so ungrateful?"

"For my part, there are too many stairs to climb," Emilie said tetchily, and I, with my hand on the door, sighed impatiently over the uncoordinated conversations of the aged.

"You have still too big ideas, Emilie. You should accept that you are now a charity. What else do you think Herre Winther should do? Put in a lift?"

"It is the least," the querulous voice muttered. "And I must correct you, Sophie. We are not a charity, we are the Greve's conscience. Gratitude is quite unnecessary. It is we who do him a favor. So."

"And the girl should be warned?"

"About his habits, of course. It wasn't only servants' rumors about poor Cristina."

"Locked up and beaten?" said Sophie as if it were the greatest joke. Her croaking chuckle was the one I had heard from my bedroom window.

"I did not say beaten," Emilie replied frostily.

"She was ill and kept in her room. That is not being locked up."

"There were tales." Emilie was stubborn and not to be denied her scandal.

"Perhaps she worked a tapestry with her hair, like the Princess Leonora Cristina? You live in fairy tales, Emilie."

"There were things that are not fairy tales at Maaneborg," Emilie insisted.

"Oh, so. In the far-off days. Every old castle has those. There is a *spogelse* in the ballroom, I am told."

"You mean a haunt, a ghost? If you speak English, speak English. Anyway, we get away from the subject. The girl should be varned."

"Oh, tch! Frue Dorothea will take care of that. It is none of your business, Emilie, if you will allow me to say so. It is getting chilly. I am going indoors."

"Vait for me!" Emilie called. "You go too fast. Oh, un-kind, unkind," she muttered.

And at that stage, I couldn't resist opening the creaking door and going into the garden.

I saw a stout woman in flying scarves walking quickly across the lawn toward the house, and limping behind her like a lame crow, a sharp-angled, small, white-headed figure in black.

I followed her, and took her arm. She looked up in surprise, her wrinkled face dominated by a pair of very alert black-currant eyes. Then she said, *"Tak. Tak,"* obviously thinking I must be an attendant. She made a comment in Danish which I guessed meant she had not seen me before, and I said:

"I'm afraid I speak only English."

"Is that true? Then you will have a difficult time. All the ladies here have not education."

She certainly was an infuriating old creature, the way she flaunted the rags of her education as her one remaining asset. I supposed others of the inmates had perhaps a diamond brooch or a tarnished tiara to flaunt.

"Will you stop a minute, please?" I said. "I heard you talking through the wall."

"Through the wall?" The black eyes blinked suspiciously.

"Yes, about me. And about my husband."

I was too agitated by that overheard conversation to be careful of my secret. It was out before I realized it. But only to this old creature who was now mumbling her jaws as if she were quite senile, and who would probably forget what I had said before she reached the house.

"The bride-to-be?" she mumbled. "And a good-looking one, too. But Herre Otto would see to that, of course. A fine-looking man, Herre Otto. I give you my congratulations, froken."

"But you said I should be warned. I heard you. What should I be warned about?"

"I was always taught that eavesdropping was not a ladylike occupation," the exasperating old woman said evasively.

"But it was not good manners you intended to warn me about. Was it?"

Emilie glanced around quickly. The figure of her friend was just disappearing indoors. Some more old women wandered in the distance, far out of earshot.

She clutched my hand.

"If you ask for advice, I will give it to you. Don't marry him. It will be trouble, trouble, trouble."

Some instinct that must have been purely preservatory made me open my bag and take out my wedding ring. I slipped it on my finger and held out my hand.

"But look! It's too late. I am already Frue Winther. In any case," I added, with a return to sense, "I couldn't be persuaded to change my mind at this stage. And especially if you won't tell me the reason why I should be warned."

"Dear, dear," said the old woman. "Dear, dear, dear, dear." She made a snatch at my hand again, then abruptly changed her mind and began to limp away, one shoulder higher than the other, more than ever like a bird with a broken wing. As she went I heard her saying, "Too late, poor thing, too late," like the worst kind of Victorian melodrama.

In her English education she must have been brought up on Wilkie Collins, I thought. Locked rooms, tortured brides, villainous husbands . . .

What utter nonsense! My poor Otto wouldn't hurt a fly. His only secret was his epilepsy of which he was so ashamed.

And there was Otto, coming through the door in the wall. I thought I detected annoyance in his face, but as he came up to me he smiled, and his face was perfectly sunny.

"What are you doing in here, Luise? Isn't there enough garden on the other side?"

"Yes, of course. It's a beautiful garden. And there is the lake, too. But I'm an inquisitive person, hadn't you realized?"

"You wanted to see how our elderly guests are treated? Did they complain to you?"

The steel behind his eyes again. He didn't like complaints. Or questions.

"I didn't talk to them, except to say good evening," I lied. "I don't expect they would understand me."

"You mustn't underestimate them. Most of them speak another language. German or English. But I did explain, Luise, that this part of the castle is entirely separate. It mustn't worry you."

"Why should it worry me?" I asked in surprise.

"Age is depressing. Rheumatism. Heart troubles. Senility. Perhaps I see it not too far in the distance for myself. So come back, and shut the door. It is only left unlocked for the convenience of the gardeners." He took my arm, and led me to the serenity and emptiness of the other garden. For a moment I thought it more melancholy than the one I had just left.

"Luise, you're looking rested, but still anxious. What is it? Didn't you like my mother?"

"On the contrary, she didn't like me."

"You were a shock to her. You must give her a few days to get used to the idea of your being here. She has been mistress since Cristina's death, and for years before that, when Cristina was ill. She's possessive and strong-minded. But you will soon charm her."

He kissed my brow. He was in one of his tenderest moods. This large gentle man with the smiling eyes a villain? How absurd.

"So now you must admit keeping our marriage a secret was wise. In a week or two Mama will come round, and we'll have another happy event. So?"

"And your children?"

"Niels isn't home yet. One doesn't know whether or not he favors us with his presence at dinner. But my daughter is waiting to meet you. She will be your attendant at our wedding. Doesn't that make you happy?"

"I suppose it does."

"Suppose? Is that all?"

"Otto, there are so many things we must talk about. Am I to be stuck in that very charming bedroom all alone?"

That pleased him, although he misinterpreted what I meant.

"You would prefer a room nearer to mine?"

"And have you sneaking up the stairs secretly in the middle of the night? To your wife!"

"My darling, it's for such a short time. I thought you understood."

"I understand nothing," I said flatly.

"Then we must talk, of course. After dinner tonight. There's a nice walk down by the lake. You shall tell me everything that troubles you, and perhaps the moon will shine."

"I sometimes think that's what it all is," I muttered. "Moonshine."

"Moonshine is what? I didn't hear you."

"It's for children. For Niels and Dinna." You're too old for it, I nearly said, cruelly, but disciplined myself enough to say formally, "Not for us."

"So the moon is forbidden?" he teased. "That's quite a problem, since you are to live in a castle named for the moon."

I suppose that was the crux of all my worrying, this great Gothic edifice that towered above us. How *could* Otto have deceived me so outrageously? Suddenly the humor of it struck me, and I began to laugh uncontrollably.

"Now what is it that you find so funny?" Otto asked, with some impatience.

I couldn't tell him. I couldn't say that most women who had been too gullible found that their persuasive lover was a ne'er-do-well, a con man, or something. I found that mine had a title and a castle. Really, whatever was I complaining about?

All the same, these surprises were rather too stringent a test of a love that hadn't been too certain in the first place.

What else? Was I going to be rash enough to probe into Otto's treatment of his first wife?

No, leave it. Shut your ears to the rumors of old women. Stick to the *status quo*. Think of all Otto's endearing qualities, and take the rest as eccentricities. You've got to live with the man. So, as the Danes said.

Chapter Six

THERE was a tap on my door when I was dressing for dinner. I called, "Come in," and the old servant, Birgitte, came in, her cosy face beaming.

She handed me a jeweler's box, said in a slow English that the master had sent it, and withdrew.

The box held the most gorgeous ring I had ever seen. At first I thought it was a topaz, then realized that it must be one of those fabulous stones, a cinnamon diamond. The setting was in an antique style that made the ring very heavy. It was really much too large for my hand, and too ornate, also, but it was a ravishing thing.

The note accompanying it, folded small and tucked inside the box, said:

"This is the betrothal ring of the Winthers. It is yours now, my darling." That was fine, and made my heart miss a beat. But the last sentence took away most of my pleasure. "Wear it tonight. Mama will be looking for it."

I slid it on the finger from which I had that morning removed my wedding ring, and then the last of my pleasure vanished as I thought of the sick thin hand the ring must have been removed from. Cristina's. And before her, all those other generations of Winther brides who had yielded up the ring to a new, probably resented daughter-in-law—or to death.

I was bitterly impatient with myself. Other people had heirlooms and took the greatest pleasure in them. They didn't see the skeletons behind them. Why must only I have these heavy, somber thoughts?

I threw the ring on the dressing table, and thought that if I must wear it this evening, I had better change my dress. I had put on the one Otto had bought for me in Stockholm. It was black with a lot of gold embroidery. It was a little too grand for my taste, but I had thought that looking grand would help me through this evening.

Now, contrarily, I wanted to look excessively simple. So I chose the short black sleeveless dress that I had wanted to be married in, in Dragor. I would wear no jewelry but the ring, and do my hair rather severely in a coil on the top of my head.

Well, I certainly didn't look like a pregnant wife that way. I didn't exactly look simple and inconspicuous, either. If I had walked into the Mirabelle or the Caprice restaurants in London looking like this, everyone would have given me approving glances. But at Maaneborg?

I got the glances, all right. Critical, curious, hostile. Even Otto's face fell as I walked into the room.

He had a more flamboyant taste than I had, and I knew at once that he was disappointed that I had chosen to dress in this understated way. He came toward me and took my arm, and practically swept me into the room.

Then I realized that he was suppressing anger, not with me, but with the group standing in front of the huge fireplace. His mother in a long trailing gray gown, a tall, fair-headed young man with pale blue eyes and light eyelashes who must be his son, Niels, and the blond girl I had seen in the garden.

They were all looking at me. I lifted my chin to hide my timidity. It was bad enough to be the daughter-in-law of that frozen woman, Frue Dorothea, but to be stepmother to these two poised young people, with their unfriendly faces, was truly alarming.

Otto made rapid introductions.

I held out my hand, and Niels and Dinna gave me quick, reluctant handshakes. At first I thought Niels was going to refuse even this politeness. He made no effort at all to hide his hostility. I had always thought the extremely fair Scandinavian men rather weak and anemic-looking, but there was nothing weak in this young man's arrogant, contemptuous glance. His lip curled and his pale blue eyes were insolent.

The girl was less bold, but I could see she took her lead from her brother. She was a delicate-looking young thing with a long slender neck, and was going to be very pretty. But at the moment she was pouting in a rude way that was scarcely becoming. I couldn't think how that elegant old woman, their grandmother, could permit them to display such bad manners.

But her own were not much better. One could not have said the ice had cracked since our first meeting. She gave me a frigid greeting, and suggested that since it was after eight (a hint that I was late coming down), we should go into dinner immediately. She had obviously given orders that all conversation was to be in English, because Dinna said, speaking fluent English, "But Grandmama, Onkel Erik isn't here."

"Yes, he is," said Erik, at the doorway. He came in without hurry, a large gray wolfhound at his heels. He put his hand affectionately on Dinna's head, ruffling her hair, then turned to look at me.

That was the first admiring glance I had had since I had arrived, so perhaps that was why I was so pleased about it.

"Why, Luise, you look rejuvenated." He turned to his mother and the two youngsters. "I must explain that I first met Luise on the ferry, and she was a little seasick. Green isn't the most becoming color for a girl's face."

Seasick on a ferry! I saw the added contempt in Niels' and Dinna's faces.

"But don't look so frightened," Erik whispered to me, as we followed Frue Dorothea to the dining room.

"Surely it wasn't that stormy today," Frue Dorothea's voice floated back.

"Luise isn't used to such small boats," Otto said.

"I'm petrified," I whispered back to Erik, indicating with a glance the magnificent dining room, which was even more overpowering than the drawing room. Imagine sitting here to eat day after day in those forbidding high-backed chairs at that massive table!

"You'll have to get over that, won't you?" Erik's voice had its quiet ironic quality. "Or else you'll have to run away."

But it was too late to do that. With an awful sinking feeling, I knew that that was exactly what I did want to do. I had wanted to from the first moment of setting foot inside this great cold castle. It was an impossible place—dark, heavy, out of date, haunted.

The branches of lighted candles on the dinner table, vying with the fading daylight, and the smell of hot food did nothing to dispel my shivering feeling of dislike.

"But you'll fit in very well, you know," said Erik. "That dress is wonderful."

I held up my hand. "And this?"

He looked at the diamond briefly. "Too heavy. I was always thankful to be the younger brother, so my wife wouldn't have to have her hand weighed down with that."

"You make it sound like a ball and chain."

I laughed. I was surprised that I could.

"Luise!" Frue Dorothea's voice pricked our small bubble of laughter. "Will you please sit here."

Otto on my right, at the head of the table, Erik on my

left. The two fair sulky faces opposite. Frue Dorothea at the other end. That was my place, really. I would see that I got it, too, before very long.

The extraordinary thing about that meal was that no single word was said about Otto's and my marriage. We talked of countries and travel, of Niels' new car, of the friend who had invited Dinna to a party in Copenhagen, to which she begged to be allowed to go, of the opening ceremony of a just-completed block of offices of which Erik had been the architect.

I sat back in the carved chair, and suddenly gave a small scream as something wet and rough touched my hand.

Erik laughed heartily. "It's only Anna. She likes you."

I saw the golden eyes of the wolfhound bitch looking up at me with something that did look a bit like adoration.

"Is that her name? Anna? I heard the old ladies in the garden today talking about a *spogelse* in the ballroom, and I thought for a minute this was it."

"Good," Erik applauded. "You have remembered your first Danish word, even if your pronunciation is a little odd."

"It means a ghost, doesn't it?"

"Luise, may I ask how you came to be talking to the old women?" Frue Dorothea asked, the usual frost in her voice.

"She only went through the garden door," Otto said. "She didn't realize it was forbidden territory."

"Forbidden? Oh, no, surely not." The food and wine, after the long exhausting day, had been exactly what I needed. I was tremendously heartened to find my spirit coming back. I had been a bit afraid I was going to turn into a timid ingratiating creature simply for the sake of peace. But Erik's conversation, and this silly groveling hound at my feet, had helped, too.

"I don't intend to ignore a charity right on our doorstep," I said. "Since my husband has been generous enough to found this home, I certainly mean to give my services in any way that I can."

"Aren't you being a little premature, Luise?" Frue Dorothea said, after a small silence.

It was Otto who was being ingratiating, not me. He said quickly, "If you mean Luise is premature in referring to me as her husband, that's simply splitting hairs, Mama."

"Is it?"

The implacable voice, and the cool stares of the youngsters opposite, nearly threw me again. I deliberately lifted my hand, and let the candlelight play on the yellow diamond.

Then I looked into Otto's eyes, and murmured, "It was a forgivable mistake, wasn't it, darling? It was only because of my impatience."

Otto lifted my hand and kissed it. Niels made a rude sound of disgust, then stood up and abruptly left the table. Dinna turned to look after him, her eyes wide and uncertain, and just a little ashamed as they flicked back to me. Erik watched Otto and me with interest. And I realized that I had just made my debut as an actress.

Frue Dorothea had said nothing more, but as if in answer to her silence, Otto made an announcement.

"I have been this afternoon to make arrangements for our marriage. It will take place next Wednesday, at two o'clock. I hope that will be convenient to you, my darling, and that you won't allow my son's extraordinary rudeness to distress you."

"Oh, Papa, how can you do this!" Dinna burst out. "Now Niels will get in his car and drive at a hundred miles an hour. You know how he is."

Otto's face had gone the dark color that I dreaded, since it could herald one of his attacks.

"Yes, I know how he is, and I also know that it will serve him right if he breaks his neck. As for you, Dinna, I thought you loved your father and cared a little about his happiness."

"Papa, I do! But Niels—and our poor darling Mama—" Dinna was suddenly a child, with a distraught face, torn by conflicting loyalties. She stared at Otto with appealing eyes, then, like her brother, abruptly fled from the room.

Otto leaned back, breathing heavily.

"Perhaps, Mama, now that the young have left us, you would like to complete the ruin of our dinner. What would you like to say? Or Erik? Perhaps you can add to this torture of Luise."

With the greatest deliberation, Frue Dorothea began. Fixing her cold gaze on me, she said, "Before Luise takes this irrevocable step, Otto, she must, of course, be warned."

Otto's face began to darken again. And I was hearing echoes of the voices in the garden.

"What am I to be warned about?" I asked.

"Nothing," said Otto violently. "Nothing that you don't know. My mother is referring to my attacks. That's all."

There was no doubt that the old woman was deflated.

"You know about them already, Luise?"

Yes, he had one the day after we were married, I was about to say. I nearly did say it, too, in pure defiance. But that would make Otto more angry, and I was alarmed about the consequences. I really rather hated those small fits he had, although he assured me that they were unimportant.

"I haven't kept them a secret," Otto was saying. "Luise isn't frightened of them. Did you think she would be?"

"I thought she may be afraid of having your children," Frue Dorothea said. I looked at her in amazement, wondering what kind of a woman she could be to make such a calculatingly cruel remark to her own son. Or perhaps, what kind of a son Otto had been to her. That last thought, of which I was heartily ashamed, made me get up and go to stand beside Otto, putting my arm around his shoulders. He immediately took my hand and pressed it affectionately. Erik was watching us. Erik hadn't contributed a word to that unhappy conversation.

"Otto told me that the trouble isn't hereditary," I said quietly. "And in any case I wouldn't be afraid."

All the same, I wasn't too sure of anything, now. I thought of the tiny foetus in my womb, and wondered if I were in the process of creating, unforgivably, another flawed human being.

"After all, Niels is perfectly all right. Isn't he?"

"Oh, Niels," said Frue Dorothea in a strange voice, which immediately made me wonder if that spoiled young man, with his bad manners and his undisciplined life, were running away from some private agony.

"I don't think you should make Luise nervous, Mama," said Erik.

"I was only telling her something she should know."

"So now you have told her," Otto said. "I was damaged at my birth, and now you damage me more."

"Perhaps Luise will refuse to believe that I was trying to help her," Frue Dorothea said. Then she, too, got up from the table, and without an apology, glided from the room.

I was left with the two brothers. Otto immediately filled his glass with the very good port we had been drinking. Erik lit a cigarette. I had the feeling that he was reluctant to leave us alone.

"Well, I didn't promise you a merry homecoming, Luise, and you didn't get one," Otto said. "Have another drink and get the chill of this place out of your bones."

Erik filled my glass, and looked at me quizzically.

"So you have exactly a week to change your mind. To be scared off."

Was he imitating his mother's tactics? I looked at Otto,

expecting him to explode with anger again. Instead, he burst into a roar of merry laughter.

"I think you underestimate Luise, Erik. Did you think I would marry a girl so easily scared? She's tougher than that. Aren't you, *mine kaer?*"

The now familiar tender address, and Otto's returned good humor, didn't reassure me. I gave a deep sigh and leaned back. Then the carving of the chairback stuck into my spine. These chairs must have been designed for the purpose of keeping drowsy, too well dined guests awake.

"I wish Niels and Dinna didn't hate me."

"They don't hate you, only the idea of you."

"Did they love their mother so much?"

Nobody answered that, but Erik said, "Get them to talk to you. Dinna will come round soon enough. She's a bit slavish to Niels at present, but it's only because she has no one else."

"But Niels?" I couldn't see myself ever liking that sulky young man.

"Niels can go to the devil," Otto said. "I am forty-six and you are twenty-six, and we will not have our plans upset by a young idiot." He got up. "Come. We were going to walk by the lake. Do you want a wrap? It might be chilly."

It was chilly in here, in spite of the warmth of the many candles. I felt gooseflesh on my bare arms. The thought of the wind over the dark water, and the reeds rustling, was uninviting. I found there was nothing more I wanted to say to Otto after all. I wanted to go upstairs and shut my door on everybody. I no longer minded sleeping alone. Indeed, the thought represented pure bliss. My week of freedom seemed suddenly much too short. I hadn't seen the room I would be expected to share with Otto, and had no desire to see it. The bed, I was afraid, would be enormous and suffocating.

I suppose it should be rather shaming to admit that one would want to lock the door on one's husband so soon after marriage, but under the present circumstances, I had no hesitation in doing so. The dubiety of my position had given me what I hoped was only a temporary aversion to Otto's touch.

So I turned the key in the lock, and some time later I was woken by a gentle tapping and the sound of the handle turning.

"Luise!"

It was my husband. Should I blame him? Yes, I should. He had invented this crazy situation, so he could make the best of it. I knew he wouldn't dare to make much noise in case he woke anyone else. I lay pretending not to hear his insistent tapping, and presently he gave up and went away. It was two o'clock. My sleep destroyed, I got up and went to look out of the open window.

The moon was shining over the still garden and the far off, darkly gleaming lake. The scene might have been English, yet somehow it was intensely foreign. That bird suddenly chattering—what was it? That cool wind in my face—had it blown over miles of marshland inhabited only by birds and wild hares and old burial grounds of Vikings? Was that faint, distant slurring sound the wash of the cold Baltic on the lonely coast?

Shivering, I crept back to bed and huddled beneath the soft quilt, as cosy as the foetus in my womb. We would both stay here and be safe, I thought, with the wild impracticability of early morning thoughts. Safe from what? I didn't know, but first and foremost I had to protect my child.

Chapter Seven

MORNING came, with the sound of the big hound barking below my window, and a girl laughing. I had intended to ring for breakfast to be brought to my room, and not to make an appearance until lunchtime. I had no desire to have a frigid conversation with Frue Dorothea or to encounter Otto's rude son and daughter. Or even to encounter Otto, heaven forgive me. Though I think I was more in need of help than forgiveness.

But abruptly I changed my mind. The sun was shining, for one thing. I didn't want to hide in a darkened room on a sunny morning.

And Dinna's laugh was infectious. For it was Dinna throwing a ball in the garden for the great lolloping hound to pursue. Niels was there, too. The sun turned his fair hair to silver. From this distance, he looked like a nice ordinary young man, shouting to the dog and joining in Dinna's laughter.

Then suddenly, both of them were still. Dinna dropped the ball she was about to throw, and Niels stood a minute looking toward the house, before he ostentatiously turned away and began walking swiftly out of sight.

Otto had come into the garden.

Neither of his children had had the grace to speak to him.

No, I was wrong, for as he walked across to Dinna, saying something I couldn't hear, she bent her head and mumbled something. She looked very young, a schoolgirl caught out in a misdemeanor. She was about to cry. Otto ruffled her hair with his big hand. I knew that affectionate gesture; my own scalp tingled with remembered feeling.

Dinna looked up at him with anguished eyes. And then I heard what she said, for she raised her voice in her emotion.

"No, I can't be sorry, Papa. Because it's quite true what Niels says. You're only marrying to upset him."

She spoke in English. There was an old man with gardening tools crossing the lawn. Obviously neither Dinna nor her father wanted a servant to understand their conversation.

Otto spoke sharply in reply to Dinna.

"If you don't behave I'll send you back to school. You and

74

your brother were exceedingly rude last night, and I expect you to apologize to Luise today. Anyway, Niels is talking nonsense. Why should he object so much to a stepmother?"

"For one thing, Papa, he's nearly as old as she is. It's ridiculous."

"Do you find it ridiculous?"

"Not for myself. I think Luise is very nice and very pretty, but apart from everything else, you have to remember how Niels felt about Mama."

"I remember," said Otto in a curious voice.

"Then how can you expect him to accept someone in her place so soon?"

Dinna's voice rang out passionately. I thought Otto would speak angrily to her again, but he surprised me by taking her hand, and saying, "Now, now, my dear, don't get excited. You know it isn't good for you."

"Or you!" Dinna said, in a kind of angry despair.

And I stood gripping the window ledge, a feeling of cold dismay making me shiver.

I could only guess at Dinna's meaning. If what I guessed was true, she also had Otto's disease. And that meant that, contrary to his assurance to me, this particular form of it was hereditary.

Which meant that my baby, of which I was already passionately protective, might have its life marred by this unpleasant disability.

Was Niels afflicted too? Did this explain his difficult nature?

Was this why Otto had insisted on marrying me quietly, before I heard too much?

I guessed this must be the answer to everything, just as Frue Dorothea had tried to tell me last night.

And here I was, caught.

I noticed, as I went to sit in front of the mirror, to do my hair and make up my face, that the tilted glass reflected the water of the moat. The dark chill of it came right into the room. And at that moment, into my bones.

How was I to go on loving Otto now?

Yet at that moment, I didn't blame him as much as myself for being led into that hasty marriage before I had met his family. Look before you leap. That had been my own mother's favorite precept. Knowing my impatience and impulsiveness, she had said it so often that I had stopped listening. I had certainly forgotten it when I had loved Ivor, but I had scrupulously heeded it with Otto. Until Dragor. Dragor, with the white geese and the blue sea, and Otto's urgency . . .

Did Otto think I was the one woman who could give him an unflawed child? Perhaps I was. I *had* to be.

The day had to be faced. It might as well begin at once.

I finished doing my hair, put on a jumper and skirt and low-heeled shoes, and went downstairs.

I thought I would find Otto and Dinna at breakfast, after their small altercation in the garden, but the only person in the big gloomy dining room was Erik.

He said, "Good morning, Luise," smiling at me. He was the only one with pleasant manners in this house, but then, of course, it didn't matter to him whether Otto married again or not. He was only an onlooker. I was glad that he was there, all the same.

"Coffee or tea?" he asked.

"Coffee, please. Black."

He lifted his eyebrows. "What does that mean? That you had a bad night?"

"No, I just prefer black coffee."

"Then you had a good night, I hope."

He poured coffee from the silver pot on the sideboard, and handed the cup to me.

Then he sat opposite me, and gave me a steady inspection.

"Yes. You look more rested than last night. I think we were all too much for you yesterday."

"You were, more than a little. Have you seen Otto this morning?"

"No. He had breakfast and went out early, I believe. He wanted to see Niels' new car. If you ask me, he's just as mad about cars as Niels is, though of course he won't admit it."

"Then he and Niels have made up their quarrel?"

Erik shook his head. "I think not that. It's an old quarrel. It has been going on a long time. It isn't all to do with you, Luise. You mustn't let it upset you."

The kindness in his voice made me say, "Erik!" in some urgency, and he looked at me closely.

"*Ja,* Luise?"

"Is Niels also an epileptic?"

"Also?" He paused a moment, before he said, "No, he isn't an epileptic." Then, still looking at me with that close, steady gaze, he said, "What are you asking me?"

"Dinna is, isn't she? I heard her talking to Otto in the garden this morning. She is, isn't she?"

"Unfortunately, yes. But very slightly. The first attack

didn't come until she was fourteen. She's very brave about it. She's a nice child. You must make her your friend. You can help her."

"Yes, I'd like to, but at the moment, it seems to be me who needs help. I didn't know Otto's illness was hereditary."

"Drink your coffee while it's hot," said Erik in his quiet voice. "Well, to give my brother his due, he thought the trouble, the Winther disease, as it is called, might have died out."

"I suppose he could think that when Niels was all right." When Erik didn't make any comment, I went on, "But how does one know he is all right? He's difficult and hysterical. Perhaps he'll have a fit any day now."

I must have seemed callous. I *was* callous about Niels, for Erik said, "You still have time to change your mind, Luise. If you are afraid to marry Otto—" That was when I nearly told him the truth. The desire to do so was very strong. It wasn't loyalty to Otto that stopped me. It was the curious feeling that that marriage ceremony in Dragor was a dream, that I really did have to stand beside Otto in the Maaneborg church and legitimize our baby.

So I said instead, "That's what Frue Dorothea hopes I will do."

"Yes. That's what she hopes."

"She's very cold-blooded about it, I must say."

"She's honest."

I looked into his own honest eyes.

"You're saying that Otto isn't. But think of him, Erik. He loves me. He really does, very much, and I expect he was terrified of losing me if I knew the truth about this disability he has."

"Then he hasn't lost you?" Erik said, contemplatively.

Would he have, but for my little foetus? It was impossible to separate the hypothetical from the *fait accompli*. I laid a hand lightly on my stomach, then moved it casually as I saw Erik watching me.

"The attacks are very slight," I said. "I've only seen Otto lose consciousness once. Usually he just goes blank for a minute or two. It's nothing to be afraid of. It's only unfortunate, and he needs sympathy. Perhaps his first wife didn't give it to him?"

That was a loaded question, and Erik had no intention of answering it.

"Poor Cristina had problems enough of her own. And I advise you, don't judge Niels too quickly. He was very close to his mother. Now, if I haven't cheered you up, let me give you some more coffee to do so. Then, perhaps, since your intended husband is conspicuous by his absence, you will permit me to take you on a little tour of the house and the garden."

The coffee, or Erik, had cheered me up, although nothing had changed fundamentally, and I knew I would begin to wilt again if we encountered Frue Dorothea on our tour.

"How often do you come here?" I asked.

"Not too often. This weekend, only by chance, because Mama said the roof of the other wing needs attention. I am not the owner, but I am the expert, the man of all jobs, around here."

"Otto says you are a successful architect."

Erik shrugged. "Then all the better to fix a few tiles on the roof."

"I'd like to see some of your work."

"So you shall, the next time you are in Copenhagen. Call me on the telephone. I shall have pleasure in taking you on a tour there, also. But come alone, eh? Otto gets bored with architecture."

I laughed. "Then I will try to come alone."

"Make it soon," said Erik, and whether intentionally or casually, his eyes were on my waistline again. He had seen me seasick on a not very rough sea; he knew I was not going to change my mind about marrying Otto, although he was quite observant enough to be aware of my disillusionment. So he had probably enough perception to have guessed my secret.

But he would never mention it. Already I was certain about his integrity. So I had one friend, even if he was a fairly inconstant visitor to Maaneborg. He was, at least, in Denmark.

We didn't meet either Otto or Frue Dorothea on our exploration of the castle. Erik could, of course, show me only the unoccupied rooms. They were on the second and third floors, room after room furnished with four-poster beds, tapestries, heavy furniture. The floors creaked and the faded curtains billowed slightly in draughts. Some of the painted ceilings were beautiful, but the overwhelming impression was one of Gothic gloom.

"Fifty-eight bedrooms altogether," Erik said. "Isn't that absurd for one family? But now Otto has given up the east wing to the aged ladies, there are only twenty-four bedrooms left. Mama thinks that is to be poor." He flung out his hands, laughing. "I have three bedrooms in my house in Copenhagen, and that is two too many. Until I marry and have children, of course."

I wanted to ask him why he wasn't married already. Instead I said, "Are you a Socialist?"

"Well, yes, if having only three bedrooms is being a Socialist, I suppose I am. Actually, I am only a lazy person who thinks too many possessions are a trouble. So it was lucky for me that I was the younger brother and didn't inherit this great ugly castle."

"I don't suppose Niels feels like that," I said casually.

"No, Niels enjoys possessions. And he loves Maaneborg. So does Otto. You must be prepared to take a great pride in this ugly house if you are to be a successful wife."

I didn't want to talk about that. I had hoped this exploration of the castle would make me excited and proud to be its mistress, but so far all I had felt was a shrinking from all the empty rooms.

"Is the castle ever full of people? Are all these beds sometimes slept in?"

"Not often. They were at the time of Otto's marriage to Cristina. And when there was a party for Dinna's christening."

"Not for Niels'?"

"No, that was just before the war ended. Nobody had parties in those days."

"I suppose not. It must have been terrible."

"Yes. It was terrible." Erik added, after a pause, "For most people."

I suppose he meant that the remarkably few Danes who had collaborated with the Germans had had an easy war, although they had later received their punishment. I asked him how old he had been at that time, and he said that he had been only a schoolboy. His face had grown hard, and it was a little while before he told me that he had been with Otto one day in Copenhagen when they had seen a crowd and heard shots, and had learned that two members of the Danish resistance had just been executed by the Gestapo. Scenes like that were not uncommon, but always horrifying. Even Otto, a grown man, had been terribly upset and had had to be helped into a café, on the verge of one of his seizures.

"It was a bad time. I shouldn't tell you about it. You look distressed."

"You have told me a distressing story."

79

"Yes. Let's talk of better things. Who are you going to ask to sleep in all these rooms?"

I looked wildly down the long stone corridors.

"I don't know. It scares me."

"Then shut them up. Come, I'll show you the turret rooms. They have views on three sides."

I was remembering Frue Dorothea's subtly insolent look yesterday when she had suggested that I be put in the usual room. I was sure now that she had meant one of these.

"Otto sleeps in the one on the first floor," Erik explained. "Then the stairs lead up three floors to the tower. There's a clock at the top. It was stopped years ago because the chimes disturbed the occupant of the top room."

The stone staircase was circular and narrow and rather forbidding, although the walls were hung with occasional pictures in dusty gold frames, or with weapons and pieces of armor. At each twist in the stairs there was a slit window set deep in the stone. These gave a narrow jewel-like vista of beechwoods and sky.

The first room into which Erik took me was surprisingly attractive. Unlike the other ones I had seen, this one gave the impression of having been used frequently and recently. The bed had a cheerful blue linen covering, the curtains at the three long windows were gold silk, there were fresh towels hanging on a rail, books on the bedside table.

"A guest room," said Erik, noticing my inquisitive interest. "It is very popular."

With whom? I wondered silently.

"You see that the view is really superb, but it is better still higher up. Come along. Are you tired?"

He was hurrying me out, as if he regretted having shown me this room. Perhaps he hadn't realized it was kept prepared like that. He could have guessed that I wouldn't have criticized Otto for having an occasional friend when his wife had been an invalid for so long.

But in his wife's house? my niggling mind was saying.

The room on the next floor had clearly not been in use for a long time. There was dust on the furniture, and the remains of a birds' nest lay on the wide stone hearth. The windows were uncurtained, and the wonderful expanse of lakes and beechwoods and sky hung like a shining backdrop. This was the best view so far. But there was one more room above. It must have the best view of all.

I said so, and was about to climb the remaining flight of stairs when Erik restrained me.

"You can't go any farther."

"Why not? Isn't there another room?"

"Yes, but it's locked."

"Why?" I thought a window must be broken or the room in too much disrepair.

"If you must know, it was Cristina's room. Otto prefers to keep it locked now. He has done so ever since she died."

I couldn't explain my deep uneasiness. Why should Otto lock the room of his dead wife, keeping it private to himself, when he hadn't even loved her. Or so he had told me. *Ill and kept in her room . . . Locked up and beaten . . .*

The disjointed conversation overheard in the garden yesterday ran through my head. The clattering of crows' wings.

"Wasn't it a very inconvenient room for a sick woman?" I murmured.

"Yes, I suppose it was, but Cristina had a faithful old servant who looked after her. Of course, towards the end, she had to be brought down. The nurses refused to climb all these stairs. Then she complained that she couldn't breathe, she was too far from the sky."

"I would like to have seen her view," I muttered childishly.

"This one is exactly the same." Erik took me to the window. "Beyond the woods, on the seashore, there's a bird sanctuary. The woods are full of hares that the farmers trap alive and send to France for breeding."

I wondered if Cristina had heard the snared hares screaming as she lay in that lonely room, dying.

How often now did Otto climb the stairs, with the key of the door in his pocket, to gloat over the room's emptiness? Or to grieve.

I must have become rather pale, because Erik said, "Let's go down. You look tired."

I wondered if he was surprised that a healthy young woman should be tired from climbing a circular stairway. Other dark thoughts were absorbing me.

There was always abortion. If I could persuade a doctor that my child would be imperfect, or find one who didn't question morals . . .

But it was *my* child, curled warmly inside me. And mine alone if I chose it to be that way, if Otto could not succeed in banishing all my muddled fears.

I would go back to London and have it in a bed-sitter in Fulham or Chelsea or Earls Court, or anywhere that was ordinary and safe. And I would never let it see its father. If I found I wasn't dreaming this Gothic nonsense, if he really couldn't, or wouldn't answer my questions . . .

Now I urgently wanted to take that private walk by the lake with him.

But now that I wanted him, he could not be found, and there was only Frue Dorothea sitting in the drawing room, stitching on a long piece of tapestry.

She was wearing a curious string-colored garment of heavy linen, not unlike a monk's cassock, and had a long string of amber beads, imperfectly matched, as if she had picked them up on the beach and threaded them herself, around her neck.

In spite of her slightly eccentric attire, she looked very much the grande dame. When I saw the rings glinting on her fingers as she plied her needle, I suddenly remembered that I had forgotten to wear the heavy yellow diamond Otto had given me.

Perhaps I would never wear it again.

I said good morning to Frue Dorothea, and Erik said, *"God morgen, Mama."*

She put aside her work and gave us her frosty attention.

"What have you two been doing? Where's Otto?"

I replied that I didn't know. I thought she would know.

"Perhaps he's riding with Dinna. She usually persuades him to."

"Should they?" I couldn't help saying, and saw her gaze flick sharply from me to Erik.

Was I being overimaginative? I asked myself in sudden anguish. For it seemed to me that there was something conspiratorial in that glance, as if it had been arranged that Erik should take me on that tour of the house and quietly alarm me.

And I had thought he was the one person I could trust. I bit my lip, wondering why this discovery, if it were a discovery, should hurt so deeply.

But Erik was answering in his calm and completely believable way, "Luise knows about Dinna. It was a shock to her. Otto should have told her, of course."

"Of course," said Frue Dorothea, picking up her work again. "But now she has found out, so it isn't too late." Her needle glinted in the sun. As it went swiftly in and out of the tapestry, trailing its tail of crimson wool, I thought, "Now she will prick her finger and fall unconscious." But that was the Sleeping Beauty, and Frue Dorothea was no Sleeping Beauty. She was the Snow Queen, quietly waiting to freeze everybody around her.

"I have always encouraged Otto to lead a perfectly normal life," she was saying conversationally. "He rides, shoots, drives cars, water skis. There's always a slight risk, but I wasn't going to allow his misfortune to blight his life. Not all women could live with this constant strain."

"I'm strong enough," I said shortly. Now I believed that this old woman would drive me from sheer stubbornness into living loyally with my husband, no matter what his misdeeds.

"And you understand, Luise," she said slyly, "that the countesses of Maaneborg never use their title."

My face flamed. I permitted myself the ineffable pleasure of losing my temper.

"If you think I want a title and this bloody castle, you couldn't be more mistaken! I didn't even know about it until Otto brought me here. You won't believe that, of course. You won't believe anything good about me. I can see very clearly that we're never going to like each other, or agree on anything. But your precious Maaneborg is big enough. If we can't keep out of each other's way in this wing, then you had better move to the other. Hadn't you?"

Then we outstared each other, and I had a childish feeling of triumph when her eyelids flickered and her lips gave a faint twitch. I wondered if she was feeling outrage at my unforgivable suggestion that she was old enough and senile enough to join the ladies in the east wing. But, exasperatingly, it seemed that she had enjoyed my outburst.

"Well, I had thought you were a pretty kitten with no claws, Luise. I was wrong. That certainly makes things more interesting."

So she was deciding that I was a worthy enemy! How ironic.

Erik said, "Sometimes, my mother dips her tongue in acid. Don't you, Mama?"

"I say what is in my mind," the old lady retorted calmly. "Why don't you sit down, Luise. You look tired. Didn't you sleep well?"

"I never do on my first night in a strange house."

"No. There are sounds one isn't used to. Perhaps you heard a trapped hare screaming in the woods."

I drew in my breath.

"Does one, sometimes?"

"Sometimes. It shouldn't happen. The traps aren't meant to maim."

Chapter Eight

OTTO hadn't been riding with Dinna, but trying out Niels' new car. He came in a little later looking as pleased as could be, although he pretended disapproval.

"Do you know what speed that little toy can do, Mama? I've given Niels strict orders. He's never to take her above eighty kilometers, but of course he will."

"How much did you take her to?" Frue Dorothea inquired drily.

"That's beside the point. I'm a far more experienced driver than Niels. Luise, my darling, have you been up long? I hope you had a late sleep, and breakfast in bed." He bent to kiss me. His skin was glowing, his eyes bright. In this genial mood, he was the man I had fallen in love with. My resilient spirits improved. I believed I could be happy, in spite of Frue Dorothea, in spite of Maaneborg, if he stayed that way.

But first I was going to have to spoil his present sunny temper with my questions.

"I'm fine," I replied. "What is this wonderful car?"

"A Mercedes, sports model."

"Oh, that really is something." And so was Frue Dorothea's generosity toward her spoiled grandson. It seemed out of character, because she looked such a frugal person, with her plain dress and her cheap amber beads. "Why can't I try it?" I asked. "I mean, why don't you drive me somewhere in it? If Niels will allow us to, of course."

"Of course he'll allow us," Otto said, a bit shortly. "There's nothing I'd like better. I want to show you the church, anyway. You'll want to see where you're to be married."

"I'd like that," I said, and saw Erik looking at me with his sober dark eyes.

What I intended to do was get Otto alone for a little while. He could stop the car somewhere on the road, and we would thrash out all the problems. Or try to.

The big gray hound barked as the car roared away across the cobblestones and over the bridge of the moat. The top was down and the wind tore invigoratingly at my hair.

"Should have put a scarf on," said Otto, as strands came

loose and blew across my face. "You slept soundly last night."

That was not a question but a statement.

"Yes, I did."

"You locked your door."

"Yes."

"Against me, against your husband."

"I'm only playing the game you told me to play."

"It doesn't need to be carried to that extent," he grumbled, but still good-temperedly. "I was a little cross with you. Are you going to behave like this until after our wedding?"

"If we have another wedding," I said equably.

He looked at me in surprise, then had to give his attention to the road. We were traveling at a good speed already.

"Are you making comments about my driving, Luise? I'll go a little slower if you're nervous. Or is it something else you're hinting at?"

"I suppose if I had had the turret room on the second floor, you would have insisted on coming in, anyway," I said.

He shot me another look, then laughed with complete good temper.

"So that's it. You've been exploring. My mother has been dropping some hints in her friendly way? Well, I admit that room did have a certain convenience for me. Cristina was a complete invalid and no longer a wife to me for several years before her death. But I make you a promise that from now on the room will be closed."

"And locked?"

We went around a curve in the road too fast. We were coming into the beechwoods, the road a long dark aisle beneath the overhanging boughs.

I went on, "Otto, why do you keep Cristina's room locked?"

"Who told you that? Mama again? She might have gone on to explain that the room has unhappy associations for me, and by keeping it locked I can pretend it isn't there. Childish, perhaps? But I am a simple man in many ways."

Oh, no, not simple, Otto. *Devious* is the word. And insensitive, too. Couldn't he have had his women in Copenhagen, or somewhere else far away from his sick wife? Dragor perhaps, the thought slid into my mind.

"Luise."

"Yes?"

"You're looking unhappy."

"There are things I'm not happy about."

"And I, too, if you must know. You refused to come for a walk with me last night. You locked the door of your room. Is this the way to treat your husband?"

"Husband," I said, testing the word.

"Oh, come now. Aren't you enjoying our secret? I think it's tremendous fun. I'll be quite sorry when it's over. Only, you must unlock your bedroom door to me, of course."

I unsnapped the catch of my handbag and looked inside for my wedding ring.

"If you find this situation titillating, I don't. I may put this on at any time and tell everybody the truth. Or, on the other hand," I added, eying the gold circlet thoughtfully, "I may never put it on again."

"You're teasing me, I think," said Otto. "Little fox."

It was not foxes, but hares, that were snared in the woods, I thought irrelevantly.

"Otto, please stop the car for a few minutes. I can't get your attention while you're driving."

At once Otto pulled the car to the side of the road, stopped it, and took me in his arms.

"Like this?" he said, kissing me. "Is this the kind of attention you want?"

I shook his big hands out of my hair. I felt stiff and prickly, unable to bear his touch.

"What's the matter?" he asked. "Why don't you like me to kiss you this morning?"

"Because there are several things I want to know the answer to first."

Otto sighed exaggeratedly. "I must say, I don't care for you in this inquisitive mood."

"The mood is your fault. I wouldn't be in it if you had told me the truth at the beginning."

"Yes, my love? The truth about what?"

It was beautiful in the beechwoods. The great trunks of the trees were dappled with sun. Birds were singing. The grass was starred with small flowers, dog violets, wood anemones, the impossibly pure gold of dandelions. It was a pity to talk about an ugly secret in such a peaceful place.

"Otto, why didn't you tell me that your daughter, also, was an epileptic?"

"Dinna? But this isn't true! She has had one or two fainting turns, that's all. What girl in her teens hasn't? Adolescence. That sort of thing."

I looked into his blue eyes and saw that they had gone as

cold as his mother's. The Snow King, I thought. And I hadn't had the wit to see it.

No, that was fanciful. He couldn't be like that. I couldn't allow him to be.

But I had to go on with this small inquisition.

"It isn't any use telling lies about it, Otto. Because I've heard the truth about the Winther disease, both from your mother and Erik. You really should have told me before you married me."

"And then you would have had nothing to do with me?"

There was a pathos in his voice that made me suddenly terribly sorry for him. He had struggled all his life with his disability. Who was I to judge him?

"No, I'm not saying that, Otto. But I wouldn't have allowed myself to become pregnant."

"But I think that is my business. If I want another son, I will have one. That is what marriage is for, isn't it? To beget children."

"But not flawed ones! That's selfish. Cruel."

He began to laugh, putting his arm around my shoulders and his face close to mine. "You look so outraged. You don't know me very well. Perhaps I am cruel. I want a healthy child as much as you do, but if it isn't quite healthy, even if it is an idiot, or a cripple, I still want it. So long as it's a boy. If you give me a string of daughters, Luise, I will put up with them, but you must in the end give me a boy." He kissed my brow. I tried to pull away from his embrace. The chill was in my blood again. I was beginning to think his disease had affected his brain.

"You have an obsession about children. I believe you would have married the first healthy girl you met."

"No. No, you underrate yourself. It happened that I also fell in love with you. Your eyes, I think. And your hair. Green and black. So different from our monotonous blue eyes and blond hair."

"Otto, you're changing the subject. Why do you so much want another son? Maaneborg already has an heir."

"Yes, it has, hasn't it?" said Otto, smiling into my eyes. "But I want your son, my darling. Didn't you understand that?"

My cherished little baby an idiot, I thought, my mind going dark. Had there been other idiots at Maaneborg?

"So now, what was bothering you has been cleared up," he went on confidently, and I had the baffled feeling that I was being swept into this euphoric dream again, all realities ignored.

"I have the answers to some questions, if that is what you mean. You married me secretly in Dragor because you were afraid that if I came here first and found out the truth about certain things, I would never have married you."

"Oh, no, I think you will enjoy being mistress of a castle, and a countess," Otto said with such smugness, that at last I came out of my cloud of worry and lost my temper.

"And being locked up and beaten! Will I enjoy that, too?"

"Luise! Why do you say that?"

I should have been warned by the slow dark suffusion of blood in his face, the swelling of a vein in his temple. But his voice had been calm enough. So I went on, recklessly.

"I heard some remarks made by your elderly guests in the other half of the garden yesterday. They were saying that I should be warned, I don't know about what. Perhaps you will be kind enough to tell me."

"We Danes have had some pretty little habits in the past, I admit," Otto said tightly. "For instance, you might care to see the dungeons at Maaneborg, too. There is one where a Swedish captain of the guards was chained by the ankle for several years until he died. That was a long time ago, of course, when we fought wars with the Swedes. But no doubt you see that same cruelty in my face." Otto had started the car. It had automatic gears. His foot was on the accelerator. "No doubt you believe that I locked up my wife, and she had to sew tapestries with her hair. I thought you loved me, Luise." The car was now in motion, and moving swiftly down the road, Otto's hands clutching the wheel as if he were thinking it was my neck.

I don't know what brought that grisly thought to me. I was too sick and despairing to listen to him, or even to be afraid.

"But now I find you're ready to believe any lies, those told by Erik, too, I expect, and my—"

I heard the words slur, but caught only a glimpse of the dreaded distortion coming over his face before the car swerved sharply. "Otto, stop!" I reached for the wheel. Otto's head slumped forward. The car tilted against the road verge. I tried desperately to get it under control, but Otto's body fell across the wheel.

The next moment there was a crash, a tremendous crackling of branches as if all the forest had fallen. Splintering pain. The high scream of a caught hare. Or was it me? Then darkness . . .

Chapter Nine

THERE were myriad colors over my head. Reds, greens, golds and rich blues in a mosaic pattern that quivered and shone. I could only look at them for a moment at a time. Then I had to rest my eyes, because they hurt so much. Although, on reflection, I found that the ache wasn't in my eyes but in my head. It was a steady pulsebeat of pain.

I turned on the pillow—I seemed to be lying in a bed beneath that rainbow-colored ceiling—but this was a mistake, for the movement sent a splinter of pain through my body. It finally lodged itself in my back and remained there, an ache that kept company with my throbbing head. I didn't dare to move again, although I could hear voices.

Someone was saying, as if it were a great achievement, "The English lady has opened her eyes."

There were flutterings around my bed, and in spite of the pain, I had to open my eyes again.

I saw a nurse in a white cap and apron, and behind her a curious assortment of wrinkled faces and gray locks. There seemed to be so many of them. Or perhaps I was seeing double. Or perhaps they were not there at all, but only part of a nightmare. For a nurse suggested a hospital, but not a bevy of octogenarians.

The nurse, who had a pleasant young face, spoke sharply to the faces, and they resolved themselves into three separate black shadows that moved reluctantly away. One of the shadows limped and had angular shoulders, one tipped higher than the other.

I had seen that person before. But where? The small triumph of realizing that the shadows were real people vanished in the anguish of not being able to remember. I searched my mind and found nothing but the fact that the limping old woman had a vague familiarity.

"*Drik,*" the nurse was saying.

"What?" I thought I had spoken clearly, but the nurse merely said, more imperatively, "*Drik,*" in the same incomprehensible language, and put a hand beneath my head to raise it.

Liquid touched my lips. *Drink,* I thought, again with a feeling of having achieved a major triumph. I still had some fragment of a brain, even if it hurt a great deal.

I swallowed the warm liquid and realized I was exceedingly thirsty. My stomach felt hollow.

Hollow . . . The word gave me a vague alarm. I pursued it, but it floated away.

I didn't realize I had slept until I opened my eyes again and found the lovely colors over my head merged into the deepest gloom. There was only a faint light on my left side, but it hurt too much to turn my head to see what it was. There was a strange noise, too. It sounded like a kettle bubbling. It went on and on, monotonously. I drowsed, only on the borderland of sleep now, and a little later I heard a clock strike. I counted the strokes. They seemed to go on forever. Ten, eleven, twelve . . .

But the clock didn't strike any more! Someone had told me that it had been stopped because it made too much noise. Someone was sick, dying. Who? Surely not me!

The feeling of panic, curiously enough, stirred the fog in my head. I was beginning to remember. Cristina. The name floated in and out of my mind. The kettle on my left side went on bubbling. A stab of light began moving toward me. A voice murmured querulously and footsteps slap-slapped across the floor.

Unintelligible words were said, someone coughed, the phlegmy cough of the old. A glass clinked. I turned my head, feeling the familiar splinter of pain, and saw a vague shape behind the shaft of light. The shape moved toward me, and bent over me. In careful English a voice said:

"How are you feeling now, Miss Amberley? Would you like a warm drink? A cup of tea?"

"I could hear the kettle boiling," I said. The thought of a cup of tea was comforting.

"The kettle boiling?"

Was she deaf? The noise was going on all the time.

"Listen to it," I said fretfully.

The shape above me gave a little gurgle of laughter.

"Oh, that is Frue Harben snoring. She always does that, I am sorry to say. Does it disturb you?"

"Who is Frue Harben?" In a curious way, the foreign name was connected with my alarm about the striking clock.

"Just an old lady. She comes from Fyn."

Fyn! My alarm splintered into flashes of pain as I moved. I was beginning to remember.

"Where am I?"

"You're in the hospital for the old ladies. You've been here for three weeks. And do you know, this is the first time you have talked sensibly, so isn't that good? It means you are getting well."

"Well from what?"

"From the accident, Miss Amberley. Now you mustn't talk any more. I will go and make you a warm drink."

The light moved away, dancing like a firefly on walls that showed glimpses of gilding and tapestries. The footsteps slap-slapped over the uncarpeted floor. And I lay very still, realizing where I was. In the ballroom at Maaneborg. The ballroom that had been turned into a hospital for impoverished gentlewomen.

I don't know whether I got that warm drink or not, or whether the old lady in the bed next to me bubbled all night. I must have fallen asleep again, for when I next opened my eyes it was daylight, and I was thinking, in complete incredulity, "How could I have been here for three weeks and not known? What had happened to me? Had I gone mad?"

The nurse had talked of an accident. What had that been? Instinct guided my hands to my stomach. It felt too hollow, positively concave. My baby! Was it still there?

"Nurse!" I began to call. My voice seemed to be a scream, but no one came. Somewhere a bell buzzed. I tried to sit up and couldn't. Perspiration drenched me. What was the matter with me? Was I a cripple?

Footsteps slap-slapped down the ward. Voices spoke in Danish. A moment later a nurse stood over me.

"What is it, Miss Amberley? Frue Harben said you were calling."

"I want my husband," I said, tears rolling down my cheeks.

Why should the plain face above me look so bewildered because I asked for my husband? And then sympathetic. An awful fear possessed me. Had Otto suffered a mysterious accident, too?

"Herre Winther," I whispered.

The nurse said, "I will see," and went away.

"Herre Winther is in Copenhagen," said a voice from my right. Frue Harben, the bubbling lady, I supposed. With a great effort I turned to look at her. She was sitting up in bed, a wizened old creature with tumbling white hair.

"You're wrong, that's Erik," I said, pleased that I was

beginning to remember so well. "It's Otto who is my husband."

The old lady looked at me hard with misty blue eyes.

"So," she said cryptically.

I wanted to get more information from her, such as how long we had been lying side by side in this once magnificent room, but I was too tired and confused. I wanted Otto, who would explain everything.

It wasn't Otto but a strange young man in a neat dark suit who arrived at my bedside.

"So I hear you are better, Miss Amberley," he said cheerfully, in very good English. "That is good."

"No one will tell me what happened to me," I said fretfully.

"You don't remember anything?"

"Nothing. I just woke up here. Someone said I had been here three weeks, but that can't be true."

"It is true. You had a bad knock on the head. You suffered severe concussion. You have talked to us a little now and then, but not very sensibly, I'm afraid."

"What was the accident I had?"

"In a car. Herre Winther was driving."

Otto was dead! I knew it now. That was what the nurse wouldn't tell me.

"He is, isn't he?"

"Who is what, Miss Amberley?"

"Herre Winther is dead."

"Indeed not. Far from it. He had only a few cuts and bruises. The car struck the tree on your side, so you suffered most. But that is past, now. You are doing famously."

But there was something in the doctor's eyes. Beneath the blankets my hands lay on my concave stomach.

"My baby?" I whispered.

"You have lost it, Miss Amberley. I am sorry to tell you. We had to perform a small operation. That is what has delayed your recovery. Fortunately your pregnancy was in an early stage." He smiled brightly, meaninglessly. "So now you will get on well. You must eat, sleep, not worry. Frue Dorothea has been inquiring for you every day."

That cold-faced witch. I didn't believe it. My baby, my cherished little foetus, gone. What would Otto say?

The tears were running down my face. I tried to speak, but couldn't. I wanted Otto. The words wouldn't come.

"My husband," I at last managed to whisper, but neither the doctor nor the nurse seemed to hear. The doctor was saying something in Danish, and the nurse nodding. Then he said cheerfully:

"I will see you again tomorrow, Miss Amberley," and moved off to the next bed.

The nurse smiled, too, and said she was going to bring me a small piece of chicken which I must try to eat. And perhaps some hot soup, too?

I made no answer. I was wondering how the doctor could go on calling me Miss Amberley when he knew that I had suffered a miscarriage. Otto must have had to tell our secret. So why wasn't I being addressed as Frue Winther?

This Maaneborg place was full of nothing but mysteries, I thought wearily. I was tired of them. They had to come to an end. Everything had to be made clear. I closed my eyes and tried to remember the accident which the doctor told me I had suffered.

The shadows stirred in my mind. Otto and I had been in a car. We were driving to see the church in which we were to be married for the second time. But we were quarreling about something and Otto was driving too fast. I remembered that. I remembered the trees flashing by, and myself protesting, and Otto's face going dark . . .

That was it! Otto had had one of his attacks at the wheel, and now I no longer needed to worry about the possibility of my baby's being born with the Winther disease . . .

When the nurse came with a tray, I was crying too much to be able to eat. She was persuasive, then stern, then alarmed. Finally she went away and came back with a hypodermic needle.

And when I woke again, someone was saying, "Your white feather, Luise. It has gone."

Feather?

"The white lock of hair," said the voice, and Erik moved into view.

I looked beyond him for Otto, who surely must be there, too. But Erik was alone.

"It had to be cut off because that was where you had a wound. I hope it grows again the same color. It was attractive."

I put up my hand to feel sticking plaster on my forehead. My face must have shown my alarm, for Erik said soothingly:

"Don't worry, your face is undamaged. If you have a scar on the top of your head, your hair will cover it. My brother escaped without any scars at all. It is hardly fair, is it?"

I moved my head dumbly. It was nice having Erik there, but where was Otto? If he were really unhurt, why didn't he come to see me?

"You are frowning, Luise. You mustn't make the effort of trying to talk, but if you could just say what makes you frown . . . are you in pain?"

Yes, I was. In every sort of pain. But I lied.

"No, only a little."

Erik's face broke into a happy smile. What a nice face he had. Warm dark eyes, that pleasant smile. But Otto had warm merry eyes, too, and look at him.

What about him? Except his unexplained absence from his wife's bedside?

"Luise, I will just sit here without talking. Will that bother you?"

"No."

"Then sleep if you like."

I closed my eyes and opened them again.

"Otto has been to see me?"

"Oh, many times."

"Then why not today?"

"When you can talk? Yes, that's a pity. But he didn't know it would be today you would come back to consciousness."

"He is away?"

"He had to make a journey to Copenhagen. He will be back."

Two very bad shocks. One about my baby, one about Otto going off to Copenhagen, leaving me lying ill.

"It is you who have a business in Copenhagen, not Otto," I said flatly.

"Luise, I think perhaps you shouldn't talk so much."

"Someone should talk to *me*," I said bitterly, with all my strength.

"Then what can I tell you? I think you already know what has happened."

"Yes, I know that Otto and I have lost our baby."

"We are all truly sorry about that. It's too bad."

"You don't look shocked," I said aggressively.

"Because you were expecting Otto's baby? But that sort of thing happens all the time. Why should I be shocked? At least you were going to get married, which is nicer for the baby. Now, perhaps—"

"Perhaps what?"

"I was only going to say that now you are more free to have second thoughts, if you wish to. But there is plenty of

94

time for that, when you are stronger. Now I will have second thoughts, and not stay here, since I seem to disturb you. My mother will be coming in a little later, if you feel strong enough."

He was moving back from my bedside. I held out my hands, imploring him to stay. Someone had to talk to me, or listen to what I now had such an imperative need to tell.

"Erik!"

"Yes, Luise."

"Tell Otto—"

Erik's form was wavering. His face came clear, then faded. There were brilliant colors around him, as if he had been swallowed into the painted ceiling. I began to wonder if he had been there at all. I didn't know whether or not I finished what I was trying to tell him.

And when I floated back to consciousness, another day— or how many days—was over, and the nurse was telling me it was such a pity, I had been sleeping when Frue Dorothea had come. But she had left a message that she was very happy to hear how well I was progressing.

"And all these flowers," said the nurse admiringly, directing my gaze to the bedside table. "You will be making the other ladies jealous."

Roses, carnations, delphiniums, sweet peas, a lovely bouquet of flowers gathered from the Maaneborg gardens that ran down to the moat's edge, as if I had every right to all the flowers grown there. As if I belonged. When Otto had gone off and left me to live or die as I pleased.

I don't know why it was at that moment that I determined not only to live, but to get well as quickly as possible.

After all, I couldn't tolerate Frue Dorothea's covering me with flowers and gloating over my decease.

This determination must have contributed to my sleeping soundly and without dreams, and I woke the next morning feeling infinitely better. Even optimistic.

My head still hurt if I made unwary movements, but the constant headache had dulled. I had the courage to ask the nurse for a mirror. That was a mistake, for the face that looked back at me was not going to set the world alight—or keep my husband at my side. But I had to know about my ruined looks sometime, and it might just as well be now.

The nurse, who was a very nice girl with Scandinavian blue eyes and pale blond hair, said that of course I must expect to look thin and ill now, but that would soon go. And my hair would grow over the scar above my temples. I looked as if I had been nearly scalped.

"You are lucky to be alive, Miss Amberley," the girl said solemnly. "What is a little scar? You can arrange your hair over it until it heals. Would you like some lipstick?"

"Yes, please. And some rouge, too, and a brush and comb. If that is possible."

"It is possible, yes. Frue Dorothea packed a bag with all the things you would need. Even the nightgown you are wearing."

I hadn't noticed what I was wearing. Now I saw that my nightgown was pale blue silk and lace in the very best taste. It must be one of Frue Dorothea's own. I wasn't very happy about that. Silk nightgowns and flowers. Was she trying to make amends to me for her previous coldness?

However, I brushed my hair, and carefully applied rouge to conceal the skeleton thinness of my face. My cheekbones stuck out, and my eyes were enormous. But the rouge and lipstick helped, and I fixed my hair a bit more becomingly, although my arms quickly ached, and I couldn't do a great deal about it.

I was watched from the next bed. Frue Harben said, "Are you expecting him to visit you today, Miss Amberley?"

"Who?" I asked coolly.

"The Greve, naturally. He came at first, when he thought you might die, but not for several days now."

Two other old women, one on sticks and another shuffling along, both wearing trailing dressing gowns, had come toward my bed. I was really seeing this long lovely room properly for the first time. It had seven or eight beds, but only four were occupied. There was nursing equipment such as lockers and commodes and basins and bottles, but this was all, even the beds with the patients, dwarfed by the vast expanse of polished wood floor, high walls covered with faded green watered silk and tapestries, and the magnificent gold and crimson ceiling.

Otto had made quite a sacrifice when he had allowed such a beautiful room to be put at the disposal of sick old women. There must have been some wonderful balls here, with the orchestra sitting on the dais at the end and the dancers swinging over the polished floor. The chandeliers, with their pear-shaped crystal drops, must have shone with a thousand lights. A ghost haunted the ballroom, the old ladies in the garden had said. I wondered if I would see it before I left, or whether the now constant and depressing sight of old age had frightened it away.

The old ladies converging on my bed were not going to allow me to dream about ghosts. The tilted shoulder and lame-bird look of one of them I recognized. This was Emilie, whom I had spoken to in the garden.

"So you are going to live after all, Froken Amberley," she said, taking up a position beside my pillow.

"I never intended to die."

"Of course not. You are much too young."

"The Grevinde Cristina was also young," muttered that rather obnoxious old woman in the next bed, Frue Harben, who snored with a revolting bubbling sound all night.

"Not so young, Frue Harben," Emilie contradicted. "In any case, she had a blood disorder. We all knew that."

"And Froken Amberley had an accident."

"So."

"But it was caused by the Greve's trouble. I have always said that he should not be allowed to drive a car. It is highly dangerous. He collapses at the wheel, and this poor young woman is nearly killed."

"The accident was an accident," Emilie said.

"And the Grevinde Cristina died of a blood disorder," said Frue Harben. "Or so people say."

"What else is there to believe? You are unkind, Frue Harben. You are making poor Miss Amberley look worried."

The third old woman, who probably couldn't speak English, hadn't said a word, but the three pairs of eyes, dim lights looking out from between wrinkled lids, tortoises' eyes, infinitely old and uncaring, looked at me, and my blood was running cold.

"Froken Amberley should talk to Helga Blom," said Frue Harben, settling back into her pillows.

"Who is Helga Blom?" I asked, forced at last to join in this unpleasant conversation.

"Old Helga," said Emilie scornfully. "She forgets everything."

"Not everything. She was the Grevinde Cristina's maid for many years, Froken Amberley. But what happened to her?"

"Yes, everything she forgot," Emilie insisted. "And lost things. She worked in the kitchen here until she couldn't be put up with. They said her mistress' death had made her brain go soft."

"She was old," said Frue Harben. "Like us all."

"But where is she now?" I wanted to know.

"You must ask the Greve. Or Frue Dorothea. Perhaps you will get an answer. Perhaps not." Emilie gave a sudden cackle of laughter. "Well, I must go to play a game of cards with Sophie. She will be waiting. We old ones have our routine, Miss Amberley. It is important. Otherwise, why do we go on living?"

"Why do you say perhaps I won't get an answer?" I persisted.

The weary eyes, callous with age, looked down at me. The crooked shoulder lifted higher in a one-sided shrug.

"Perhaps it depends on how important you are, Miss Amberley. If you understand what I mean."

I did understand. I said at once, "But I am important. After all, I'm married to Herre Winther. Doesn't that make me important?"

The ancient faces were not too indifferent to show surprise.

"Then where is your wedding ring?" Emilie asked.

"Don't you remember, I showed it to you in the garden? It's in my handbag."

"I would think a woman who was married would wear her ring," Frue Harben pronounced.

"There were reasons why I didn't." My head was beginning to ache rather badly. I didn't like the skepticism on the faces of my audience. Even the old lady who didn't speak English was pursing up her mouth and shaking her head.

"But now I intend to," I said. I reached for my handbag, which I had had out of the locker when I had been making up my face. To find the ring more quickly, I tipped the contents of it onto the bed. Everything was there—money, powder compact, lipstick, handkerchief, keys, perfume, all the motley objects that a woman carries about with her. Except a wedding ring. That had gone.

And the three pairs of dim eyes looked at me skeptically, and one old face, Emilie's, held a sudden disturbing look of pity.

Frue Dorothea came that afternoon. There was a great flurry in the ward, if that great ballroom could be called a hospital ward. One nurse hurried to the door to open it, and all the old ladies, the four bedridden ones and the two who tottered about on sticks, sat up and made vague movements to pat their hair into place and straighten their shawls. But Frue Dorothea, dressed as usual in the plainest garment, walked quickly toward my bed as if she disliked any suggestion of a fuss being made for her. She stood above me, and I saw that she was actually smiling. I thought it must be a smile of triumph until I saw the sympathy in her eyes. Was I so ill that even the Snow Queen was sorry for me?

"How are you feeling today, my dear? At last I have found you awake."

"They told me you had called," I muttered.

"Yes, many times. So has Dinna. She has cried about you. She's very tenderhearted."

So what? She might have shown me a little of her tender heart earlier, but it wasn't Dinna's heart I was concerned about.

"Otto?" I asked.

"Otto has been, of course. But then he was called to Copenhagen on urgent business."

There *was* sympathy in those large pale eyes. They were not ice-locked any longer. Had she also been shedding tears for me? It seemed too fantastic to be possible.

"My dear, you mustn't worry about Otto. He was very concerned for you until the doctor said you were out of danger. You must remember he was badly shaken by the accident, too. Looking at you lying here was very hard for him. He blamed himself entirely."

I had to be fair. "He had one of his epileptic fits," I said. "It was probably my fault. I was arguing with him. I should have had the sense not to do that in a car."

If Frue Dorothea wanted to know what we had been arguing about, she concealed her curiosity. Instead, she made a strange remark.

"So now you realize what a constant strain living with Otto would have been. I had it with his father. And poor Cristina was often very unhappy. You must have thought us very unwelcoming at Maaneborg. But this was the reason."

Would have been ... Was ... Everything was in the past tense.

"If the doctor will allow it," Frue Dorothea was continuing, "I intend to have you moved over to the other side of the house tomorrow. You can't lie here with only old women for company. It's too depressing. You are welcome to stay with us for as long as you want to."

My head still ached badly when I tried to concentrate. It was doing so now, and it was this that made me think I must be completely misunderstanding Frue Dorothea. Surely she wasn't congratulating me on *escaping* Otto.

I made a big effort to hold my own in this decidedly one-sided conversation.

"I would expect to be welcome in my own home."

That remark seemed to give the advantage to me, for Frue Dorothea looked considerably startled. She was silent for a little while, then said with a gentleness that seemed perfectly genuine, "Not exactly your own home, you poor child. I'm afraid you don't know my son as well as I do. The fact is that he has been betraying you."

Betraying. Such a Victorian word. Quite melodramatic. It made me laugh. But laughing hurt both my head and somewhere in the regions of my stomach. My womb, I supposed, from which my little foetus had escaped, leaving this echo of pain.

"You mean having led me on. Leading me up the garden path. That's idiomatic English. But rather crude. Perhaps I like your word better. Although of course it isn't true."

"No?" Frue Dorothea's long face, with those big shining blue eyes like moonstones, hung over me.

"Of course it isn't," I said impatiently, before I could be hypnotized.

"Otto should have told you himself." Although her face was just as close, it wasn't so clear, and her voice seemed to come from a long distance. My heart was beating too fast, and my head really did ache very badly. I had to close my eyes, and as I did so, something cool touched my forehead.

"Poor child. Now there is to be no baby, my son feels he has no obligation towards you. I can disapprove his behavior, but I can't prevent it. I am only his mother. And he is forty-six years old. But he should have told you himself."

Cruel ... Cruel bitch ... Don't pretend reluctance. You wanted to have this pleasure ... To tell me these lies ...

"I don't mean to be unkind, Luise. It is only something you must know, and as soon as possible, before you build hopes."

Hopes of what? Living in that great haunted barn, Maaneborg? Coping with my treacherous husband?

Oh, no, Frue Dorothea, you're wrong. I don't want Maaneborg or your son. I only want to escape. But I can't. I have a wedding ring, Somewhere.

My eyes wouldn't open. I felt as if I were rocking on a black sea. All the words I wanted to say remained tumbling about inside my head.

"Nurse! I've given her a shock. I'm sorry. It had to be done." And again that sympathetic, "Poor child. It isn't fair."

And fingers on my arm, and the sharp prick of the hypodermic needle.

And dusk coming in the windows and filling the great

room when I woke again. Something cold and damp against my hand, and a girl laughing.

"It's Anna," said Dinna gaily. "Erik and I have brought her to cheer you up."

I hadn't known how enchantingly pretty Dinna was. Previously, whenever I had seen her, she had been pouting and looking sulky. Now she was gay and friendly because she thought I was not to be her stepmother after all. I had yet to find out why she and her brother were so opposed to the fact of having me as their stepmother.

Because it was a fact. As they, and Otto, my devious husband, would soon know.

Apart from my infuriating lapses into weakness, I was aware that my determination was hardening rapidly.

But just now I couldn't help enjoying Dinna's pretty face, and Erik smiling behind her. The hound was putting large shaggy paws on the bed and showing every sign of being as friendly as her master. Loud cluckings of disapproval were coming from Frue Harben in the next bed, and the nurse came hurrying down the room, only to be waved away imperiously by Dinna.

"Anna is very clean. She had a bath this morning especially for her visit to you, Luise. Didn't she, Onkel Erik?"

"And with perfume in the water," Erik said. "She now has odor of Lanvin's Arpege, or so Dinna tells me. I find it delicious, but I secretly believe Anna herself feels it something of a disadvantage."

"You are making me laugh and it hurts." But I could laugh with genuine amusement, that was the surprising thing. It was so nice to see Dinna looking friendly. And Erik.

"Sit down and talk to me. I'm getting so strong I'll soon be up."

"Yes, that's what we wanted to talk about," Dinna said. "My grandmother said she had visited you and arranged for you to come back to us as soon as the doctor said you could get up. But Onkel Erik and I have said, why should you wait for that? You can come back to your own room at once, and Birgitte and I can nurse you."

"We thought you could have a little too much of elderly ladies here," Erik said.

"They are kind," I protested. "And it isn't everyone who can lie ill in a ballroom." I wasn't sure that I wanted to be moved back to my own room, and surrounded by this eager attention. Did I trust it? Hadn't it come a little late?

I looked into Dinna's face and couldn't help saying, "Only

a little while ago you would hardly speak to me. Why have you changed?"

Dinna flushed. "I know that I was very rude. So was Niels. We're both sorry."

"Because I was nearly killed? Or because you think I'm not to be your stepmother after all?"

Erik had taken my hand. I liked the feel of his fingers around mine. I wasn't sure about trusting this gesture, either. Though it really would be difficult to read deviousness in his steady dark eyes.

"Let's not have talk about stepmothers, or any other problems. Just believe that we want to look after you. Is that so difficult?"

"Why aren't you in Copenhagen?" I asked. "It's you who has a business to look after there, not Otto."

"Yes, I have indeed, and unfortunately I must go back to it in a day or so."

"Onkel Erik stayed until he knew you were out of danger, Luise," Dinna said. "He said someone must stay. Especially when Papa had to leave. Please, Luise, you mustn't worry about Papa's bad behavior. My grandmother says it's a good thing you found it out before it was too late, and we think the same. Don't we, Onkel Erik? It's sad to say that one's own father is not a very good or honest man, but I still love him a little, although my brother doesn't. He hates him." Dinna gave a small adult shrug. "This happens in families, which is a great pity."

"But it *is* too late," I said, staring at the ceiling, letting the lovely colors please my eyes.

"Too late for what, Luise?" Dinna was asking.

"What are you trying to tell us, Luise?" said Erik, bending over me.

"I'm not trying to tell you, I *am* telling you. I have a wedding ring somewhere, when I can find it. It should be on my finger. I should never have let Otto persuade me to take it off. But we hadn't been married long. I suppose I was trying to please him, by doing what he asked and keeping our secret."

I looked up into the two pairs of eyes, Dinna's as blue as flower petals, though no doubt one day they would be faded into that washed moonstone color of her grandmother's, Erik's dark with astonishment, and what seemed to be dismay.

"Dinna and Niels have a stepmother after all," I said wearily. "They will just have to make the best of it."

Chapter Ten

∽✠ "THEY tell me you have been having hallucinations," said Otto's pleasant voice.

I was maddeningly exhausted as a result of the move from the hospital to the charming bedroom I had previously occupied at Maaneborg. I must have been asleep when Otto came in, for he was sitting in the easy chair at the foot of the bed, and looked as if he had been there for some time.

I was so relieved to see his big familiar figure that I forgot my resentment over his having deserted me while I was ill.

"You're back at last! I've kept asking for you. Did they tell you?"

"They said you had been talking a lot of nonsense," said Otto, lazily lifting his big body out of the chair and coming to the bedside. "Something about a wedding ring."

"Oh, yes, I seem to have lost it. Please find it for me, darling, and then we can prove I haven't been having hallucinations or talking nonsense."

"I'm glad you seem so much better," said Otto. "It was a good idea of Mama's to have you moved. You'll be more comfortable here, and of course you're welcome to stay as long as you want to. I believe the doctor has ordered at least a month's convalescence. That was a nasty knock you had, and it was entirely my fault. How can I make amends?"

Otto's blue eyes were at their sunniest. He looked kind and genial and sympathetic. And he was talking to me as if I were a stranger ...

"It was an accident. I don't want amends. I only ask you to find my wedding ring and put it on my finger again."

I looked up into his smiling face, and something cold stirred in me. Why was he looking so sympathetic, so humoring?

"Really, Otto, this silly farce has ended now. I won't be well enough for another marriage ceremony for some time, so we had better tell the truth at once. I've been trying to, but nobody would listen. Not even the old ladies in the hospital, but they were half daft, I suppose."

When he still didn't speak, but merely went on looking tolerant, as if he were listening to an idiot, I said with asperity, "Your mother isn't daft, nor is Erik, or your children. They think the bump I had has affected my brain, but they'll believe you if you tell them."

"About a wedding ring?" said Otto in a dreamlike voice. "But there is no wedding ring."

"You mean it's really lost?" I said irritably, and then, catching the flicker in his eyes that I had come to dread, my heart began to pump madly, and I had to lie back on the pillows and close my eyes. I was so stupidly weak, and in no condition to deal with Otto's infuriating mysteries.

He was being kind, the wretch, lifting my head to give me a sip of water.

"I'll go and let you rest, Luise. I seem to upset you."

I grabbed for his hand. "You'll upset me more by going away. You *must* tell me what is going on. Who has taken my wedding ring?"

He began to stroke my hair. "Dear girl, there *is* no wedding ring. You have been having hallucinations. It's a kind of wish fulfillment, the doctor says. You wanted to marry me. So!"

So, indeed! I could only gape at him in complete incredulity.

"I don't know what you're trying to do, Otto, but if you're telling me that not only does my wedding ring not exist, but neither does the parson at Dragor and the witnesses, that horrid little stuffy room, and the parson dropping the ring, then I'd say that it's you who is having hallucinations."

Otto listened to my confused protestations in smiling calm.

"Are you telling me we were never at Dragor?" I demanded.

"Not at all. We certainly spent a few days there." Now there was a faintly lecherous look in his eyes, and I liked that even less than his jolly smiling. "I'm not trying to deny that your pregnancy and also your unfortunate miscarriage was due to me, Luise. I'm most truly sorry about that, and I wish I could make amends. But I must tell you that we can no longer be married. My mother says I am a *skurk,* which means a scoundrel, although not so long ago she was doing her best to persuade us not to marry. But there you are. You have managed to get her sympathy, and I am the bad boy. Isn't that it?"

"Otto, I don't know why you're tormenting me with this nonsense."

"It isn't nonsense, my dear." Now the sincerity in his voice was making my blood run cold. Was he doing this to me with such cold deliberation, denying our marriage, because I was thin and ill and scarred? Was I more scarred than I had thought?

I sat up, reaching for a mirror. He put my hand back under the bedclothes.

"No, it isn't what you think. You haven't lost your looks. And I am still very fond of you. I just no longer wish to be married. Something has finished in my feelings. These things, when they die, can't be brought back to life, much as one would like them to."

"It's because I lost the baby."

"Yes, that was very sad. And the doctor has more bad news for you. It seems there's a doubt whether you can have another child. Some repair he had to do. Though of course, you must not despair. Doctors make mistakes."

Barren! That catastrophe I would have to come to terms with later. Just now I had to deal only with the strange lie Otto was telling me.

"So you deny that we were ever married."

"Luise, try to remember. Do try, I beg you. We were to come to Maaneborg to meet my family, to discuss a wedding in the church, to see if you would be happy here. We were on our way to see the church and make plans when we had the accident. But previously to that"—he looked down at me tenderly—"we had only loved, as you very well know."

When I didn't speak, he said, almost wistfully, "There was no *sognepraest* at Dragor, no witnesses, no wedding ring. Your illness has given you hallucinations. But they will go. Presently you will remember clearly."

I looked into his face and found its tenderness revolting.

"Otto, much as I now regret it, you are still my husband."

"You have clouds in your head, silly child."

"If you marry another woman you will be committing bigamy."

Did he look momentarily uneasy? I doubted it. He was too ruthless. Old Emilie had talked about the Greve's conscience, but she was mistaken. He had none.

And he was my husband, heaven help me.

"Bigamy!" he was saying in surprise. "What are you talking about? We simply spent a few weeks together. Living in sin, as the English call it. We Danes have much less feelings of guilt about things like that. After all, we didn't have your Queen Victoria for seventy years."

"Queen Victoria had nothing to do with bigamy being a crime," I said wearily. "And I have no guilty feelings about

105

living in sin. But I'm not the sort of woman who would allow myself to conceive an illegitimate child, nor will I have anybody accusing me of such a thing. So whatever you say, I intend to tell the truth."

"But, my poor child, no one believes you."

"Again and again until I am believed!"

"You will begin to be a bore, *mine kaer*."

I sat up, hot with anger.

"Don't you dare to call me *mine kaer!* How have you the face to? I'm beginning to hate you."

"Ah, that's not so nice. But I told you that accident had killed our feeling for each other."

"Otto, once and for all, I will not be cast off like one of your convenient women who spend a night in the turret room. I came here as your legitimate wife, and that I intend to prove."

"People will say hallucinations can be useful," he murmured. "Especially if they bring one a castle and a title."

"I will go to Dragor and get a copy of our marriage certificate. Did you think I couldn't do something as simple as that?"

All he said was, "You mustn't think of attempting to travel yet, Luise. You must rest. Stay with us until the end of the summer. As a matter of fact, I think my mother is going to insist on that. She is sorry your visit to our country has been so unfortunate. In any case, she admires you. She was only opposed to you as a daughter-in-law."

"Your epilepsy has affected your brain," I said.

And at last, with that cruel remark, I penetrated his smiling good humor. His face went dark, and I was afraid he was going to have one of his attacks there and then. I had to go on taunting him.

"Your mother's right, you shouldn't marry and have children. I'm glad I'm not going to have your child after all." But when he turned and went quickly out of the room, shutting the door with a heavy thud behind him, I sank back, trembling and in tears.

I hadn't known I could be so vindictive. Or so appalled and perplexed and hopeless. I was beginning to suspect Otto of anything, even that that urgent trip to Copenhagen had been for the purpose of removing all evidence of our marriage. Perhaps he had gone to Dragor and got rid of the *sognepraest!*

It wasn't surprising that my next visitor was the doctor,

who said Herre Winther had asked him to look in. He felt my pulse, asked whether my headache had come back, shone a light in my eyes.

"Well, am I going mad?" I asked sarcastically.

"The move has been a little too much for you," he said in his soothing doctor's voice. "I will give you something to make you relax."

"It wasn't the move, it was my husband who upset me."

"Too many visitors," the doctor murmured, shaking tablets out of a bottle.

"You don't believe me, do you?" I had never before heard myself speak in that ugly belligerent voice. Well, that was the way I was going to be until I had proved my story.

"I think you are suffering from a little personality disturbance," said the doctor pompously. "It is to be expected after what has happened. Now if you will just swallow two of these—"

I pushed his hand away.

"My head is as clear as yours. I remember perfectly. I am Frue Otto Winther, little as I now like it. If you want a personality disturbance, you must study my husband. He is simply not the man I married. Or else I didn't know the man I married. Doctor, it's Otto who is mad, not me."

"Yes, yes, perhaps."

I looked into his calm eyes and knew he was simply humoring me, a difficult, highly disturbed patient who must be restored to sanity.

"Please be so good as to swallow these tablets, Miss Amberley."

"I'm *not* Miss Amberley," I said despairingly.

"You will sleep for twelve hours and be much stronger in the morning."

"Will I?"

"Indubitably."

The pedantic English word came so unexpectedly from this serious young man that I had to smile.

"What English writers do you read, doctor?"

"Dickens, Trollope, your James Bond."

"Well, James Bond didn't think up this mystery."

The doctor laughed pleasantly.

"I think by the morning you will find there is no mystery, Miss Amberley. You have suffered from both concussion and a miscarriage, not the simplest illnesses for the delicate female system. But you will recover, I assure you."

My hands were on my flat stomach. I cried out sharply,

"Doctor, Otto told me I could never have another baby. Is that true?"

"Perhaps. Not necessarily."

"Which means it is true."

"When you return to London you should consult a good gynecologist. He may be of quite a different opinion from me."

I sat up. "Doctor, why did Otto ask you that question if I was not his wife? It's a question only a husband asks!"

I had thought my deduction so brilliant. But of course, the answer was predictable.

"Or a husband-to-be, Miss Amberley. I understand Herre Winther was interested for that reason."

I was defeated. I swallowed the tablets meekly, and closed my eyes. Twelve hours' sleep, the doctor had promised. It seemed an impossible paradise. But I was drowsily reaching its dark gates when I heard someone moving about my bed, and Birgitte's voice in its quaint broken English.

"You should talk to Helga Blom, froken."

I opened my eyes, trying to focus.

"Where can I find her, Birgitte?"

I thought she said, "In the turret room," but I must have imagined it. That room was locked and empty. Only ghosts lived there. *Spogelse* . . .

All the same, that serious little doctor was right, I did feel infinitely better in the morning. Well enough to get up and dress and go downstairs, although both Frue Dorothea and Dinna demurred at that.

They had come to visit me after I had had my breakfast of coffee and a boiled egg and dark rye bread.

"Now don't be in a hurry, Luise dear," Frue Dorothea said. "After lunch, if the sun is still shining, you can sit in the garden."

"I'll help you downstairs," Dinna said. "Are you really feeling better, Luise? You look better. Your eyes are quite bright again. I'm so glad, because I want to ask you hundreds of questions about London. My grandmother says I may go there when I am nineteen. Perhaps I could come and visit you."

My pleasure in the bright morning vanished.

"But I will be here."

Frue Dorothea laughed. "You may stay as long as you wish, Luise, but that is two years away. I think we may bore you a little by then."

"I will be here unless I can get a divorce," I said stubbornly. "Is that difficult in Denmark? I suppose it must be, when one's husband won't admit to being married in the first place."

Frue Dorothea said briskly, "We hoped you would have forgotten about that, now that you're so much better. Didn't we, Dinna?"

Dinna put her charming chicken-fluff head on one side and said with a precocious gravity, "Niels and I have discussed this, Luise. We think that the English are more—what is the word, Grandmama?"

"Prudish? Puritan?" said Frue Dorothea.

"Yes, I think so. I mean, guilty about making love before one is married. We don't take those things so seriously in Denmark."

"So you think my wedding ring existed only in my subconscious?" I said.

"Of course. You were going to have a baby, so you were wishing you could be wearing a wedding ring."

"Dinna is right, I think, Luise," Frue Dorothea said kindly.

I didn't want to get agitated. I kept a tight control on myself, and said quite calmly, "But I do have a wedding ring. I kept it in my handbag. Otto wanted me to hide it until we were married again in the Maaneborg church. I shouldn't have listened to him. But I did. And now the ring seems to be lost. Or stolen."

"Who would steal it?" Frue Dorothea asked, a touch of the old frostiness in her voice.

"How do I know? One of those senile old women, perhaps. But I don't think so. I think it was Otto. Probably after the accident. He was conscious all the time, and alone with me until help came. He had the opportunity. Didn't he?"

"But why should Papa do such a strange thing?" Dinna said.

"And, really, Luise, who would believe you were married because you were carrying a wedding ring in your handbag? It would much more likely be there for the convenience of wearing in hotels. You don't have to tell me that my son is not a saint."

I had thought of that. Frue Dorothea wasn't telling me anything I didn't already know. But all the same, I had to find the ring. Its discovery must surely shake Otto a little.

"Now, Luise, you are worrying again," Dinna chided.

"We must leave her to rest," Frue Dorothea said. "Is there anything you would like, Luise?"

"I would like to see Erik, please."

"Oh, but he left this morning. He had to get back to his office. He had already stayed away too long. They were telephoning for him."

"There's an opening ceremony of one of his buildings," Dinna said. "Onkel Erik is getting quite famous, you know. He has been asked to design a building in Stockholm, so he has to go there, also. He works very hard."

"Then he will be away some time?" I felt unaccountably depressed.

"Well, yes, he doesn't come to Maaneborg very often, does he, Grandmama?"

"He has his dog," I murmured.

"Niels takes care of her. She is quite happy. You will see her in the garden this afternoon."

They were gone, and I was alone and totally unable to rest. It seemed that every conversation I had at Maaneborg was going to be too upsetting. Come to think of it, it was only Erik who had been able to make me feel calm and relaxed, and he had gone. I really felt rather desolately alone. I believed I could have convinced Erik of the truth of my story, but for the rest, absolute proof was required.

I would have to get that, if only for the reason that I did not intend to commit bigamy. I had no intention of spending the rest of my life alone, a rejected wife.

Besides, I was getting vindictive. Whatever feeling I had had for Otto was turning to hate. Just thinking about him made me boil with anger and resentment. I was determined to show up his treachery. How could such a devious lying person live behind those sunny blue eyes? And I had more than a suspicion that our marriage was not his only guilty secret. There were the things the old ladies had hinted at. Poor Cristina an invalid, a helpless prisoner, in the turret room with only Helga Blom ... I slid out of bed and began to dress, my weakness making me clumsy, tears of frustration in my eyes.

It was too much. I would never be able to dress and climb all those stairs unaided. But this was my ideal opportunity, when everyone thought I was lying in bed, too weak to get up without assistance.

Where would I find Helga Blom? In the turret room ... That was what I imagined old Birgitte had said. Perhaps I had imagined it. Perhaps I had not. Somehow I would climb the twisting stairway.

I did, too, although it took every scrap of energy, and I had to rest several times, panting like someone with heart disease. But at last I dragged my shaking legs to the top and stood in front of the heavy wooden door set in the deep stone doorway.

I turned the handle, although I knew that would be useless. The door was locked, as Erik had said. So I knocked, at first softly, and then louder.

I waited, thinking I heard a faint shuffle within. The slit window on my left showed a bright scene of lake and woodland. Swallows were nesting in the stonework outside, for there was a flutter of wings and the shrill cheeping of chicks.

That must have been where the shuffling noise came from. I knocked again, hopelessly.

"Is there anyone in there?" I called.

Then I was sure I heard a slow dragging footstep. Someone whimpered. It sounded like the wolfhound Anna. It couldn't have been Anna. She was outdoors with Niels.

"Who is it?" I said urgently. "Open the door."

But now my weakness was getting the better of me. My ears were buzzing. Was that a thud behind the door, as if someone fell? Or was it the swallows fluttering outside the slit window? I had to sit down and put my head between my knees. When my faintness had passed, there was absolute silence. The door was still locked. Much as I had wanted to get into that room, it now terrified me. I didn't want the door to open after all. I was still too weak, too full of nightmares. When I was stronger I would come again. I would call more loudly.

Who would answer?

Not Cristina, because two days later I stood on her grave, more accurately, on the tablet that marked the spot where she lay in the vault beneath the paving-stone floor of the Maaneborg Kirken.

I read: GREVINDE CRISTINA SARAH MATILDE WINTHER, and the date of her death, less than a year ago. It was true that Otto had been in a hurry to remarry. He seemed to have snatched at the first willing person. Me.

Niels had driven me to the church. They had asked me that morning what I would like to do, since I was rapidly getting so much stronger, and I had said I would like a drive, to prove that I would not be nervous in a car after my accident.

Like Dinna, Niels had changed completely in his attitude

toward me. He was gentle and polite and charming. I had not seen how he behaved toward his father now that he was no longer threatened with a stepmother, as I had not set eyes on Otto since his visit to my room two days ago. I had avoided him by having meals upstairs, and deliberately not going down when I thought he would be about. I was not ready for another clash with him. That would come when I was stronger.

But Niels had been delighted to take me out in his car, repaired since the accident, and had only looked surprised when I had asked to stop at the little gray squat-towered church on the opposite side of the lake.

It was a peaceful place. From this aspect, Maaneborg looked as if it rose out of the lake, the reflection of its ochre-colored walls making a smoldering orange fire in the dark water. It looked grand and medieval, and for the first time pride stirred in me at the thought of being its mistress. But only because it stirred my aesthetic sense.

Cristina's grave was another thing. The lettering was so newly cut in the stone, and Niels' young face was so taut. I was remorseful for having brought him here.

"Did you love her very much?" I asked, knowing that he had, knowing this explained his antagonism toward his father.

"Ja," he said briefly.

I led the way out of the church and looked across at the window of the turret room.

"Did she really want to be in that room all the time?"

"Oh, yes. It was her—" he sought for a word, and I supplied one. "Refuge?"

"Perhaps. Perhaps more it was her place to be happy. My grandmother likes the window seat in the drawing room where she sews, and Dinna has the garden. And I have the stables and my horses and cars. But Mama had the turret room. She said she could see all the world from the windows. *Ja,* Miss Amberley, she was happy there."

I was pleased about that. Unaccountably pleased. My picture of Cristina being a wan prisoner was false.

"Niels," I said impulsively, "I know it was awfully soon after your mother's death for your father to marry again, but surely that wasn't the whole reason for your being so abominable to me?"

"Abominable?" he repeated, grinning as he tested the unfamiliar word. Or was he only pretending not to understand?

"You know what I mean. Rude. Horrible. And now you're so sweet."

"Well, you see, Miss Amberley, it was never you I disliked."

"But just someone taking your mother's place?"

"Perhaps."

"You are hardly being fair. Your father is only in his forties. When you are that age, you won't think your life is over."

Niels' face changed subtly. It had a tinge of his grandmother's arctic cold.

"Perhaps it would be a good thing if his were," he said, and walked abruptly toward the car.

I followed at a slower pace. My legs were still unsteady.

"Look here, Niels, you can't say a thing like that without explaining it. Whatever you may think, you're speaking of my husband."

He had started the engine and was revving it noisily. The roar seemed to relieve his feelings. His voice was more in control when he said, "My father says he never married you, and for that you can count yourself fortunate. Why don't you leave it there, Miss Amberley? Believe me, you should be glad to escape. Or is it Maaneborg you want, after all?"

I wanted to slap his impudent young face.

"It just happens that I was very fond of your father. I even thought I loved him. If I don't any longer, that's beside the point. All I want to do is avoid being a bigamist in the future. Or perhaps—I have a perhaps, too—I can prevent your father playing this trick on another woman."

Although the car was moving, Niels turned to me with the greatest urgency.

"Then prove that you can, Miss Amberley! Prove it!"

I hadn't got over my nervousness in a car, after all. I begged Niels to turn his attention to the road, and then asked him quietly, "Why do you hate your father so much?"

The handsome profile was cold, stubborn, implacable.

"Because he hates me."

"But why?"

"Because I am healthy. Because I didn't inherit the Winther disease."

"Niels! That couldn't be!"

"It is. My grandmother will tell you. It is the reason."

With this new picture of a vicious, slightly insane Otto, I was almost tempted to take everyone's advice, and simply go

113

back to England and keep my Danish marriage a secret forever more.

But my necessity to justify myself, as well as my sense of tidiness, instantly dismissed this idea. I would have to take the long dreary course of the divorce court. I could never make another marriage with this situation hanging over me. Otto's strange mentality might take a more sadistic direction, and it might be he who accused me of bigamy.

But who would want to marry me, barren and with two unhappy love affairs behind me?

The thought of this depressed me so much that Niels began to tease me about my long face.

"You should be happy and laughing, knowing what you have escaped."

"But I didn't escape," I insisted wearily. "Your father did marry me. As soon as I am strong enough, in a day or two, I hope, I intend going to Dragor to ask the parson for a copy of the marriage certificate."

"We call it an *aegteskabsattest*."

"That sounds like another form of torture."

Niels laughed. "Our language is always strange to foreigners. And do you think you can get this marriage certificate?"

"Of course. I should have got one at the time. It was only that I trusted your father then."

Niels was silent for a moment. Then he said, "Well, that will certainly be more proof than a ring that has been lost. Anyone can wear a ring."

That remark made me think of the old ladies' gossiping in the garden, and the remarks about the Greve's conscience, and the Grevinde's old maidservant, Helga Blom.

I asked Niels one more question.

"Has the turret room been empty ever since your mother died?"

"Yes. My father has ordered it to be kept locked."

"I thought I heard sounds in it the other evening."

Niels looked at me sharply, and I thought he was going to accuse me of snooping. But he only said, "It must have been swallows. A pair come every year to nest on the windowsill. My mother used to enjoy watching them."

"And perhaps mice?"

"Oh, I don't think mice. The room is cleaned every now and then."

What animal's feet could make a shuffling noise? I said, quite casually, "What happened to the servant who used to

114

look after your mother? I heard the old ladies talking about her."

"You mean Helga. Oh, she became *forrykt*—what is the word?"

"Crazy?"

"Yes, queer in the head. She was put in the old women's home."

"But they said she wasn't there now."

Again Niels gave me a sharp glance. This time I thought it was a little disturbed.

"How would they know? They're all more or less crazy themselves."

We had come up the long winding drive to the bridge over the moat. Niels stopped the car and pointed to the strange stone faces set at intervals in the high walls of the castle.

"Those are the faces of the enemies of the Winthers, embalmed there to be looked at by coming generations. When I was a small boy, I had a nurse who used to frighten me with the stories of what happened in the dungeons here."

"But that's long ago."

"Yes? We are the same family."

The castle looked so peaceful, with the sunlight warm on the red walls and gilding the windows. The extravagant thought came to me that it was like Otto, his smiling serenity covering the dark dungeons hidden within him.

"My grandmother loves Maaneborg," Niels was saying. "She came to it as a very young bride, only seventeen. My grandfather died a long time ago. I never knew him. But he was one of the good Winthers, I think."

"He didn't have ep—the disease?"

"Yes, but he was still good. Like Onkel Erik. I will marry and have a good son, too."

He was speaking with the optimism of youth. I sat with the sun falling on my face, feeling sad and resigned and suddenly peaceful. I was glad for the first time that my little foetus had not grown.

My peaceful feeling lasted into the evening. For the first time since the accident, I felt well enough to dress and go down to dinner. I was glad I did so, because Otto didn't come in, and as a consequence, Niels and Dinna were gay and uninhibited. and Frue Dorothea looked gentle and benign. I could see what a charming life one could have in this old castle if the shadow were removed. Frue Dorothea wanted to show me, from the drawing-room windows, how the sun lingered on the lake. Niels had put a record on the gramophone, and he and Dinna began to dance. They looked so handsome, with their pale hair and fine features. Frue Dorothea let the curtain drop, and clapped her hands softly in time to the music.

"My husband and I loved dancing," she said. "We had some wonderful balls here. When Niels announces his engagement, we will turn the conservatory into a ballroom. It won't be like the old one, but one can't have all that magnificence in modern times."

"Is Niels planning to marry?" I asked.

"It isn't settled, but I think it soon will be. Such a sweet girl, from Odense. Her name is Liselotte."

"Does she know about the Winther disease?" I couldn't help asking.

Frue Dorothea's mouth tightened. "No. And there is no need for her to know. It won't affect her. She will make a very suitable mistress for Maaneborg."

Well, there it was. I had to ruin the peaceful evening.

"But *I* am the mistress of Maaneborg."

Chapter Eleven

I DIDN'T see Otto again until I was leaving Maaneborg.

Everyone said it was too soon for me to travel. This was true, because I was still weak and I still got headaches. But I couldn't stand this ambiguous position any longer. My last feeble attempt at proving myself failed. This was when I had asked to see the old woman Emilie whom I had talked to in the garden on my first day.

She obviously enjoyed her visit to the private half of the castle. She accepted coffee from Frue Dorothea and held her sharp little chin high, to emphasize that she was just as much a lady as her hostess.

But when I asked her if she remembered my showing her the ring on my finger and telling her that I was Otto's wife, her face went blank.

She had no recollection whatsoever of such an event. All we had talked about, she insisted, was the poor dead Countess Cristina. Then she wagged a bony forefinger at me in an infuriating way and said, "But you will remember that I gave you good warning about taking Herre Winther seriously. I said that he gave too much unhappiness to his poor wife." She turned to Frue Dorothea. "My apology for making that remark, Frue Dorothea, but you must agree that it is true, and I and my friend, Sophie Holberg, were concerned about this innocent young woman."

For all her outspokenness, however, she had an unpleasant undercurrent of servility. She was a penniless old woman dependent on the Winthers for the comfortable home she now occupied. She was not going to risk losing that.

Anyway, what did it prove if she admitted my story? Simply that I was being too eager to become the new countess.

I said tiredly, "You have a bad memory."

Her old eyes snapped frostily.

"And you, Miss Amberley, if I may say so, have been too anxious to get a father for your child."

"Oh—" I began to rise in anger, but Frue Dorothea's hand on my arm held me.

For the first time, I enjoyed the arctic chill in her voice.

"I think you can find your way back, Frue Andersen. Thank you for coming."

The old woman, disliking being dismissed so summarily, went off muttering to herself. Frue Dorothea said quietly, "It really is time you realized that my son Otto is an unscrupulous person. When I, his mother, who should defend him, have to say this, it must be believed. So why don't you stop hurting yourself, and accept things as they are?"

"I am Otto's wife," I said stubbornly. "That is how things are."

Frue Dorothea smiled tolerantly. At least I knew that she and Dinna and Niels didn't think I was telling this story because I wanted to have a title and a castle to live in. They thought, bless them, that I was singularly innocent and wronged, and wanted to whitewash my character.

Otto didn't think that. He thought that I wanted revenge. I saw him once more before I left. He was sprawling in his big leather chair in the library, and looked at me with half-closed smiling eyes. Like a fat sinister tomcat. Contemptuously I threw the ring he had given me on my first evening at Maaneborg into his lap.

"You forgot to ask for this back."

For one moment he looked abashed. But only for a moment.

"Thank you, Luise. I imagine you don't want it as a keepsake."

"I never cared for it, anyway. I don't enjoy dead women's rings. But don't imagine this means I'm going off meekly and giving up."

"Then go to Dragor, Luise. No one is stopping you."

"We signed a register," I insisted. "No priest or parson is going to destroy a register."

"Then go and look at it, if you can. But I can tell you now you're wasting your time. This is all a hallucination. I wish you would believe me."

"Perhaps you think I have forgotten which house it was," I said. "But I haven't. I particularly remember it. It had yellow walls, and geraniums in pots."

"So have a thousand houses in Zealand."

"It was the second from the corner on the Strandlinien."

"I congratulate you on your observation. One can dream yellow houses with geraniums, of course. But you insist on seeing for yourself. So I wish you luck." He stood up and held out his hand. "Will you be coming back to see us at Maaneborg?"

"Yes," I said wildly. "To see Helga Blom."

"Helga Blom!" He was astonished. "Whatever has she to do with this fantasy of yours?"

"I don't know. But I would like to see her."

"Then I must tell you again that you will be wasting your time. There is no secret about her. She is being cared for, as are all the old women whom I have given a home. But she has become senile, so has to have some constraint." He gave his attractive smile. "Sad, isn't it? Now do you wonder that I go off to gay places like Majorca to amuse myself?"

My face was stiff with dislike.

When Otto put out his hand in a familiar gesture to touch my hair, I moved back so sharply that he burst into his great jolly laugh.

"Good heavens, Luise, I won't eat you. But I am truly sorry our little affair has ended this way. You are getting your looks back, too. The scar on your forehead is fading. I would never have forgiven myself if I had marked you for life."

"A little scar!" I cried. "What is that compared with the rest?"

"You blame me too much. Would you have had us go ahead with a marriage that was bound to be unhappy? I didn't think you would be so dishonest."

"Dishonest! *You* can use that word about me!"

In that moment my motive for seeking the truth did change. Now I really wanted revenge on this large smiling man whom I had thought I had loved.

Maaneborg. Moon Castle. The castle that was nearly mine. Although a better name would be Cloud Castle, since that was what it had proved to be. I spent a long time, on my last night, looking at the moon shining on the lake, and listening to the sad sough of the wind in the beechwoods. An owl began hooting, then, in a moment of pure magic, it floated absolutely noiselessly past the window. I saw it hang over the black and gold water of the lake, before moving off on an upcurrent of air out of sight. All at once, far off, there was a thin high scream, a primitive cry of agony. The hunting owl had made its kill. The odor that came in my window was composed of roses and stagnant water. Beautiful, primitive, cruel, faintly diseased . . . That was Maaneborg. I should be so thankful to be getting away.

I knew this, yet I could not get over my obsession with the

place. It was with reluctance that I prepared to leave in the morning.

Niels said he would drive me to the ferry. Frue Dorothea kissed me, with a great show of affection. "We have grown very fond of you, Luise. It is a pity we made such an unfortunate start." And Dinna threw her arms around me and begged that I come back one day. "This place gets lonely. It's all old women. And I'm not permitted to go to Copenhagen except with my grandmother."

She had her father's limpid blue eyes, and the hint of tragedy at the back of them. Poor child, she lived under the Winther shadow, too. But perhaps she would find a sympathetic husband.

"We're going to have a party when Niels announces his engagement. You must really come to that."

"What as?" I asked. "A shadow stepmother? Your father's shadow wife?"

Everybody laughed as if I had made a huge joke. Then Niels helped me into his car, and we were off.

It did not take long to flash down the winding road, through the lovely beechwoods and the quiet green fields, to the little town of Kolby Kaas, and the jetty where the ferry was already loading with passengers, cars and cargo for the much bigger island of Zealand, and Copenhagen with its million inhabitants.

Niels shook hands with me, and apologized again for his behavior on my arrival.

"But I am forgiven? I have made amends?"

His charm had nothing to do with Otto's. He must have taken after his mother's family entirely. When he smiled like this, he gave no hint of the petulance and rudeness of which he was capable. He was just a nice ordinary young man whom it really was absurd to imagine as my stepson.

"We Danes like to keep our reputation for being hospitable," he said. "I really would like you to come back for my and Liselotte's party."

"And if I come with proof of my marriage, will you be just as beastly to me again?"

He frowned. "I wish you would leave all that nonsense alone. You will only find what a rogue my father is."

"Have you always hated him?"

"I was born in the last year of the war. I suppose from the time I first went to school, yes."

"Why then? Was it because of things the other boys said?"

"That is nothing to do with you," he said with a return to

120

his old rude manner. "If you want to catch this boat, you had better go on board."

I was not seasick on this crossing, although the sea was far from calm. The summer was almost over, and the wind blowing across the Kattegat had a distinctly Siberian chill. I took refuge in the small saloon, and sat at a table to write a letter to Tim.

I should have written it days ago. I had put off facing the reality of my position. If I couldn't prove my marriage, I was on my own and more or less penniless. Even if I could prove it, I had no intention of living on a reluctant husband. So I had to swallow my pride and ask for my old job back.

It was impossible to go into the whole story now. I hadn't enough writing paper, the boat rocked, two women with a restless child sat opposite me and began a long conversation in their curious throaty language. They kept looking at me, and I was sure they knew who I was, and my ignominious story. Then I realized that they were looking at the scar on my forehead, and my wing of white hair which was growing again since my accident. When I caught their eyes they smiled in sympathy. The child crowed and knocked over his mug of milk as the boat lifted in a swell. I rescued my writing paper and mopped off the milk, thinking that Tim would believe it was tears.

"Can you send me some money quickly," I had written, "to the Hotel d'Angleterre in Copenhagen? I can't tell you the whole sad story now, you wouldn't believe it anyway, but can I have my job back? You can call me all the things you want to—gullible, innocent, simple—but do it before I see you. I can't go on being told I'm a semi-idiot, or I'll really become one. I'll be back in London after I have done one or two rather important things. Did you, by the way, do any more research on my delightful husband, Count Otto Winther? Fifty pounds will do, in the meantime. I have some traveler's checks left, but not enough for my air fare."

I signed the scribbled stained note, and on an impulse wrote a postscript. "Oh, what a tangled web we weave, when first we practise to deceive." I might as well make Tim thoroughly curious. Then he would try hard to remember the reason for the small faint bell that rang in his head at the mention of the name Otto Winther.

Dragor. It had lost its charm. There were still the same narrow streets of yellow and terra-cotta houses, the Dragor Kro was exactly the same—a few weeks were not going to add much to its extreme antiquity—the sea gulls still swooped and cried over the fishing boats, and the fat white geese picked at the turf on the foreshore.

Perhaps the charm had gone because the sun wasn't shining and the wind was just as chilly here as it had been crossing the Kattegat. More likely it was because I felt so lonely.

I had loved Otto, damn him. At least, I had enjoyed a happy cozy relationship, wrapped in his protectiveness, his affection and his good humor. I had walked along this windy Strandlinien arm and arm with the man I was about to marry, and the wind had never seemed cold or the sea this dreary mud color. Although I had to admit, there had been a slight chill in the air after my discovery of Otto's illness. But only a slight one.

It was hard to believe that this had been only a few weeks ago, only time for the petunias and lobelias in the little neat gardens to fade, and for dahlias and nasturtiums to take their place. How could I have lost so much optimism so quickly?

It wasn't difficult to find the modest house where the parson lived. I recognized its yellow walls and brown door, and the pebbled path leading up to the door. The same lace curtains hung in the windows, and there was the same fat tabby cat curled up among the geraniums in the windowbox.

Naturally I expected the fat elderly woman who had picked up the ring when her husband had dropped it to open the door.

But I should have known scenes never repeat themselves. The woman who opened the door was young and sharp-faced, and I had never seen her before.

She said, *"Ja?"* in a quick sharp voice that matched her face. Yet she wasn't unattractive. She was slim, and had fine, pale blond hair. Her eyes were cold, though. As she looked at me, their expression became suspicious.

"Do you speak English?" I asked.

"Yes, a little."

"I've come to see the parson. He'll be your father?"

"Parson?"

I was sure she understood the word. But for some reason she pretended she didn't.

I attempted the difficult Danish pronunciation. "The *sog-nepraest.*"

"A priest!" Her voice was full of surprise. I couldn't be sure whether it was assumed or not. "You have come to the wrong house, I think."

"An elderly man," I insisted. "And his wife was rather fat. She did her hair in a little knot on top of her head."

I looked helplessly at the young woman as her pale eyebrows went up.

"No such people live here. You have made a mistake."

"You mean they have moved since the middle of summer?"

"Oh, no, I have lived here with my husband since we were married five years ago."

A flat feeling of inevitability settled on me. I looked at the brown door, the low eaves, the windowboxes, the tabby cat. It was the same cat, I could swear.

I saw the young woman (Now why was she so hostile? For I wasn't imagining that!) begin to close the door. I put my hand to my forehead and said faintly, "I'm so sorry. Could I have a glass of water? I've been ill."

No woman, unless she was a downright enemy, could refuse that request. Neither could she keep me standing on the doorstep. Albeit reluctantly, I was asked to come in. A chair was pushed forward in the little passage.

"Sit down. Excuse me."

The girl darted away, presumably to the kitchen for the glass of water, and I, seizing the opportunity, had the door into the little front parlor where Otto and I had stood to be married open in a flash.

The girl came back with the glass of water as I stood there, staring.

If she were really innocent of the whole affair, my actions must have seemed very suspicious. Indeed, her expression indicated that.

Very coldly, she said, "Are you really ill, or is this an excuse to come into my house?"

I just stared into the little room, unable to reply.

It had been newly decorated, there was no doubt about that. The very modern wallpaper was hardly suitable for such a small room, and I had much preferred the cosy plush-covered sofa and chairs to the functional ones that stood there now. But if I looked carefully, I would find something familiar remaining. The lace curtains? But they were of a kind that hung in every second window in Denmark. The carpet? No, there had been only rugs on the floor, because I remembered that when the parson had dropped the ring, it had rolled away with a little clatter over the wooden floor. So the carpet, with its faded pattern of roses, had probably been bought economically, secondhand. The bribe hadn't run to everything.

The bribe?

"I was admiring your new decorations," I said.

"*Ja?*" came the hostile voice.

"I suppose I'm old-fashioned. I really liked that nice faded furniture better. What happened to the stuffed canary on the mantelpiece?"

"I don't know your name, or what you want, but you are certainly in the wrong house. A stuffed canary? My husband would throw it on the fire."

Was she protesting too much?

I heard some thumping overhead, and a child's voice calling.

"*Ja*, Peter," the woman called back. To me she said, "That is my little boy just woken up. I must go to him."

She stood impatiently, waiting for me to leave.

"But don't you want to know why I came to this house?" I asked. I couldn't believe she was so incurious.

"*Nej.* It is nothing to do with me."

"Can I speak to your husband?"

"Only if you come back in two weeks' time. He is out with the fishing fleet."

"A fisherman!" I said excitedly. "But that's right. Is his name Jens Larsen?"

The pale eyes flickered. "*Nej,*" said the woman.

But she didn't go on to say what her husband's name was. Surely, if she were telling the truth, she would have said it was Hansen or Andersen or whatever.

"I believe it must have been your husband who was a witness at my marriage. If the priest doesn't live here, did he use your front parlor? Perhaps my husband paid him to perform the ceremony here. Or did he pay you? Is that how you got the money to buy all that new furniture?"

More disturbing than this young woman's hostility was the faint pitying smile that now played over her narrow face.

"I notice you have an injury to your head, froken. Has it perhaps affected your brain? A marriage ceremony here!" She suddenly began to laugh. "Why, my husband doesn't even go to church. He has no time for religion."

"This wasn't exactly religious," I said stiffly.

"It couldn't have been lawful either, froken." She was using the term for an unmarried woman with insolent deliberation. "A marriage ceremony here! Oh, dear, I must tell my husband. He will be much amused."

The child upstairs began to cry loudly.

"I have to go, I am sorry." I was being edged out of the door politely but firmly. The woman turned to call up the steep narrow stairway, something in Danish that I didn't understand, and the child's crying stopped. Someone began singing to him, then gave a low rollicking laugh in which the baby presently joined.

I was out on the chilly doorstep. "You have someone looking after your baby? Your mother?"

I wasn't told that this, too, was none of my business. Instead, the door shut in my face. The fat cat in the geranium box stretched and yawned and stared at me, and as I took some steps backward the lace curtains in the tiny window in the eaves parted, and someone looked down at me. Seeing herself observed, the curtains were dropped in a flash. I had only a vague impression of a plump rosy face and a topknot of gray hair.

It was really so vague that I was afraid it was only wishful thinking. Perhaps Anna Hansen was crooning to a restless baby today instead of scrabbling on the floor for a dropped wedding ring. It was possible. But it was more probable that many grandmothers in Denmark had plump rosy faces and gray hair, and I was merely looking at one of these.

The only thing that was certain was that I was not going to be allowed inside that house again.

I had to investigate the possibility that I had made a mistake about the house. I spent a weary hour walking up and down the streets near the seafront, willing there to be another exactly similar house with yellow walls, a brown door, a cat among the geraniums. If they had gotten rid of the parson, they really should get rid of the cat, too, I thought tiredly. If they had thrown away the canary, it wouldn't break their hearts to give away the cat. There was no point in not being thorough.

I wondered if the woman and the baby had been in the house the afternoon that Otto and I were married. If so, they had kept very quiet.

Or had I really imagined the whole thing, as people wanted me to believe? I was so tired and dejected that I was beginning to think that everyone was telling the truth except myself. Even Otto. For mine was such an unlikely story. A marriage ceremony in a fisherman's cottage. How could I have been so naïve and bemused as to think this was the way things were done in Denmark?

But it *hadn't* been a fisherman's cottage then. There had

125

been a Bible on the table, I remembered. And apart from his breath smelling of schnapps, the parson had had a solemn air and an educated accent.

In any case, I hadn't the faintest reason for thinking that Otto would want to deceive me. He had behaved impeccably until then. And he really had wanted to marry me. I was absolutely certain of that. So why indulge in something so far-out as a bogus ceremony, which must have cost some trouble and money to arrange, apart from anything else?

Why, why, why?

I was sure I could get to the bottom of this the moment I found the parson. He, surely, would not lie to me.

It was late afternoon and the wind was rising, driving muddy hanks of cloud across the low sky. I had one more thing to do before I caught the bus back to Copenhagen and the Hotel d'Angleterre, where I had left my bags and booked a room.

It was pretty hopeless, and wouldn't really prove anything, but I wanted to check whether they remembered Otto and me at the Kongelige Hotel. They had known we were married. Otto would have signed the register to this effect. That, at least, would be some evidence I could produce.

I was pleased to see the same stout gentleman, Herre Frolich, sitting at the desk. When he saw me, he gave a broad smile of welcome and held out his hand.

"Ah, Frue Pedersen, how good to see you again. But alone? Where is your husband?"

"What did you call me?" I asked stonily.

"Frue Pedersen." He began to laugh heartily. "Is it that you want to be called *Mrs.*, as in English?"

"You're making a mistake," I said. "My name is Winther."

"But I thought—you are so like another lady—" He was staring in perplexity at my white patch of hair, a rather unique peculiarity that he was unlikely to forget.

"I am the same person," I hastened to explain. "It's just that you have the wrong name. Probably it's my husband's bad handwriting. I'd be interested to see how he could make Winther look like Pedersen."

Herre Frolich was so apologetic about his mistake that he couldn't produce the hotel register quickly enough.

"Let me see, it was about the end of June, I think. As you see, I have an excellent memory. Now then, here we are. But I am right, Frue—" Now the poor man could call me nothing at all. He could only show me in the clearest hand-writing the signature "Otto Pedersen and Luise Pedersen."

It was there in black and white, Otto's deliberate treachery.

Had he anticipated every move I was going to make? Had he never meant us to be married properly at all, not even in the church at Maaneborg?

Oh, he was clever. No wonder he had been so unperturbed about my trip to Dragor. He knew I would be thwarted at every turn. He was a sadist, my so loving husband.

"So? Is it correct?" Herre Frolich was asking anxiously.

"No," I said. "It seems my husband was anxious not to be recognized. He is very modest. He refuses to use his title, too. He is Count Otto Winther of Maaneborg. Perhaps you have heard of him?"

Herre Frolich's light blue eyes seemed to grow more prominent in his surprise. Then, in a very curious way, they became cool and aloof, as if, all at once, I was a complete stranger.

"*Ja,*" he said briefly. "I have."

He slammed the register shut. "Then if madam doesn't require a room—"

She can be on her way. He didn't actually say those words, but I could read them behind his unfriendly gaze.

"And why would Count Otto Winther not have been a welcome guest in your hotel?" I asked.

Herre Frolich showed no surprise at my question, but was not to be drawn.

"That you must ask him yourself, madam."

And a fine chance I had of being answered, I thought.

I puzzled about this new development as I wearily walked off to catch the bus. Had Otto used a false name, not because he wanted to hide my identity, but because he must hide his own?

Herre Frolich would be about the same age as Otto, or a little older. Did he remember some scandal about Otto? It seemed that I was as little likely to find that out as I was to sort out my own affairs.

On the half-hour bus ride back to Copenhagen, I was near to giving up. As soon as Tim sent me some money, I would fly to London. I would put all this out of my mind. Much as I had grown to love Denmark, I would forget it.

But a skein of geese moving across the late evening sky reminded me of the swans at Maaneborg. I shut my eyes and saw the wind moving the reeds, and sending black shadows silently across the water. I remembered the high rosy red walls of the castle, and the ash-colored faces petrified in their niches. I heard the long mournful *whoo-oo* of the owls at night, and the lugubrious voices of the desiccated gentlewomen drifting over the garden wall. And knew that I would never forget any of these things. Indeed, I believed I had suffered some kind of trauma, and they would haunt me for the rest of my life.

I walked wearily into the Hotel d'Angleterre thinking of nothing but a hot bath, and some supper in my room. The clerk at the desk, handing me my key, said that a gentleman had been telephoning. He hadn't left a name. He said that he would call again.

Otto, I thought with distaste. He was curious about what I had been doing. A little nervous, perhaps. I hoped he was more than that. I would like him to be in a state of complete funk at the possibility of being stuck with a barren wife, after all.

Barren! I truly believe that as I walked across the elegant foyer of the hotel toward the lift, I realized clearly for the first time the disaster that had happened to me.

"What floor, madam?"

The lift boy was looking at me with some bewilderment, the strange lady who had stumbled into the lift as if she were drunk.

"The third, please," I said, wondering by what desperate effort I could control the tears that were trying to break forth.

We reached the third floor, and the nice little pink-cheeked boy held open the door of the lift and gave me a small stiff bow. I mumbled thanks, and went blindly toward the sanctuary of my room.

I didn't remember ever longing hungrily for a baby, as some girls did. I think I had too much ego for a strong maternal instinct. But there had, of course, always been the thought that a child, or two or three children, were waiting for me in some not too distant area of my life. I had certainly never contemplated marriage without children. But now I felt like those women in the Bible who were spoken of so contemptuously for their barrenness, as if they were less than worms. I was no longer complete. I was a thing to be scorned, not only by Otto Winther, but by other men. I was only twenty-six, and ruined.

Well, have a good cry and stop being melodramatic, I told myself, sobbing into my pillow. All those tears must have been inside me since my accident. It was time they came out. Lucky they were doing so when I was alone, locked in my room and with no one to tap at the door, lucky this profound uncontrollable misery hadn't hit me when I was on the bus, or sitting in a restaurant, or on the street.

The telephone beside me buzzed, wrenching me out of my self-absorption.

I automatically picked it up, then wished I hadn't as the voice of the clerk said, "A call for you," and immediately the other voice came. "Is that you, Luise? This is Erik Winther speaking."

"Erik," I said faintly. "How did you know I was here?"

"My mother telephoned me from Maaneborg. She said you had left, and they were a little anxious about you, as you were still not very strong for traveling."

"I am perfectly strong for traveling, thank you."

"So she asked me to see you in Copenhagen," Erik went on calmly. "Perhaps we could have dinner this evening?"

"Are you being a watchdog?"

"Yes. That is right."

"You want to find out what I've been doing today."

"I am very interested in what you do, certainly."

Could I trust another Winther? They all changed face so bewilderingly. So far, Erik had been quiet and serious and convincingly sincere, but how was I to know that he also hadn't another unpleasant face? Families closed ranks when threatened by trouble. I was beginning to wonder how much Frue Dorothea's sudden change to friendliness was genuine. And also Niels' and Dinna's.

As if he had heard my thoughts, Erik said, "Don't you trust me, Luise?"

"You are my beloved husband's brother."

"A fair comment. So you don't wish to see me?"

"I don't wish to be seen," I said crossly. "The day I've just had shows on my face."

"I understand. You have been crying some tears. That explains your unfriendly voice."

He needn't have sounded so relieved or so sympathetic. My eyes were filling with tears again. I blinked them back painfully and heard Erik saying, "Wash your face and I will meet you downstairs in thirty minutes."

Before I could refuse, he had hung up, and I was left staring at my bedraggled image in the mirror and wondering how I was ever to make myself presentable. Erik had seen me a shattered wreck in the hospital, so I supposed this variation of red eyes and haggardness didn't matter too much. All the same, I madly drenched my face in cold water, then did my hair with as much care as time permitted before changing into the little black dress which Erik had admired at Maaneborg. That seemed years ago.

I certainly looked ten years older, although the cold water had brought some color to my cheeks, and my heart was jumping a bit. I supposed I must be quite excited about seeing Erik, in spite of my distrust.

When I was ready, I lost confidence in my appearance and hid behind dark glasses.

That ploy, however, was useless, for as soon as Erik had shaken hands with me, he calmly removed my glasses.

"Excuse me. I never could talk to a woman wearing dark glasses. I am always afraid she might have fallen asleep behind them, in boredom with me. I have my car outside. We'll go to Tivoli. It's very pretty in the evening."

If anything, Erik had made an understatement, for the colored lights and the fountains cascading in golden jets, and the night-dark trees dropping dry rustling autumn leaves were as near to fairyland as anything I could have imagined. But I wasn't in the mood to enjoy any of this gaiety or even my serious, courteous companion until I had swallowed the dry martini Erik had ordered, and felt the knot of misery inside me miraculously begin to loosen.

We had a table overlooking the little theater where Harlequin and Columbine were going through their complicated affairs for no doubt the thousandth time that season. A little distance off, the balloon seller was struggling to hold his airborne wares. The wind was tugging at them, and swirling fallen leaves and little girls' skirts. A band composed of little boys in red and white uniforms marching very upright and stiltedly, like Hans Andersen's toy soldiers, went by, playing noisily. When the sound had died, Erik discussed what we should eat, gave the order to the waiter, then said in a businesslike voice, "Now, Luise. My mother said you intended going to Dragor today. Did you?"

"Yes, I did."

"This is where you say Otto married you."

"This is where Otto married me."

"I'm sorry. I didn't mean to put it like that. I wasn't doubting you."

"But you were. You still are. You didn't believe my story any more than anyone else did."

"It was a strange story," Erik said. "You must admit that. And since you had had such a bad knock on the head, we could surely be forgiven for being a little surprised by it.

After all, why didn't you tell it when you were in full possession of your senses? Why not the morning I showed you over the castle, for instance?"

"It was a secret. I was respecting Otto's wishes. Now I no longer have to do that."

"It didn't occur to you to distrust Otto?"

"Why should it? He had been courting me pretty assiduously since we met in Majorca."

"Courting?"

"An old-fashioned word we use in England."

"It means serious intentions?"

His voice was gently humorous, and I thought he was laughing at me. I said shortly, "I am neither naïve nor a prude. It just happens I wanted a husband, not a lover. And Otto made it pretty clear he wanted a wife. I had to follow the law and be a resident here for six weeks, and at the end of that time we found ourselves in Dragor, and Otto simply didn't want to wait any longer. Neither did I. So Otto was clever enough to find a parson, a *sognepraest*, as you call him, who would marry us privately, and there it was."

Erik had listened attentively, his eyes fixed on my face. I thought his expression had become a little grim; otherwise, he expressed no disbelief.

He just asked if I hadn't been surprised that Otto could find a parson so quickly.

"I didn't think about it. Dragor is a small place. I suppose anyone could tell him where to find one."

"But today it wasn't so easy?"

"How did you know?"

"Well, for one thing, you had to wear dark glasses to hide your eyes which were not full of triumph. Mind you, you are foolish to waste tears on Otto, who is a traitor, anyway."

"You mean trickster."

"Whichever word. Neither is pleasant."

"Perhaps. But I don't know whose side you are on, either."

He gave me a startled and reproachful look. "Why, yours, of course."

"So are Niels and Dinna and your mother, now. But they weren't when they thought I was going to be Otto's wife. Why was everybody so opposed to his marrying again? Even you were when you first met me. You looked sad and sympathetic."

"That was because you were seasick. I was suffering with you. You know, I am waiting for the day when you look well and happy. First you were seasick, then you were just becoming conscious after a bad accident, now you are full of pain at discovering my brother's treachery."

I meant to make an apology for my constantly unfortunate appearance, but the martini I had drunk on an empty stomach had addled my wits even more completely.

I heard myself saying in a dreamy voice, "When I first saw you, you were with an attractive girl, and Otto told me you were a womanizer."

I liked the way his eyebrows raised themselves into beautiful black half-moons.

"Is this another of your strange stories?"

"Oh, no, this one is as true as the other. We were at the opera on my first evening in Copenhagen. Otto seemed very anxious not to be seen, even by you. Now, of course, I realize it was I he didn't want seen."

"Perhaps not entirely," Erik said slowly. "Otto hasn't many friends in Copenhagen. Now, will you please stop worrying about him for a little while, and eat your food."

I took a mouthful of smoked trout and put down my fork.

"The man in the hotel at Dragor looked just as you do when he talked about Otto. I asked him if he didn't recognize the name Count Otto Winther, and he became furtive. Why?"

"Well, perhaps my brother doesn't endear himself. You know that already. He had found someone to pretend to be a *sognepraest*, to pretend to sign a marriage certificate. Doesn't that prove his bad character?"

"But why did he do it?" I said again, successfully diverted back to my own problem. I went on to relate the story of the young woman, and the baby upstairs, and the tabby cat, and the newly decorated parlor in the cottage on the Strandlinien. "It wasn't real," I said. "It was something out of a Hitchcock thriller."

"Luise, my darling, will you please me by eating a little?"

My darling, he had said.

"But Otto told me most specifically that you were a womanizer."

Erik began to laugh, his plain face suddenly delightfully merry. I *could* trust him, I thought.

"So I am. So are many Danes. Why not? It adds to life."

"But you have never married?"

"Not even once. Certainly not falsely."

I ate a little more of the very good smoked trout, wondering whether to pursue the subject of Otto's or of Erik's equally fascinating affairs of the heart.

"You must be very eligible," I murmured.

"Eligible?"

He was pretending not to understand the word. Or was he? Behind his facetiousness, I sensed pain.

"It means a desirable *partie*."

"Oh! Desirable! Now you are flattering me. I have no title, no castle, no wealth."

"And don't tell me you have suffered from being under your brother's shadow, because I won't believe you."

"Thank you, Luise," Erik said quietly, suddenly serious again. "I am glad you see that."

"And you haven't the Winther disease."

"No. I am lucky."

"So?"

"So we will keep to your problems this evening, if you please. We have now established that Otto has almost certainly bribed someone to play the part of the parson. Did the old man do it convincingly, may I ask?"

"Not really. He dropped the ring and the fat woman had to scrabble for it." I don't know why, after all those weeks when I had regarded the affair with such deadly seriousness, that it should now seem very funny. But it did, and I began to giggle. "It wasn't the way I had imagined a wedding. Nothing could be less like one."

Erik joined in my laughter.

"Weddings should be amusing. They may never be again, after the first day."

"But we didn't laugh when it was happening. It was just embarrassing and rather sad. No wonder Otto wanted it to be done again properly at Maaneborg."

"Then why did he change his mind?" Erik asked, all the skepticism back in his voice.

I hesitated, still finding what I suspected to be the reason too painful to talk about. "For one thing, everyone was so hostile. They were, you know. Your mother would have liked to see me dispatched pretty quickly. So would Niels. That boy is two people, did you know? One is charming and sweet, the other simply abominable. Is that the Winther disease, again?"

"Perhaps," said Erik. "And what happened after this strange marriage ceremony? You went to the Kongelige Hotel? Did Otto sign his own name in the hotel register?"

"You know that, too," I said drearily. "Of course he didn't. But why was he so secretive?"

"I expect you had kept him waiting too long," Erik said in

a factual voice. "Otto usually takes what he wants rather fast. You must remember that although he had only been a widower for a short time, Cristina had been ill for several years."

"You're not suggesting that he was sexually starved!"

The disbelief in my voice made him give a half-smile, and say quickly:

"No, no, no. But neither was he used to that little word, *nej*."

"It was more than that," I said slowly. "It was an obsession about wanting children."

"No! You can't expect me to believe that! Otto! With two children already."

"I'm telling you that this was his reason. I doubt now if he even loved me. He was just fairly certain that I would have children. That was all he wanted. A woman to bear a child. And now I can't."

Erik put his hand over mine. The waiter came to take away our half-eaten fish. The wine waiter filled our glasses with the claret Erik had ordered. When he went away Erik said, "Do you mind very much?"

"Of course I do. It makes me a cripple." I glared at him, incredulous that he should think I didn't mind, and he said very gently, "Poor Luise. Don't look so savage. Drink some wine."

"Do I look savage?"

"Yes. I am trembling."

So I managed to laugh, and didn't do that most unforgivable thing a woman can do to a man, burst into tears at an expensive dinner he has bought for her.

"Let us talk of something more pleasant," Erik said.

"You mean I am to forget Dragor and all that?"

"Yes, forget it. You will only discover more of my brother's treachery."

I couldn't let the subject go.

"Assuming that ceremony at Dragor really was a fake, do you think that Otto genuinely intended to marry me at Maaneborg? Before the accident happened, that is."

"It seemed so. I don't know."

I put my hands to my face, feeling the boniness of my cheeks and the forked scar on my forehead.

"I suppose it's because I have lost my looks, as well as my baby."

I wasn't seeking a compliment, and I didn't get one.

"You need time to recover, that's all."

Erik filled my wine glass once too often, for when we got ready to leave the restaurant, everything swam a little, the colored lights threaded like a necklace around the hoary tree trunks, the golden cascade of the fountains, the faces of the people pressing past. The balloon seller, I noticed, had had a successful evening. He had a bare dozen of his airy treasures left. He thrust them toward Erik and me as we came down the steps of the restaurant, urging us, in a hoarse, slightly drunken voice to buy one. The crimson and yellow globes waved in front of my eyes. Erik took my arm firmly, and walked me past the too-eager vendor.

I looked back. I was about to say that he had a face vaguely resembling the long-nosed, endearingly ugly one of Hans Andersen when I observed that the man was watching us. I encountered his bleary gaze. For a moment we stared at one another. My brain, muddled with weariness and too much wine, struggled with a vague signal of alarm.

"Come this way, Luise." Erik was saying. "It's less crowded. This is almost the last night of the season. That's why there are so many people here. Next week the Gardens will be closed for the winter."

I walked a little way beside him until, like light piercing fog, the signal in my brain interpreted itself.

"Erik, that balloon seller! He looked awfully like the witness to that ceremony at Dragor. I've just realized it."

Erik stopped sharply and looked back. Crowds of people pushing by had hidden the balloon seller from view. Erik took my hand and hurried me back. I had time only to think with gratitude that he hadn't laughed at my fantastic statement before we discovered that the man's place at the foot of the restaurant steps was empty. He had moved on.

But why so suddenly, and before he had sold the last of his wares? Standing on tiptoe, I caught sight of a bouquet of balloons waving in the distance.

"There!" I said excitedly.

But the crowds impeded our progress. Erik pushed people aside relentlessly. We covered a few yards in the direction of the ornamental pool and the golden fountain. Then Erik gave an exclamation and said, "Look!"

Other people looked upward also. They began to point, and to laugh in mirth at the fate of the poor balloon seller who had lost his impatient merchandise to the tug of the wind. The balloons sailed over our heads, yellow and red and blue, rising higher and higher until, somewhere in the direction of the skyscraper hotel opposite, they were lost from sight.

Without his distinguishing wares, their owner was lost from sight, too. He might have had the bad luck to lose them accidentally, but I was pretty certain he had let them go deliberately, and was now ducking and diving through the crowd almost as swiftly as his balloons had floated away into the night.

"Wasn't that queer?" I said to Erik.

"Very."

"Do you think he did it purposely?"

"If he recognized you, and he is who you say. This is very strange. But it shouldn't be difficult to have him traced. People here will know him. Tomorrow I'll make inquiries."

I slipped my hand inside his arm.

"Then you do believe me at last?"

My hand was pressed firmly against his side.

"Let's say that I am anxious to prove that you are not married to my brother. Will that answer do?"

Chapter Twelve

✍ I SLEPT badly, as I had done ever since my accident, and woke with the now familiar nagging headache. I automatically took two aspirins, and picked up the telephone at my bedside to ask for coffee.

I had no sooner put it down, my request made, before it rang. The time was only half past eight. Who would be ringing me so early?

With a feeling of apprehension I put it to my ear again, and a strange thick voice, speaking in heavily accented English, said, "I am the man you looked at last night."

"Who?" I could hear heavy breathing, as if the caller were very old, or out of breath, or drunk. "Who is that speaking?" I asked sharply.

"At Tivoli. You looked at me."

"The balloon seller!" I was beginning to breathe a little heavily myself. "Jens Larsen!"

"Ja."

"If you want to talk to me, why did you disappear in such a hurry?"

"You were not alone."

Thoughts flashed through my mind. The man had recognized Erik. It was Erik, not me, whom he hadn't wanted to see.

"I am alone now," I said quickly. "So you can tell me what it is you want to."

"Not on the telephone. I wish to see you."

"Then come to the hotel. How did you know I was here, anyway?"

"That is easy, Countess Winther. I knew you would be either at the d'Angleterre or the Palace."

I drew in my breath sharply as he called me *countess*. "Then you at least know the truth. I must see you!"

"That is what I am asking you to do. Meet me at the Viking Café on the Klerkegade. It is not far from Kongens Have."

"The king's garden. The Rosenborg Palace."

"Ja. At ten o'clock. I will buy you some schnapps." The

137

man gave a rich drunken chuckle. "But come alone, if you please. Otherwise, I will not be there."

My headache had gone. When my breakfast came, I swallowed two cups of coffee in a great hurry, but could eat nothing. I showered and dressed, putting on my warm tweed coat because there was a cold-looking fog outside. I decided on a scarf around my head. This covered my wing of white hair and made me look inconspicuous. Not that anybody at the Viking Café was going to think me anything but an English tourist.

I would have something to tell Erik when I saw him again, I thought with excitement. But I had an inner trembling that came more from fear than triumph that my marriage seemed about to be proved, at last. I was beginning to be afraid that I would find I really was Otto's legitimate wife. Revenge was one thing. A marriage that had begun so disastrously was another.

As I had expected, the café was a very modest one. It was in the old part of the city, where the buildings were of a dilapidated antiquity. Crumbling brick walls blackened with age, carved sloping doorways set so low that one would have to stoop to enter the little dark basements behind them, greengrocers' shops and shoemakers and junkshops, the inevitable lace curtains and windowboxes and cobblestones and bicycles. It was hardly a street one would come to dressed in mink.

But I sat quite happily in the little dark café waiting for Herre Jens Larsen. Since he was not there when I arrived, I ordered some coffee and smoked a cigarette, and enjoyed watching the simple scene out of doors. Housewives shopping, children bouncing a ball, a white cat settling itself in an empty packing case at the greengrocer's.

I noticed a plaque set in the grimy brick wall opposite, and asked the proprietor of the café what it was.

His pleasant rosy face stiffened. His little twinkling blue eyes went opaque.

"It is from the last war, froken. It marks the spot where two of our resistance fighters were shot by the Gestapo."

He looked for a long time at the small brass plate, then added gratuitously. "I could speak very good German when I was a young man. Now I will never speak a word of it again. It is not even taught in the schools. Our children speak English today."

"Yes, I had noticed that. But the war has been over a long time."

"*Ja*. But it is never entirely over. Not until all of us who remember it are dead."

"Were you in this café when"—I pointed across the street to the innocent cobblestones—"that happened?"

"I was at sea on a British freighter. That is where I learned to speak good English." He laughed, and his face became jolly again. "You are in Kobenhavn on holiday, froken?"

"More or less. What is the time, please? I think my watch must be fast."

"It is twenty minutes to eleven."

"As late as that!"

"You are waiting for someone?"

"Yes."

"Then he has got lost. Tourists get lost very easily. Can I give you another cup of coffee?"

I nodded. My tension was growing again. I would remember this morning chiefly for the coffee I had drunk, I thought. But where was Jens Larsen? Had he floated off with his balloons again?

I would wait until eleven o'clock, I decided. I lit another cigarette and made it last. The proprietor, giving me surreptitious pitying glances, thought my boyfriend had let me down, and this was hardly surprising, for it must have been a clandestine appointment to have been made in such a place. The clientele now consisted of two old men drinking Carlsberg beer, and myself.

Somewhere a clock with carillon bells chimed, the sound floating sweetly and peacefully over the old street. Eleven o'clock. I had stopped being nervous, and was conscious only of intense anticlimax. The elusive Mr. Larsen was being elusive all over again. Or had that telephone call been a hoax?

I stood up, angry and disappointed. There was nothing to do but go back to the Hotel d'Angleterre and see if a message had been left for me.

But I had a strong feeling that Jens Larsen was not the kind of person to leave messages. Neither did there seem to be any reason for him to play a trick on me. So he must have been prevented from keeping this appointment. Probably, I thought disgustedly, he was too drunk to do so.

There was a message at the hotel. I snatched the piece of paper from the desk clerk and read, "Call me as soon as possible. Urgent. Tim."

Only Tim. But why the urgency? I was curious enough to

obey Tim's request, and asked for the call to be put through to London at once.

I didn't want sympathy or recriminations over the telephone, and said so as soon as I heard Tim's voice, although I hugged the receiver close to my ear. His familiar voice sounded so nice and so safe.

"Look here, Tim, I'm paying for this call and I haven't much money, so come to the point."

"You have some more money at Handelsbank. I cabled it this morning. It will pay your fare home. Get the B.E.A. flight this afternoon. I'll meet you at the airport."

"Tim, I'm only in a muddle, not deadly danger."

"I'll say you're in a muddle. Since when do you go marrying foreign counts? If you'd told me Otto Winther was a count at the beginning, I'd have remembered him."

"What have you remembered about him now?"

My heart was skipping beats as I waited for him to answer. But he didn't intend to tell me anything over the telephone.

"It will keep until you get home. Don't miss that flight. It can't be full at this time of year. I'll see you about six. And all I hope is that you're not pregnant!"

"Far from it," I said wryly.

"Well, that's one blessing, at least."

A blessing? Problematical, Tim, my friend.

So that was the end of my Scandinavian adventure, I supposed. My passport still showed my innocent maiden name. It was sufficient to establish my identity at the bank in order to collect Tim's remittance. At the B.E.A. offices I found I was able to book a seat on the London flight that afternoon. And that seemed to be that.

But I still had to cope with nostalgia.

After I left the airways office, I crossed the street and looked through the gates into the Tivoli Gardens. The balloon seller, I noticed, was not in his usual place. Otherwise, everything looked as gay and colorful as usual. I had come in the spring at the beginning of the season. Now the tulips had gone, the leaves were falling, the season was over.

I decided to walk back to the hotel across the Radhuspladsen and down the Stroget, the narrow, winding shopping street that cut through the center of the city. My footsteps began to flag. I felt awfully tired, reluctant to get back to the hotel, reluctant to pack. I took the opportunity to rest in the Amagertorv, sitting on a seat under a slender beech tree that dropped an occasional yellowed leaf on my lap. The flower sellers were selling posies of old-fashioned pinks and corn-flowers. Pigeons circled about my feet. The fog had cleared sufficiently to let a little sunlight fall on the peaceful scene: the flower market, the pigeons' rosy feet, the strolling shoppers, the fountain with storks, the pastel-colored buildings and the twisted green spires piercing the mist.

I didn't want to go back to England, I realized. When I had decided to marry Otto, some mechanism in my mind had made this my country. Now I couldn't put the mechanism into reverse. I was stubbornly clinging to my new world that I had found so enchanting.

But what was I worrying about? Denmark wasn't going to sink into the Baltic the moment I left it. I could come back. In the meantime, I had to start watching the time. Go back to the hotel, have some lunch, pack, ring Erik, catch the bus to the airport, stop dreaming, stop staring into the face of every elderly man who approached in case it should be that of the elusive balloon seller who was probably at this moment sitting in one of the small, shabby drinking parlors on Nyhavn, getting steadily more drunk and more forgetful.

I was saved one chore, for the moment I entered the hotel, Erik grabbed my arm.

"Where have you been?"

"Doing things. I was just about to telephone you."

"What things?"

"Booking a flight to London, among other things."

My feeling of exhaustion had come back. I disliked being cross-examined. I hardly looked at Erik. But his next words jolted me into looking at him, and then I saw how tense his face was, how hard his mouth.

"Thank goodness for that. Thank goodness you're safe."

"Safe?" I repeated. "Whyever shouldn't I be?"

"Our friend the balloon seller is not."

He had an early edition of the afternoon newspaper in his hand, and he thrust it at me, pointing to headlines.

How was I to read that outlandish language? I thought irritably. I could only see the name Jens Larsen and something about Tivoli, and inset in a box in the column, a small picture of an elderly man holding a bunch of balloons.

Drukne, I read. I pointed to the word.

"What does that mean?"

"Drowned. He was fished out of the canal at Nyhavn a little while ago. He must have been drunk and stumbled in in the fog this morning."

"But he telephoned me! He asked me to meet him at a

café. He wanted to tell me something." A wave of heat went over me, and then I felt very cold. I hoped I wasn't going to faint.

"Nyhavn has a bad reputation," Erik was saying. "Sailors come ashore and get drunk on schnapps or vodka. So do people like our friend Herre Larsen. Perhaps he got into an argument."

"He wasn't drunk when he spoke to me. Or only a little. Why should he immediately go out and tumble into the canal?"

Erik looked at me, and I tried to read his guarded dark eyes. They had an element of hostility I hadn't seen before. It upset me. I disliked it as much as I disliked the news of the balloon seller's death. I had a stupid hazy idea that the two facts were connected.

"I waited in that café for an hour," I said. "It was a dreary place, too. The owner kept telling me about the Danes shot by the Gestapo just across the street."

"That happened in more than one place in Copenhagen," Erik said aloofly. "Didn't I tell you about it once? Anyway, that isn't the question just now. The question is that you must go back to England."

"I'm going. I told you I had just booked my flight. You said, thank goodness I was safe. Why?"

"I've been waiting for you. I was getting alarmed. I thought, perhaps in the fog you had fallen into the canal, too."

"Or been pushed?" I said slowly. "That was what you meant, wasn't it?"

"Nothing of the kind. What nonsense! And don't begin to think that Jens Larsen was pushed, either. It was a well-known fact that he was always drunk, and the real marvel is that he had not fallen in the harbor long before this." However, the news that I had a flight booked seemed to have eased Erik's tension. He was becoming more animated. "What time do you go?"

"I have to be at the airport at four thirty."

"Then you have two hours to wait. Have you eaten?"

"No, but I'm awash with coffee. I don't think I want to eat."

"Nonsense. Come to my house and I will make you a sandwich."

"I'd like to, but I must pack and pay my bill."

"And that will take you how long? Half an hour? My house is only five minutes' walk. It is on Nyhavn."

142

"Nyhavn!"

"Not among the tattoo shops. The more respectable side. It is very old, some parts of it, three or possibly four hundred years. I have my office downstairs, and I live on the floor above. From the attic windows you can see across the Sound to Sweden. I thought you would be interested to see it."

"I would, very much."

"Then hurry with your packing."

I don't know why Erik wanted to take me to his house. I suspect it was to keep me out of trouble, but it may have been that he genuinely wanted me to see such an interesting and charming place.

There was a grand piano, flowers, a log fire burning, paintings and etchings of old parts of the city on the paneled walls, armchairs covered in faded crimson damask, carved doors and doorframes.

It was Maaneborg in miniature, a cosier, shabbier Maaneborg without the gloomy corridors and the battle scenes.

"Do you like my house?" Erik asked. He was more friendly now that I was warming myself at the crackling fire, but there was still something distrait in his manner. "I suppose you will say, like everybody else, that it is strange for an architect who designs modern buildings to live in such antique style. But I do have a very modern summer house on the coast, so I make the best of both worlds."

He had come in with a tray and now proceeded to pour whiskey into two crystal tumblers.

"Two houses and you live alone," I said.

"I have a housekeeper. And an office staff. Am I right in thinking whiskey the only drink for this kind of day?"

"Yes," I said, looking out of the window that faced the canal and shivering. "Was it down there that Jens Larsen— the accident happened?"

"On the other side."

"Did you see it?" The thought had just occurred to me.

"No, no, I only heard the commotion afterwards. I didn't known the identity of the man until the newspaper came out. Come away from the window. Have your drink. I will be back in five minutes with the sandwiches."

The feeling of peace I had had on the street bench in the Amagertorv came back to me as I sat in front of the fire watching the logs burn, and thinking what a peaceful room this was. It was as I had imagined the house in the Hans Andersen story "The Old House." "Det Gamle Huus" ... I thought dreamily. I was glad to be here. I had wanted to see where Erik lived. I wished he hadn't this shut-in, constrained manner. It made me think that he knew more about the balloon seller's death than he was telling me.

Don't think of it. Think of the fire, and the warmth of the whiskey, and of someone playing that piano, and how this dusky room must have looked when it was lit only by candles or lamps. There would have been a mother and several fair-headed children, and a father who came in from his work in the city . . .

I realized Erik was standing in the doorway looking at me. For a moment he was the father in my fancy, a serious, good-looking man, not too young to have those rosy-cheeked children, not too old to have a youthful pretty wife . . .

"You haven't time to go to sleep," he said.

"No. But for a moment I had forgotten the invention of the airplane. I always want to fill old houses with ghosts."

"And this one has ghosts?"

"Oh, certainly."

He put down a plate of caviar and smoked salmon sandwiches, and picked up his whiskey to swallow it.

"There. Unlike ghosts, we can eat. There isn't much time. We must leave in an hour." I nodded, but I was wondering how I was to reconcile myself to flying back to London with so many unanswered questions.

"I'll have to come back," I said.

"No!" The tight look was back in his face instantly.

"But for something I've been so involved in—"

"Your involvement is finished."

"What *is* it about Otto? The old women at Maaneborg talked about his conscience, his son hates him, people's faces change when his name is mentioned, you yourself hope I'm not married to him. This all makes him a sort of leper. Why?"

"There's no reason any more for you to be concerned with him, Luise. You can go away and forget him. And all of us." His frown was so forbidding that I couldn't, for a moment, make any protest.

"We're an unlucky family," he said. And again, "Forget us."

"You must think I have a very incurious mind," I said at last, "if you think I don't want a few things cleared up. For instance, why that wretched old man wanted to see me at the Viking Café."

"Well, that's the easy one to answer. That was only to tell you he would keep your bogus marriage a secret so long as you gave him a little money to buy schnapps now and then."

"You're guessing."

"Have you a better guess?" His voice was so flat, so disillusioned, that again I was without words.

We ate for a little while in silence. The peace had left me, and I had an annoying desire to cry. The fog must be coming up again because it was getting darker outside. What was the long, cold, dark winter like, when the canals were frozen, icicles hung from eaves, the wind howled across the Sound?

"This really is a charming house, Erik. I wish I could see your beach place, too."

"Yes. It's a pity you can't."

Silence again. A log collapsed on the fire and sudden flame illuminated our faces.

"I'm sorry I can't clear up the other mystery for you," Erik said. "I went to Dragor this morning, but the young woman in the house you described told me no more than she told you. Indeed, she shut the door in my face."

"Then she must have been frightened."

"No, just busy with her own affairs. Her baby was crying. She said I was the second person to make a mistake about that house, and what was the game. Or words to that effect."

"So you will do no more?"

"You are on your way back to your own country. No, there is no reason to do any more."

And he didn't want to. His cool voice told me that.

Yet when he said goodbye to me at Kastrup Airport, before I began the long walk down the corridor to the waiting plane, he held both my hands hard, and his eyes were brilliant with some unexpressed feeling. I remembered that flare in them long after we were above the clouds and the green islands lying in the foam-tipped sea were gone from sight.

Chapter Thirteen

᠆᠊ LONDON outside Tim's window. Pigeons quarreling on the windowsill, Nelson's Column hazy in the fog, the fountains playing green water that looked icy cold, red buses circling Trafalgar Square.

"Stop wandering about, Luise," Tim said impatiently. "Come and sit down and tell me more of this extraordinary story which I must confess I only half believe. You're adding your own Gothic trimmings, aren't you? Denmark must have gone to your head."

"If those fountains were in Copenhagen," I said critically, "they would be decorated with some charming comic nonsense like storks or fish with lovely twisting tails or mermaids. They might not suit London, but they would make people smile."

"From what you've just told me, you didn't smile too much while you were there."

"Oh, yes, I did at first. It was all so enchanting, like a fairy tale."

"All fairy tales have sinister undertones."

"I suppose so. And don't look at me like that. You would have been taken in by Otto, too."

"Not enough to marry him, darling. Well, go on. What happened after the balloon seller was fished out of the canal?"

"There's no more. That only happened this morning. Just after I had talked to you and promised to catch the afternoon flight."

I had sat down, and Tim came over to touch the scar on my forehead and ask if I had been assured it would disappear.

"As nearly as makes no matter," I said indifferently. "The other thing is the one that matters. I must make an appointment with a good gynecologist."

"You said you weren't pregnant!"

I had to laugh at the dismay on Tim's face.

"No, love, I'm probably sterile. I hate the word *barren*. It makes me think of parched desert and rocks and thorns and vultures."

"Luise!" Tim was shocked.

"It's all right, I'm not going to have an emotional seizure or anything. Leave that to Otto. Now it's hardly fair that you've made me tell all my side before you tell any of yours."

"It's not mine, exactly," Tim said drily. "This side of the story belongs to a chap called Alan Melbourne. Flying officer Alan Melbourne, D.F.C. who parachuted from his blazing plane into the Kattegat after the R.A.F. raid on Aarhus University, which was the Gestapo headquarters. He was picked up by some fishermen and taken to the island of Samso and hidden there until an escape through the Danish underground to Sweden was arranged."

"The fishermen took him to Maaneborg!" I said excitedly.

"You know!" Tim said disappointedly.

"I don't know a word. I'm only guessing. Where else would he be hidden? The castle is a perfect place. All those rooms, even dungeons. Do go on, Tim. When can I see Alan Melbourne?"

"You can't. He's dead."

"Oh, Tim! Then what?"

"He died a year ago. He was an antiques dealer in Salisbury. I only remembered about him when you told me Otto was a count. After the war a lot of stories came out about miraculous escapes, and Melbourne's was one. He talked about a Danish countess whose husband, Count Otto Winther, was suspected of being a collaborator with the Gestapo. But the countess was a loyal member of the Danish resistance. She undertook to hide Melbourne and nursed him herself—he had been fairly badly burned—until he was well enough to escape. I looked up the story on the files. The *Sketch* ran it."

"But Alan Melbourne is dead!" I wailed.

"Is that so important?"

"Of course it is! He could have told me about Maaneborg—about Otto— Now I know why everyone got chilly when Otto's name was mentioned. A friend of the Gestapo! The man I married!"

"He was only suspected of being a collaborator," Tim pointed out. "Otherwise, I expect he would have been shot when the war ended."

"I think it must be true," I said feverishly. "That's why Niels hates him. And why Erik speaks of him so guardedly. I expect that's what Jens Larsen wanted to tell me." I banged my fist on the desk in frustration. "*Why* is Alan Melbourne dead?"

"If you would stop talking for a minute," Tim broke in, "I could give you another small piece of information."

"What?"

"You shouldn't be so interested, love. You're finished with the Winthers."

"No, no, tell me!"

"Well, how did you think I found out Melbourne was dead? Because I went to Salisbury to see him. Since I couldn't talk to him, for obvious reasons, I talked to his wife, although at first she didn't want to know about it."

"Whyever not?"

"I don't think she cared much for that episode in her husband's life. Apparently he had a bit of a fixation on Countess Winther. He said she was beautiful and sad, and unhappily married to an epileptic."

"And a traitor!" I said fiercely.

"That didn't come into it, except that Melbourne was told to keep out of sight while he was in the castle. He apparently never left the room he was hidden in during the whole of his stay. It impressed itself on him pretty thoroughly, because when he was dying his wife said he kept talking about tapestries, and a mural with a dwarf on it. He thought he was back there, and used to keep saying, 'Don't draw the curtains,' or 'Who's that on the stairs?' Well, that's by the way. The only bit of evidence that might be of some use is a letter his wife found after he died. He had kept it rather carefully, in a sealed envelope, so she thought it might be important. She was rather shattered when she found it was just a very brief letter written on crested paper."

"What was in it?" I asked in a breathless state of suspense.

"Well, nothing very much. It was just a few words. 'Your gift has arrived. It is beautiful, and I will treasure it all my life.'"

"Gift?"

"Yes. Since Melbourne dealt in antiques, his wife thought it was probably a painting or some *objet d'art*. He was grateful to the countess, who had undoubtedly saved his life, and naturally he would want to send her a gift."

"But what would Otto say when he saw it?"

"Perhaps he never did see it. Perhaps she hid it."

"In the turret room," I breathed.

"The turret room?"

"That's where Cristina chose to spend all her time when

she was ill for so long. Now it's kept locked. There must be something in there Otto doesn't want seen."

"An innocent antique? Couldn't he throw it away?"

"I suppose so. My reasoning's gone a bit peculiar." I pressed my hands to my head. "I've had too many things to puzzle about. I wonder how many other British airmen the countess hid. That must have been when their marriage went wrong. Cristina must have despised Otto, even if his helping the Gestapo was never proved. And that's why the old ladies talk about the Greve's conscience. Half of Maaneborg has been turned into an old women's home, did I tell you?"

"Your Otto attempting to reinstate himself, no doubt, since the wrong side won the war."

"I wish you had met him, Tim. He was such fun, always laughing. And handsome, too, although he was getting a bit overweight. And he kept his epilepsy as a surprise for me on our wedding morning."

"Teach you to run off and marry a foreigner. I had always thought you were an adult person."

"But impulsive," I sighed. "And don't tell me I've learned my lesson. Those nauseating words should be expunged from the English language. I'm the kind who never learns a lesson, anyhow."

"You're looking a bit scarred, certainly."

"Oh, I know. I look a mess and I'm in a muddle. I'm still not absolutely certain I'm not married. I feel like a *spogelse*, a ghost, a shadow."

Tim's usually cheerful face was grim. "Do you want some advice?"

"No, but I can see that you're going to give it to me, anyway."

"Take a week's rest, then go off on another trip. The sterling countries are in at present. What about the Bahamas? Or Australia, to see your brothers."

"So far!"

"The farther the better. At least you won't find any Gothic castles in Australia. Marry a sheepfarmer, if you like."

"And commit bigamy?"

"Oh, for God's sake!"

"No, Tim, it isn't as easy as that. I've got to clear this thing up first."

"You don't mean to go back to Denmark!"

"I expect so. I don't know. I'll take your advice about a week's rest."

"Luise, for sticking your neck out—"

I cut him short.

"For one thing, I'm enormously curious about what you've just told me. I want to know what Cristina's gift was."

"It's nothing to do with you," Tim said exasperatedly.

"You thought it was when you told me to come home so urgently."

"That was only to get you home. I was worried about you. Your letter shook me. It did Barbara, too. We both decided we must get you home."

"So I'm home," I said wearily. "And all you've done is heighten the mystery."

Tim's sharp eyes surveyed me.

"What about the brother?" he asked suddenly.

"Erik? To tell you the truth, he gave me the same advice as you. To go back to England and stay there."

"I meant, what is he like?"

"Oh, very different from Otto. He's ten years younger, and he has that sort of nice plain face that can look distinguished. I believe he's quite a distinguished architect—" I caught Tim looking at me in an odd way, and said, "No, I haven't fallen in love with him. I've had enough of the Winther family."

"Have you?"

"Well, you must admit they're a fascinating study," I qualified.

"For a sociologist. Or a psychiatrist."

"Oh, not Erik. He couldn't be more sane."

"You thought that about his brother, once."

"I know I did. But Erik's entirely different. You only have to meet him—" I broke off to say exasperatedly, "What are you doing, Tim? Cross-examining me?"

"I'm trying to keep you at home. Honestly, love, with that setup—a Nazi sympathizer, a history of mental instability, a suicide—"

"You mean Jens Larsen? Oh, no, it wasn't suicide. He was a happy drunk, not a depressive one. It really must have been an accident."

"Or murder."

"Now you're just being melodramatic, Tim darling. You, a good newspaperman whose religion is facts!"

"Change the venue of all this to London and I might be interested."

"Wouldn't you like to know what's hidden in that turret room?" I wheedled.

"Of course I would. I'm bursting with curiosity. But what can be done about it? Your so-called husband has thrown you out after nearly killing you. What excuse have you to go back?"

"Niels' engagement party," I said serenely, the idea coming to me on a wave of inspiration. "I was warmly invited to come to it."

Tim scratched at his writing pad. He didn't look up, a sure sign that he wanted to hide his growing interest.

"When is that?"

"At the end of the month."

"Would you stay in the castle?"

"Of course. That was the invitation."

"And do some off-the-record exploring?"

My weariness had vanished. I hadn't realized how much I had wanted to go back to Maaneborg until this minute. I leaned forward eagerly.

"There was an old woman called Helga Blom, who was the countess' maid for many years. She must have been with her during the war when Alan Melbourne, and probably other British airmen, were helped to escape. Now that old woman is still alive, and they say she's senile, but I believe she's kept hidden so she won't talk. Probably she's just senile enough to have lost her discretion. If I could talk to her—"

"Hold it," said Tim. "Aren't you getting off the track? Helga Blom and her secrets are no business of yours."

"They are if they explain Otto's behavior toward me," I maintained stubbornly. "I'm sure it's tied up with all this secrecy about his first wife. Frue Dorothea will help me. I told you she had got friendly towards me. So had Otto's children. And Erik."

"I thought Erik couldn't wait to kiss you goodbye."

"At the end, yes. But he was upset about the balloon man's death. That will have been sorted out by the time I get back."

Tim came around the desk to lay his arm over my shoulders.

"Luise, sleep on this, for goodness sake. Spend a week or two sleeping on it."

"Oh, sure. I told you I want to see a gynecologist, anyway. And I'll have to see to my flat. I'm thinking of giving up the lease."

"Don't be rash."

"I'm not being rash. I only know I can't face that place again. First Ivor, and then this. If I come back to England I'll make a fresh start."

"If?"

"I mean when." I was suddenly tired of Tim's interference, or interest, or curiosity, or whatever it was. "You're trying to run my life," I grumbled.

"Somebody needs to. Have you written to your brothers about any of this?"

"Good heavens, no. I was going to wait until I was happily settled down in what I thought was going to be a cosy Danish farmhouse. But it never happened."

"Barbara and I care," said Tim.

"Well, don't make me feel a beast," I shouted nervously. "I know you care. But you're unsympathetic."

"And you have an obsession."

"Yes," I said quietly and thoughtfully. "I have. I admit it. Though I'd call it a trauma. And I have to get over it. Somehow."

Chapter Fourteen

MY bed was strewn with lingerie, silk blouses, stockings, cosmetics. The muddle of packing had become an occupational disease in my life. I had thrown out all the clothes I had worn both preceding and after my sick-joke marriage to Otto. I was behaving like someone with an extremely healthy bank account, which was a piece of fantasy. But caution had become a commodity of which I had even less than money.

I had bought one of those wildly expensive couturier coats in Irish tweed, to brave the chilly winds over the Baltic, and a simply ravishing party dress. I had had to sell the remaining shares from my father's estate to do it, and from now on I would be more or less penniless. But I didn't intend to look penniless. None of the "poor unwanted wife" look for me.

I was still deep in that damned fairy tale.

I had written to Niels, "Can I really come to your party? Would love to," and the answer had come by return mail. "Wonderful! *Vidunderlig!* My sister and I and my fiancée will warmly welcome you. Let us know the day and time of your arrival."

Although so unmistakably welcoming, Niels' letter was exasperatingly without news about anything, so I supposed the reason for the death by drowning of a drunken man on Nyhavn had not been of sufficient importance to reach Maaneborg. Otto might have been privately interested. And Erik. But the letter I had hoped for from Erik had not come, and it wasn't until I had begun to pack that I was released from that particular tension. By then, I no longer needed to listen for the postman.

Tim and Barbara, of course, were disapproving, although I suspected that Tim the newspaperman wanted this unfinished story tied up neatly as much as I did.

I had found my flat so abysmally depressing that without hesitation I had given up the lease, and was arranging to have my furniture stored. I thought I might live in a residential hotel for a while. I didn't know. I couldn't plan for anything beyond Maaneborg.

I had had a consultation with a reputable gynecologist, and

although he hadn't been encouraging, he had not entirely dismissed the possibility of my being able to have a baby at some future date. He had said the usual cliché about the human body being a wonderful invention, and its own best healer. If I were patient for a year or two, and then took the greatest care in the early stages of pregnancy, it was possible I might produce a living child, though I would probably need to have a Caesarean delivery. He was a nice man. He made no comment at all about my ringless fingers, but treated me as a normal woman who wanted a child, and who had had a piece of exceedingly bad luck.

After that my headaches stopped and my looks improved. I felt ready to cope with anything.

Tim came with me to London Airport to see me off. He had a lot of last-minute things to say, such as, "Don't get personally involved, for God's sake. Otherwise you won't be a good reporter. I really might make a reporter of you, love—if you get back safely from this."

I looked at his shrewd monkey face and complained that he was more interested in a story than my happiness. Or my safety, if it came to that.

"Anyway, apart from indulging in a personal hate for my ex-husband, or whatever one should call him, I have no deep involvement with the Winther family. And I don't expect anyone is going to tip me in the moat. For goodness sake, Tim, here I am with a suitcase full of party clothes. I'm supposed to be having a ball."

"You look like it, too, love," Tim said affectionately. "That's a smashing new coat. Who is it designed to impress?"

"Myself," I said shortly.

"I fancy it will make you a little conspicuous."

"Does that matter?"

"I hope not. You may have got a bit uncomfortably close to some people's secrets, that's all."

"You're thinking of that balloon seller again. But he's dead."

"The priest isn't."

I looked sharply at Tim. It was the first time he had suggested that that fumbling, rather doddery old man, the elusive priest, might be part of all this. The thought had sometimes come to me, but I had dismissed it. He was a clumsy fellow who might have been pretending to be a parson to make some easy money, but surely for no other reason?

Tim kissed me, and held my hand. "I don't suppose I

should be letting you do this, but I doubt if I could stop you, so I'm giving you my blessing. Telephone me or cable me if you have anything to report, have fun, and keep away from the moat."

At Kalundborg, as I climbed the gangway onto the little ferry I accidentally bumped into a man wearing dark glasses. Or he bumped into me. He murmured an apology in Danish, and hurried ahead of me. He had gray hair, but walked briskly, belying his elderly look, and he certainly was not blind behind those dark glasses. I forgot about him immediately. I was scanning the passengers for a familiar face. I had had a vague feeling that Erik might have been crossing over on the ferry today.

It was chilly as we left the harbor. The sea was iron gray and the little white ferry looked like a seabird dipping up and down on the waves.

I had been seasick on a summer crossing, but only through nervousness and pregnancy. I had no fears of a similar catastrophe today. I intended to enjoy the wild gray sea and the wind sweeping icily across the Kattegat. And no stuffy saloon for me, either. I wrapped my coat around me, and stood on the upper deck feeling a quite unreasonable exhilaration and anticipation.

Someone had to meet me with a car at the little port of Kolby Kass on Samso. Perhaps this time it would be Erik, and he could get rid of his disapproval of my arrival on the drive to Maaneborg.

Of course, it might be Otto, but I doubted that. No one needed to tell me that Otto wouldn't want me back.

As it turned out, it was neither Erik nor Otto, but Niels and Dinna. They waved madly to me from the jetty. Dinna looked pink-cheeked and pretty in a coat with a furry hood, and Niels held out his hand welcomingly as I went toward them.

"Luise, you look marvelous," Dinna exclaimed. "We're so happy you came. Aren't we, Niels?"

"Yes, indeed. You have quite recovered, I see, Luise."

"Completely. Tell me, have you a lot of guests staying?"

"Oh, millions," Dinna answered. "And Grandmother took me to Copenhagen to shop. I have a fantastic dress to wear to the party."

"My sister is exaggerating," Niels said. "We have about twenty people staying."

"And the bride? Where is she?" (The new bride who was

155

so welcome at Maaneborg that a big party was being given for her, I thought sadly.)

"Oh, she was a little shy," Dinna said.

Or tactful? I wondered. She was probably full of amazement that someone who had been as shabbily treated as I had been could come back to Maaneborg. I would tell her some time that my curiosity excelled my pride. Though I couldn't actually analyze what had brought me back. I was full of unidentifiable emotions as we drove down the winding road through the familiar green countryside, and then entered the beech forests that were awhirl with yellow leaves. My heart was beating constrictedly as we made the turn in the road that brought the castle into view. It seemed more impressive than ever now that the surrounding trees held only bright rags of foliage, a great rosy-red structure against the gray sky. The lake, I noticed, was like black glass, with a few sandy-colored reeds sticking out of it. It looked wild and melancholy.

Anna began barking before we crossed the moat. She bounded excitedly to welcome us as the car entered the courtyard. Old Birgitte was crossing the courtyard, and stopped to give a smile and a little curtsy. Then Frue Dorothea, who must have been watching for the car, came hurrying out, her hands held out in welcome.

"Luise, it is so nice to see you again!"

I believed she meant that. This reserved, cultivated woman and I could develop a great sympathy, and this made it the more odd that she should have so much disliked the thought of my being her daughter-in-law.

Neither Niels nor Dinna had asked me what had happened regarding my investigations in Dragor. I am sure they were both being tactful, since they must have guessed I had met only failure and humiliation. Now Frue Dorothea made no comment, either, but simply led me into the great room that looked over the lake. A fire of enormous logs was blazing. In the summer, when the sun had streamed in, this room had still looked cold, but now it was alive with the blaze of the fire, with lamps burning, and great bowls of autumn leaves and hothouse flowers. I fancied that the figures in the tapestries and pictures moved in the flickering light, like guests arrived for the party.

"How good of you to be still our friend," Frue Dorothea said. "This is a very generous gesture you have made."

"Oh, no, I wanted to come. It was for my pleasure. Where is everybody? Dinna says you have millions of people here."

156

Everybody, to me, meant Otto and Erik. Frue Dorothea guessed this quickly enough.

"Erik has taken a party out shooting. They will be back presently. Liselotte is upstairs with the other girls. I think she would like to dress for the evening before she meets you. She is anxious to make a good impression. She thinks that since you come from London, you must be very sophisticated."

And Otto?

Frue Dorothea's large moonstone eyes read my thoughts, and took on the cold look I had known too well.

"Otto, I think, has taken Froken Bergson to see the Viking graves, although she didn't seem the kind of young woman who would be interested in antiquities. Did you think so, Niels?"

Niels shrugged. I realized that a strange thing had happened. I had been drawn into what had once been the enemy's camp. Otto was out climbing over the strange grave-mounds by the seashore with his next victim—for victim I was sure she would be—and I had to join Frue Dorothea and Niels and Dinna in attempting to save her from that fate.

Did they all know, secretly, that Otto was mad? If they did, they should make it public knowledge, and protect other women. I saw that Dinna was looking upset, and I put my arm around her waist.

"Did you have a nice time in Copenhagen?"

Her face regained its liveliness at once.

"Oh, yes. We stayed with Onkel Erik. He said you came to his house, Luise, and sat on the floor in front of the fire."

"For a very short time," I murmured.

"Well, he has remembered. He said it was sad you had to go back to London."

Sad? Had to? But he had practically pushed me onto the plane!

"Then perhaps he will be pleased I have come back," I said lightly.

The three of them exchanged glances, and Dinna began to giggle.

"But he doesn't know. We have kept it a secret."

"From your father, too?" I said sharply.

Dinna looked distressed again. Niels said coldly, "Haven't you made the discovery that my father has no heart? He would just simply not be interested."

"Now he has his new woman," Dinna said, and Frue Dorothea looked angry.

"I don't like to hear you talking in that flippant way,

Dinna. Now why don't you take Luise to her room? She would like to have a bath and rest, I am sure. The party begins at seven thirty, Luise, with drinks in here and dancing in the conservatory. We decided, also, to invite any of the old ladies who are able to come to the party. It isn't often they have any excitement. But there will be plenty of young people to dance."

The castle was full of life. I had been given my old room and was pleased to have Birgitte unpacking for me. As a background to her conversation, which was limited to words she knew in English, I could hear snatches of laughter and running feet, and a constant undercurrent of excited voices.

"It's nice having Maaneborg so gay," I said.

Birgitte nodded and smiled, and made an exclamation of admiration as she shook out my party dress.

"That is pretty, froken."

"I'll look a bit better than I did the last time I was here, I hope."

Birgitte shook her gray head.

"That was bad. Bad."

"It was my own fault. I was too trusting."

"*Ja*, it is wrong to be that at Maaneborg, froken," Birgitte said, then seemed afraid that she had been indiscreet, and buried herself with hanging up my clothes.

"There are too many secrets," I said. "And no one told me the truth. Not even you, Birgitte. You told me I should talk to Helga Blom, but you never told me where I could find her."

"*Nej, nej,*" said Birgitte in alarm.

I could read her face, just as I had read Frue Dorothea's. She was thinking that my curiosity had led to my downfall, and that if I wanted to have a quiet and peaceful time at Maaneborg, I should mind my own business.

The secrets had been my business when I had thought myself married to Otto. Nevertheless, if I had left them alone and not provoked that fatal quarrel with him, I might now have been the Countess Winther, in all truth, and still comfortably pregnant.

The thought of that was enough to make me abandon any caution.

I pulled the old woman around and made her face me.

"Birgitte, how can I get into the turret room?"

She looked even more alarmed, and had difficulty in finding the right words in English.

"There is nothing to see there."

"How do you know? When were you last in that room?"

"There is no key. No one goes there."

"There must be a key. What would Herre Winther do with it? Throw it in the moat?"

This had the old woman thoroughly evasive. She shook her head and said something about its being nothing to do with her.

"Were you here during the war, Birgitte?"

"*Nej.*"

I thought that answer was made too quickly to be the truth. But the poor woman looked so distressed that I had to stop. It wasn't fair to upset her tonight. We were all supposed to be gay and lighthearted. Anyway, she probably couldn't tell me much more. She had told me enough, by her alarm, already. The keyless turret room was, in itself, the key to the mystery.

Then what should I do? Play it by ear, I supposed. Keep my eyes open, seize opportunities, get myself thrown in the moat . . . I suddenly wondered where the elderly man in the dark glasses had been going to on this small island. Now, why should I have a feeling he would turn up again?

"Will that be all, froken?" Birgitte was asking formally.

"Yes, thank you," I said absently, for I was looking out of the window onto the moat that was black, except for patches where light streaming from uncurtained windows shone on the water. I thought I had heard a scream.

It must have been a water bird calling. It wasn't a trapped hare because that kind of scream was high and human, like a child's. This sound had been deeper, more prolonged. It wasn't repeated. And, with my nose flattened against the windowpane, I was impatient with myself for getting so quickly affected by the shivery atmosphere of Maaneborg.

Chapter Fifteen

⟨ I HEARD Anna barking in the garden as I went downstairs, an hour later. I was early, but I wanted to be first down. I had become nervous about walking into a crowded room.

I wasn't the first down, however, for Otto, still in his outdoor clothes, was at the sideboard, helping himself to a drink. He spun around in a guilty way as I came into the room. I don't know who he thought was going to catch him having a perfectly legitimate whiskey, but it was certainly not I. His face went blank with surprise.

But his poise was admirable. He said instantly, "Luise! Nobody told me you were coming," and held out his hand.

"Your son invited me," I said stiffly, ignoring his hand.

"Niels, the young scamp."

"I understood that this is his party."

"Oh, certainly. He is free to ask whom he likes. And don't be so distant with me, Luise. You are looking wonderful."

I made no answer to that, but turned away and went over to the fire. I hadn't thought Otto could still humiliate me. The very admiration in his eyes did so, as if he thought I could still be mollified by it. Or what did he think? because his next words were, "I hope you have got over that extraordinary hallucination of yours, and that your memory isn't playing any more tricks on you. You must have had a baffling time in Dragor, looking for houses and people who only existed in your imagination. Concussion—"

"Spare me the medical lecture," I said shortly. "At least I was recognized at the Kongelige Hotel."

"Well, my darling, your face isn't exactly forgettable. That was a very pleasurable episode."

I wanted to hit him. I was greatly tempted to pick up an onyx ashtray on the table beside me and throw it at him. But I was held back by something in his eyes. I realized he had been talking only from the surface of his mind, that something else was occupying him more seriously. The Bergson woman, perhaps? Whatever it was, he had seemed to need a drink. I noticed a splash of mud down his jacket. I thought he must have had one of his epileptic attacks, and was just recovering. This thought made me calm down and keep my temper.

"Will you excuse me, Luise? I have to bathe and change. I'm late. My mother will be annoyed. Not to mention my son, who never confides in me. I would like to have been warned of your arrival."

"Warned?" I said.

He didn't like the inflection in my voice.

"Oh, my dear Luise, we are not to have more wild accusations from you, I hope."

"No, only a little unfinished business," I said gently.

My softness made him far more uneasy than my moment of visible rage. He murmured something about it being splendid seeing me looking so well, and left the room rather quickly, though with a slight tumble, as if he were very tired, or ill, or a little drunk.

At least, our awkward first meeting was over. Now I ought to be able to relax and enjoy myself. I knew I looked as well as I would ever look in my new dark green velvet dress. It was long and flowing, in the lovely exaggerated style that was being worn this season, a style that looked rather absurd in a small London flat, but absolutely splendid in the setting of a medieval castle. I simply didn't want to look inconspicuous tonight, though I really didn't know why I was being so flamboyant. Like Ophelia, I was wearing my rue with a difference.

But all the same I couldn't relax. I had the evening planned as well as possible: polite chatter to Frue Dorothea's guests first, a few words with Erik, and some more with the bride-to-be, then a little conversation which I hoped might be illuminating with the old woman from the other half of the castle, the wrong side of the tracks, so to speak, and after that, when the party would be well launched, an exploration of the turret room.

I didn't intend to be timid about that this time. I intended to bang on the door until even the dead could hear. And if Helga Blom—or anyone else—was within, she, or they, would simply have to turn the key and open the door.

Anna was still barking outdoors. I wondered if she had found a hare in a trap. A servant came in with a tray of drinks, and stopped to mend the fire, throwing on more logs with splendid lavishness. The light and warmth, however, could not altogether distract me from the night outside. I looked out again through a parting in the curtains, and heard voices in the distance. I thought there was someone moving down by the lake. It might only have been a clump of reeds bending in the wind.

"What are you doing, Luise?" came Frue Dorothea's voice.

I dropped the curtain guiltily. Frue Dorothea had spoken with all her old cold hostility, and I was startled and upset.

"Only looking out. It's dark. The moon isn't up yet."

"So there is nothing to see. Come back to the fire. You look cold."

That was better. Frue Dorothea was a friend again. She looked magnificent in a long straight black gown with diamonds at her throat and in her hair. But I noticed, with some curiosity, that her hand shook as she poured two glasses of sherry. Otto's hand had shaken, too.

"Will you have a drink, Luise? The champagne will be opened when Niels and Liselotte come down. Liselotte is a charming child. She will make Niels a very suitable wife."

"She will be the next countess," I said.

Frue Dorothea nodded. "But as you know, we never use the title."

"And what about Froken Bergson?" I couldn't help asking.

I suppose there was an ironic satisfaction in seeing the glacial look that I had once aroused come over this strange old woman's face. At least now I knew that the enmity hadn't been for me, but for what I represented.

"That woman has gone."

"Gone? At this time of night?"

"She was not invited to my grandson's party, so naturally she had the good sense to leave. I believe she is staying somewhere on the island. I didn't inquire where."

"But didn't Otto object? I mean—what an extraordinary man he is. I don't begin to understand him."

Frue Dorothea patted my bare arm. I noticed that her hand was shiveringly cold.

"Of course you don't. But I, his mother, do. And I can tell you this—that Niels' wife will be the new countess. No one else."

"You did believe me about Dragor, didn't you?" I couldn't help saying.

"Perhaps. But only that you were badly deceived. I hope you will do no more about it, Luise. It isn't safe."

"Safe!"

I had scarcely repeated the word before Niels came in with the prettiest fairy-tale child on his arm. At least she

162

looked a child, with her long yellow hair that hung to her waist, and her scrap of a pink dress, and her slim legs.

Yes, I could see that in ten years or so she would make a very suitable mistress of Maaneborg. The charming face behind the curtain of hair had breeding. I had a fancy that the Countess Cristina might have looked like this when she was eighteen.

"Luise, this is Liselotte," Niels was saying happily, and I had another private thought. How did he dare to be so happy in this house?

I took the doll-size hand in mine and murmured a greeting. Niels was saying, "What are you doing drinking sherry when we have champagne? I'll have some opened. Everyone will be down in a few minutes."

Erik, I thought, my heart beginning to beat uncomfortably. Would he be surprised and pleased to see me, or surprised and angry?

Dinna came flying down the stairs and into the room.

"Luise, have you met Liselotte? Isn't she fantastic?"

That was Dinna's word for everything that pleased her. She looked fantastic herself in a very chic blue dress, the exact color of her eyes. The shadow had left her face tonight. I believe she was thinking that after all, some nice sensitive young man might fall in love with her and marry her. Why not? All the Winthers married, in spite of their inherited disability.

Almost at once the room was full of people. I saw a little group of white haired old women being shepherded in and seated near the fire. They were very grand in their old-fashioned velvet or satin dresses, with the sparkle of jewels pinned in scraps of lace at their breast, or on their arthritic fingers.

I didn't pay too much attention because I was still looking for Erik. A hearty voice speaking in Danish sounded near the door, but that was Otto's. He had made a swift change into evening dress, and was now being the smiling host. From where I stood, I couldn't see whether that queer look of strain was still in his eyes. The champagne fizzed in my glass, and I thought I could hear Tim's voice telling me not to waste my time being polite and guzzling champagne, but to start looking behind doors, and into cupboards for the Winther skeleton.

Where was Erik?

"But isn't that the young lady who lost her wedding ring?" I heard a hoarse old voice.

"Froken Amberley! The poor young lady who was so ill."

"Imagine that she would come back!"

"There never was a wedding ring, of course."

"Oh, but there was. She showed it to me in the garden."

"Which doesn't mean to say, Emilie, that it was a *wedding* ring."

"The poor girl was deceived."

"*Ja.* She should have been warned."

The old ladies, who were all a little deaf, must have thought they were speaking in low tones. It was they who should be warned that their conversation was perfectly audible to people with normal hearing, and it was hardly the thing to talk this way in the house of their host.

But old ladies have always gossiped on the fringes of parties. I decided to join them.

They gave me surprised greetings in their twittering voices. Emilie, the only one with a fur wrap, a tatty old gray squirrel, pulled it ostentatiously around her bony shoulders, while the others made do with their various fringed silk shawls or woolly comforters.

"We hope you are quite recovered, Miss Amberley," said Emilie, who was obviously the leader of the little group. She had the fur, and the superior number of jewels. Even at this single step from the grave, possessions obviously mattered a great deal. One old crone was clutching a bulging handbag. I couldn't help wondering what curious collection of objects it contained.

"Yes, I am well again," I said politely.

"That was a bad accident."

One of the old women leaned forward to say something in Danish, and Emilie, the spokeswoman, answered her, then explained to me in her infuriatingly smug voice, "Frue Skansen has no English, but she likes to hear what is going on."

"Are you enjoying the party?" I asked.

"It is nice. It is a change for there to be a party here. It must be the first since before the war."

"As long as that!"

"But you must know, Miss Amberley, that there would be no parties while the Countess Cristina was ill for so long. Indeed, who was there to come? These, you see, are all young people."

"Except us," interposed another old woman with a sad titter.

Were they saying that Otto and Cristina had no friends?

"But it is Niels' and Liselotte's party," I said. "Of course everyone is young."

"Nevertheless."

I scanned the upturned faces. Three or four were familiar, the rest strange.

"I don't know your names," I said, and as I had expected, old Emilie was eager to make introductions.

I shook hands with each in turn. With the pathos of the aged, they were grateful for my attention, and I felt completely false as I smiled and held the dry old hands in mine. I said casually:

"I thought that Helga Blom might be here."

They all fell abruptly silent. The excitement and animation left their faces. They seemed to move closer together. Trembling hands fumbled with shawls. One began wheezing with a cough, another fumbled in a beaded evening bag and brought out a pillbox from which she extracted a small white pill and swallowed it. I got the impression that they were closing forces against an enemy. What was it about the name of Helga Blom that always caused secret consternation?

Then, "Here!" said old Emilie in her cracked voice. "That's not very likely. She's in the hospital. She is not expected to live more than a few days, or a few hours, perhaps." She cast a quick furtive look at her companions, and added, "But who knows whether she will even be the first of us to go. We all sit waiting."

I felt foolish standing there with a glass of festive champagne in my hand. I could read the expression on the old faces now. It was vulnerability. They were not interested in any secret surrounding Helga Blom, but only that she was facing their mutual enemy, death.

"Can anyone talk to her?" I asked.

"Anyone can try, but they will get no answer. She is beyond idle conversation, Miss Amberley. She will soon be joining her late mistress. That is all there is to say."

"I'm sorry," I murmured. I thought of Tim training reporters to stand over accident victims or murdered bodies to get a story, and I steeled myself to pursue the subject.

"Then she must have been brought down from the turret room when she became so ill."

Emilie's eyes lost their brooding look and became surprised.

"The turret room? You are getting confused. That is only where the late countess chose to live because of the view. She felt like a bird in a high nest, she said. She could only breathe properly up there."

"But I thought Helga Blom chose to be there, also, as she got old."

Emilie shook her head violently.

"Nej, nej, nej! The room was locked on the Greve's orders. Was that not so?"

Her friends, appealed to, nodded their heads in confirmation, but Frue Harben added that because of Helga's loyal service to the Winther family for so many years, she had had special treatment.

"Frue Dorothea looked after her herself, it was said. Until yesterday, of course, when she had her stroke. So now she is brought down to our level."

I don't know whether Frue Dorothea had heard her name or not, but suddenly she was beside me, giving her frosty smile to the old women, and saying to me, "Luise, the young people are going to dance in the conservatory. I think you should join them."

"Perhaps she will begin by dancing with me," Erik said, and I spun around to see him behind me.

I smiled because he was smiling. He wasn't angry with me after all, I thought, and the party was suddenly much more gay. Even the row of old ladies, hands trembling over fans or gloves or sticks, were looking at me with a certain benign goodwill. Or perhaps it was Erik who provoked this kind of friendliness.

"You don't seem surprised to see me," I complained.

"No, but I admit someone whispered to me that you were here."

"Nor angry?"

"And why should I be angry, for heaven's sake?"

"You were very anxious to say goodbye to me at Kastrup Airport not so long ago."

"I admit that, too. But certain things have changed, perhaps. Or are about to change. Anyway, let's just say I am happy to see you. Will you dance with me?"

I discovered that my hands were trembling as much as the ancient ladies'. How ridiculous. Erik must have noticed it as I put my right one in his for he held it quite hard to steady it.

"Now," he said. "Are we to dance or go into the library where it is quiet?"

"Why the need for quiet? I am perfectly well."

"I can see that, I am glad to say. It wasn't your health I was thinking of. I thought we had things to tell each other.

You have been to London. I have been to Dragor and other places." He looked at me with his serious eyes and said thoughtfully, "Other things, too. But the unfinished business first?"

"How funny, those are exactly the words I used to Otto to explain my being here."

I scanned the crowd for Otto, and our glances met simultaneously. A strange little shock went through me. I was seeing, in that moment, the stranger inside his skull, the cold schemer who had used me to suit his devious purposes.

"Let's go to the library," I said quickly. Erik followed my glance, and understood at once.

"Yes, that's my brother," he said grimly. Then he took my hand and we left the room.

In the library the curtains were drawn and a fire blazing. Erik shut the door behind us, and surprised me by turning the key in the lock. I was even more surprised when he turned out the light, after which he crossed to the window and drew back the curtain an inch.

"Come and look," he said in a low voice.

This room faced on the wilder part of the garden that sloped to the edge of the beechwoods. Only a corner of the lake was visible. I noticed that the moon was up and that the water glimmered. Otherwise I could see nothing, though I believed there was something moving. As my eyes became accustomed to the darkness, I was sure I could see two figures at the bottom of the garden. At the same time I heard Anna barking again.

"Are those men down there? Why is Anna barking so much this evening?"

"It isn't Anna. It's a police dog."

I dropped the curtain. "Why?"

Erik switched on the light. After the darkness, it was so brilliant that now I could see his composed voice didn't begin to match his appearance, which was strained and haggard and too alert.

"Erik, what's happening?"

"Nothing that our guests are meant to know about. But it's fitting that you of all people should be here at the denouement."

"The denouement of *what*?"

"I suppose of my brother, among other things."

I remembered Otto's mud-stained jacket, his desperate effort to maintain an air of normality.

"This can't just be the sequel to that crazy marriage!" I

waved toward the window and the darkness outside. "Not police and police dogs."

"It should amuse you, Luise. It's your elusive priest from Dragor who is being chased."

"Peter Hansen! The *sognepraest!*" He had never been a genuine priest to me, so I called him by the unfamiliar foreign name.

"Ja! Det sognepraest." Erik lapsed into Danish, too.

"But can he be arrested for performing a bogus marriage? Is there any proof? I could find none." I was suddenly cold with doubt. "Am I really married to Otto after all?"

Erik gave a small half-amused smile.

"Not so long ago I thought you were very anxious to prove that."

"But now I am not. At least, I am anxious to prove it wasn't so. If Peter Hansen is an imposter, he couldn't perform a legitimate marriage, could he?"

"But he isn't an imposter. He is a priest. Or was."

In the conservatory the band was playing dance music. There were bursts of laughter and clapping, and then, in a little silence, I could hear the wind moaning over the lake. And the dog barked again.

"Erik," I said nervously, and with an apprehension that made me feel as if the cold lake wind were blowing directly on me, "you must tell me the whole story. This is something to do with the death of the balloon seller, isn't it?"

"It goes back much farther than that. It goes back to the end of the war, when a certain man called Hans Oller, a priest, was known to be guilty of having been a collaborator with the Germans. He disappeared before he could be arrested and was never discovered. He had had an accomplice who also could not be found. Between them, they were responsible for the betrayal and death of two of our bravest resistance leaders."

I could see the cobbled street in Copenhagen, the plaque on the wall opposite, and the fog hanging over the ancient rooftops as clearly as if I were sitting in the little café at this moment. And I remembered Erik telling the story of Otto's collapse after the horrifying shots . . .

"The balloon seller was going to tell me!" I breathed.

"No, I don't think so. I think he only wanted to get some money from you one way or another. But there's no doubt Oller thought he was going to be betrayed. So poor drunken Jens Larsen never got any farther than the canal."

"And the accomplice? You haven't told me his name."

My voice was cold and dry, and so was Erik's as he asked me why I bothered to inquire. Wasn't it all quite clear?

"For some reason my brother wanted to have you go through a form of marriage, so he was tempted to look up his old friend, the unfrocked priest, who had been living quietly under an assumed name in Dragor for the last ten years. He was a fisherman. No one recognized him as a wanted traitor. I suppose Otto paid him handsomely for this service. Perhaps he was tired of being poor. He had a wife to keep, and a daughter with a child, whose husband had left her. He was living a seedy, dull existence. I expect this bit of trickery enlivened things for him, if nothing else. As for the balloon seller, he was just a drunk who always wanted money for schnapps. But a drunk should never be trusted. Their thirst makes them cunning."

"Well, go on," I said impatiently.

"I hoped you could go on. I hoped you could tell me why it was so urgent that Otto should go through a false marriage with you. Were you expecting the child then?"

I flushed.

"No, I wasn't, but that's not to my credit. I had gone a bit Victorian, if you understand that expression, and insisted on a wedding ring before bed. It was only that I had had an unhappy love affair that I couldn't forget. I had got cautious, rather cold-blooded, to tell the truth. I really deserved what happened. I think Otto wanted to prove that I could have a child before he married me. As soon as he knew I was pregnant, he was perfectly happy to do the thing properly at Maaneborg. Then when I had a miscarriage and the doctor said another conception wasn't likely, he backed out again. Now if you can explain why it was so essential for him to have a child, when he has two already, we might have the answer to the whole impossible affair."

"Don't you have the answer to that? Didn't you find it out in London?"

"Not really, although both Tim, my editor, and I thought we had found out enough for me to come back here."

"Then you had better tell it to me, hadn't you?"

"Of course. I can tell you very quickly. Otto's wife, the countess, helped British airmen to escape during the war. I can see now why she had to keep it such a secret from him, since she must have suspected he was helping the Gestapo."

"Yes?" Now Erik was as impatient for more as I had been.

"There was one, a flying officer, who was burned rather

badly and had to be nursed before he could be got away. She hid him for several weeks—in the turret room, I think—and some time after he got back to England, she wrote him a letter which he kept until he died. It said that his gift had arrived and she would treasure it all her life. Now I think that gift must be in the turret room, and that's why Otto keeps it locked. Isn't there any way we could get in—"

I stopped as I saw Erik's face.

"What was the date of that letter?"

"I don't know exactly. Just before the end of the war, I think."

"Then how could a package have been posted from England and arrive here safely, unless it came through the Red Cross? And it was hardly likely to have done that."

A burst of excited barking from the beechwoods diverted me from the immediate problem.

"Erik, how do the police know the *sognepraest* is at Maaneborg?"

"It's believed he crossed over on the ferry today."

"The man with dark glasses!" I cried. "I thought for a moment that he was following me, and didn't want to be noticed."

"He certainly wouldn't have wanted to be noticed by you," Erik said. "You must have given him a shock."

"But why would he be coming here?"

"Because he knows he's being hunted. The police have been on his trail ever since your last visit to Dragor. However, I must say they didn't take the strange story of your marriage very seriously until the accident of the balloon seller's death."

"And then you wanted me out of the way."

"For your safety," said Erik. His dark eyes watched me. "For your safety only."

A great tremor ran over me.

"And now that awful man is here, hiding in the forest!"

"He probably came to Otto, his old accomplice, for refuge. There are plenty of rooms in the castle including the dungeons. A dungeon would be quite suitable for a rat like that."

"The turret room?" I said.

"No, Luise, I think you have an obsession about that room."

"Then why is it always locked? Is it really because Otto wants it kept unchanged and untouched after his wife's death?"

Erik shook his head.

"That would be very strange, since Otto hardly spoke to or visited Cristina during the last ten years of her life."

"The old ladies said he beat her!"

"Not exactly, I think. He just ignored her, and had other women. He has plenty of attractions. Even you knew that."

"Yes. I knew it," I said shortly.

I moved nervously toward the window and held the curtain, afraid to pull it back.

"Erik, should we be safely in here while—that—goes on out there? Does Otto know?"

"No. And he mustn't know. He is to stay here, looking after his guests. It's only if Oller is caught and can be made to talk that my brother can also—"

"Be arrested?" I said, when Erik seemed unable to finish what he was saying.

He nodded, his face gaunt and sick. After a little while he said, "This is how they told me it had to be. We really ought to go and dance, Luise. Perhaps we can look as if we are enjoying ourselves."

I gripped his arm.

"No, Erik, no! Now is the time for us to explore the turret room. You can get some tools and break the lock. With all this noise going on, no one will hear."

Chapter Sixteen

HE behaved as if he were humoring me, but I believe he was now as curious as I was. We stood at the closed door and Erik examined the lock. It looked heavy and solid, but age had probably worn it. Erik thought he could break it with the tools he had brought.

The wood cracked and groaned under his pressure. Suddenly I wanted him to stop. I had the overpowering feeling that within, some frightened little creature was cowering in a corner in the dark, afraid of being brought out into the world.

Erik saw me biting my knuckles and laughed.

"What do you think we're going to find in there?"

"I don't know. I guess I'm a coward."

"Well, this is it, I think." Erik put down his tools and put his shoulder to the door. "I don't know what my brother is going to say about my damaging his precious castle, but it has survived many things. I expect a broken door won't cause its downfall."

With a long-drawn splintering sound the door gave. Suddenly it was wide open, and with a crack of thunder something enormous flew over my head.

I screamed. The air was full of dust. The clatter of wings went on as a huge white owl tried blindly to find its way out of the bewildering light and the confined space of the stairway. Finally it settled in a curve of the stairs, folding its wings and blinking its big blind golden eyes.

"So that's the family skeleton," Erik said. "I wonder how it got inside. Oh, I see. A windowpane has broken. Probably blown in by a gale last winter."

The circular room was dim with moonlight. Glass crunched beneath our feet as we went inside. The owl, of course, had been the shuffling inmate I had heard when I had once listened at the door. It seemed as if the room were innocent after all.

A cold wind came through the broken window. Dusty curtains stirred.

I whispered to Erik to put on the light, and wondered why I was whispering.

I didn't want to set that great owl fluttering again.

The ceiling light didn't work. The bulb had been broken. But a reading light by the fireplace sprang on when Erik pressed the switch.

Then I saw that the room hadn't been used for a long time. The floor was covered with owl droppings. There was very little furniture—a broad bed covered only with a shabby brocade spread, a table with heavy carved legs in the center of the room, some chairs, a huge painted wardrobe. Everything of value, or small enough to move, had been moved.

This was no hallowed sanctuary kept by a grieving husband. It was an empty room, derelict and neglected. The long windows on three sides gave views over the lake and of beechwoods that must be magnificent by daylight. Now there was only a stretch of darkness beneath the sailing moon. The wind moaned against the windows and down the chimney.

"It's *sad*," I whispered.

I explored a narrow doorway that led to an old-fashioned bathroom. Here, too, the uncovered floor crunched with dust and debris.

"Why is it kept locked when there's nothing special to see?"

Erik was peering up at the carved ceiling which the one dim light left in gloom.

"I don't know. It was a comfortable place when Cristina was here. She had it filled with color and luxuries. Pictures, rugs, small treasures. That was less than a year ago. Now it's not a place that even a ghost would stay in."

"The broken window and the owls have made it look like this. I don't suppose anyone has come in to find the damage that has been done." I walked about, the broken glass crackling under my feet. "But it's all very mysterious, since there's nothing here to be kept secret."

"No, not even any treasure that a British airman is supposed to have sent my sister-in-law. I think you were wrong about that. And that broken window should be mended. Everything is getting damp."

Erik wasn't very interested now that the turret room had proved to be such an anticlimax. He kept going restlessly to look out of one or another of the windows, much more occupied with the drama that was taking place on the fringe of the beechwoods, although even that seemed to have moved away, for there was no sound but the whistle of the wind.

Then he turned to look at me in a half-humorous half-tolerant way.

"I believe your imagination has been too strong this time, Luise. You have filled this room with skeletons that don't exist. The real Maaneborg skeleton is hiding out there"—he pointed out of the window—"and that is something you have nothing to do with."

But his gaze stayed on me, and he smiled a little.

"You look very pretty standing there in your green dress. A little like the figure in the mural behind you. She is a queen, and dead long enough not to be of interest to anyone. That is why I look at you instead."

I hadn't noticed the mural. The light was too bad, and the colors had faded so much that even now that Erik had drawn my attention to it, I had to go close to study it.

It was a descriptive painting: a bearded king and his queen, both wearing small gold crowns, walked in a garden, followed by a troupe of courtiers. In front of the royal couple a dwarf cavorted in a grotesque dance, his disproportionately large head turned back to look at his master and mistress with a merry grin.

He was, I supposed, the court jester, and it should hardly have seemed so significant that his was the figure Alan Melbourne remembered, and talked of as he lay in the strange half-world of the dying. But it did, in this moment, as light exploded in my brain.

"I know. I know, I know!" I exclaimed. "This is the room where Cristina hid her British airman." I pointed at the dwarf. "That's the secret."

"Now, just a minute, Luise, your imagination is running off with you again. That picture has been there about three hundred years. It has nothing to do with the history of the last war."

"Oh, you're too slow!" I cried. "Why should Alan Melbourne talk of this room when he was dying if it hadn't meant a very great deal to him, if it hadn't the sentimental association that it never had for Otto!"

Erik was not so slow after all. "The gift!" he said.

"Yes. You see it, don't you? It arrived nine months later, and Cristina said that she would treasure it all her life."

"A child, of course! How stupid we were not to guess. It would have to be hidden. I wonder where it is now."

"Helga Blom knew." I said, with certainty.

"And Otto, no doubt. That explains a great deal about Otto's behavior to his wife. Although, as I remember it, it was only after Dinna's birth that they became so unhappy together."

"Perhaps he only found out at that time," I suggested.

"And so, poor Cristina took refuge here, in the room where she had had her short happiness."

"And when she died, Otto locked it up so that no one would discover her secret, although how anyone could, I don't know. The dwarf can't speak."

"You are wrong," came a voice from the door. "It was not Otto who locked up the room. It was I."

Frue Dorothea stood there in the half-light. She must have come up the stairs very silently, so silently that she hadn't even disturbed the crouching white owl. How long had she been standing there listening to us? I wondered. In her long black gown, with her frozen face, she looked a figure of doom.

"You, Mama!" said Erik. "Then perhaps you can tell us the reason."

"And perhaps," said Frue Dorothea, looking at me, "you can tell me why you have so rudely left a party which you came all the way from London to be present at. I should have guessed your motives were not all from friendship."

"There are things I'm entitled to know!" I said hotly. "I've been hurt enough at Otto's hands. I can live a bit better with my injuries if I know the reason for them."

"Luise is right," Erik said in his sane, calm voice. "Otto has behaved unforgivably towards her. She is entitled to know why."

For a moment it seemed as if Frue Dorothea was going to keep her hostile attitude. Then suddenly she broke down, her face in her hands, her shoulders shaking. I had to listen hard for the muffled voice.

"It has all been so bad for so long. Poor Cristina—watching her having to be a wife to a man whom she suspected of being a traitor—watching her gentle spirit break. It was too heartbreaking. She was only unfaithful to Otto once, and that for such a short time. I believe it was her single happiness in all her life at Maaneborg. She could have told of her suspicions of Otto as Hans Oller's friend, but she never did. There was only that one infidelity. She was a brave and tragic woman." I understood now the years of strain that had brought the granite look to Frue Dorothea's face.

I said warmly, "So that is why you tried to stop my marrying Otto. You knew I wouldn't be happy."

"It wasn't you I was protecting, Luise. I must confess that."

"Then who?"

Instead of answering, Frue Dorothea stretched out her arms. I heard the owl on the stairs flutter, and half-expected it to come swooping in over the old woman's high gray head.

"I love Maaneborg," she was saying. "I came here as a bride when I was seventeen and I loved it from that moment. I had a good husband. I would have been completely happy but for one thing. The Winther disease."

"But didn't my father die from a fall off a horse?" Erik asked.

"No, he died of the Winther disease. He had an attack while out hunting, and so had that fatal fall. It was quite unmistakable. His face was still in the throes of his fit when he was discovered."

Frue Dorothea walked across the room and stood against the wall, the mural behind her.

"Otto's and Erik's father was a kind and good man. His illness hadn't twisted his mind. With Otto, unfortunately, it has, to a certain extent. I think you have found that out, Luise."

I nodded.

"Cristina found it out, too. Before Otto, there have been other Winthers who have had reputations for cruelty and violence. I knew this when I married. But I loved Maaneborg, and I began to have a dream. If only the shadow could be removed. I've suffered very much for Otto, and now for Dinna, poor child."

"But not Erik? Not Niels?"

"Erik is lucky so far."

"So far," said Erik, the tight look back in his face.

"But Niels," said Frue Dorothea with deliberation, "will be perfectly all right. Liselotte will have nothing to worry her. She can be something unique, the first happy wife at Maaneborg. And she need have no fears about her children."

The long, angular, resolute face was turned to Erik and me. The strange pale eyes glowed.

I felt for Erik's hand, and curled my fingers within his palm.

"I think I guess," I said.

"You only guess?" said Erik. "You are not usually so slow, Luise. Mama has been telling us something in very plain language. My nephew Niels is not my nephew at all."

"He is Alan Melbourne's gift," I breathed.

"He is the heir to Maaneborg," said Frue Dorothea, and she sounded like Moses reading the first of the Ten Commandments.

It was still not clear. Otto hated Niels because he was not his son. That was why, as soon as Cristina died, he wanted desperately to have a legitimate son so that Niels could be deposed, or exposed, or whatever was necessary to remove him as Otto's heir. But how had he ever been accepted as the heir?

"You know so much, I suppose I must tell you the whole story," Frue Dorothea said. "But I must ask you to give me your promise you will never tell any of this to anyone. I have often been tempted to tell you, Erik. But Luise? Can I trust you?"

"You can trust me," I said quietly.

"The only people who have ever known are myself, Otto, and Cristina's loyal and faithful maid, Helga Blom, who is now dying. There have been rumors, of course, but no one ever guessed the truth. Least of all Niels. He loves Maaneborg even more than I do. He was only rude to you, Luise, because he knew his father hated him and would be unbearable if he had another son. He was afraid it might somehow make him lose Maaneborg. Now he is to be the next Greve, and nothing must be allowed to change that."

I had a swift thought about my lost baby, a sort of shadow Greve of Maaneborg in limbo. Although it might have been a girl, and Otto would have wanted to kill me for that.

"Otto himself had no idea that Niels wasn't his legitimate son until a little while after Dinna's birth. Unfortunately, Cristina was ill with a high fever, and talked in delirium, and Otto heard and guessed her secret. From then on he never touched her again or spoke to her. He simply waited seventeen years for her to die. This is where his touch of madness comes in, I am afraid. He had this terrible patience, this determination to strike Niels down when the time came."

Erik's fingers pressed on mine. He said quietly, "And that time would have come when Luise had her baby. But can it be, Luise, that Otto wouldn't even risk marrying you legitimately until he knew you could be made pregnant?"

I nodded. "He talked all the time of having more children. I thought he had an obsession about it, proving his virility and that sort of thing. He must have been pretty angry when I wouldn't go to bed with him until we were married. So he had all that trouble of arranging a fake ceremony. He was terribly pleased when I was pregnant. That's when he said we could go at last to Maaneborg, and there was all that talk of another marriage in the family church, when, of course, it would have been our real marriage." I was almost crying. I don't know why I should have been so affected now that the mystery was solved. "Otto should have been more careful of me! Driving so carelessly, ruining my life as well as his own!"

"No, not entirely," Erik said gently.

"You do promise there will be nothing mentioned of this," Frue Dorothea was saying. "I am sorry you have had to find out these things, but perhaps it is best. For Luise, anyway, poor child. She is the one who has been wronged."

"And I should have been told long ago, Mama," Erik said reprovingly. "You could have shared such a worry with me. Or did you think I was not to be trusted?"

"No, no, dear boy. You were too young, and you might have learned as well that your brother had friends among the Gestapo."

"There were always those rumors. Even now, Otto has very few friends in Copenhagen. We Danes have long memories," Erik said to me.

"Everyone has long memories for things like that." Suddenly I began to shiver. I looked around in distaste at the desolate room. "Couldn't we go downstairs? Haven't we found enough skeletons? Dear Frue Dorothea, of course I am to be trusted. Forever. I hope I may come to the wedding of the heir of Maaneborg."

"More immediately, perhaps you would like to drink his health now," said Erik. "Mama, come downstairs. Luise is cold, and there's a very frightened owl somewhere on the stairs who would like to return to his quarters."

"And a very frightened man downstairs," he added under his breath. "That fake marriage you talk about, Luise, is the thing that has led my disastrous brother to his own fate."

"It's all so melodramatic." I was trying to reduce the strangeness to something acceptably trivial.

But that was impossible. Outdoors, a long-wanted criminal was being hunted. At any moment, I imagined there would be a dramatic thundering on the doors of the castle. It wouldn't be the first time in its long history that that had happened. Nor the first time that the moat had lapped about the barred windows of the dungeons, or the head of another enemy been carved in stone and set in a niche in the wall.

Wasn't Frue Dorothea being too optimistic? Could there be happiness in a place so soaked with emotions, from the fear and cruelty of the past to the long, long diminishing of the gentle lady in the turret room?

Chapter Seventeen

✍("PLEASE behave as if nothing has happened," Frue Dorothea said over her shoulder to me. At the foot of the stairs she paused to wipe the dust off her shoes on the carpet, then proceeded, her head held high, the diamonds around her neck blazing, toward the brightly lighted room and the gaiety.

"You will be kind enough to have the next dance with me?" Erik said, tucking my arm in his.

"Erik, how *can* we, with a bomb about to explode at any moment! Otto must know what's going on outside."

"He can't unless he has seen Oller already, and is putting a good face on it. No, he is unaware, I think. But if the chase moves closer, the castle will have to be searched."

"The old ladies will be alarmed."

"If they find a man hiding under one of their beds, I expect they will. Now, please my mother and smile, Luise. And I will see that you get decorated with the Order of Maaneborg!"

"I think you deserve it yourself. After all, it's you who is making the sacrifice. I have just realized it. If Niels is not Otto's son, you are the heir to Maaneborg."

"I!" He threw back his head, and it really was good to hear him laugh.

"It doesn't appeal to you?"

"This great place! Didn't you like my little house on Nyhavn?"

"Oh, yes, very much."

"I am glad, because that is me. And there has also been a little of you in it ever since you were there."

Now we were talking party language. I sighed, relaxed and moved into his arms, and we began to dance. I don't suppose we had been away more than half an hour, for no one looked at us strangely. Dinna, dancing with a tall young man with floppy fair hair, waved to me. I saw Otto across the room making a request to the band leader. He had a girl who looked no older than Dinna in his arms, and was giving her his merry smile. I wondered if he had loved me at all, or had I never represented anything but a brood mare?

I continued the light conversation.

"Nonsense, Erik, you were very glad I was leaving Denmark. You couldn't get me on that plane quickly enough."

"Yes, you told me that earlier. I didn't think you were so easy to deceive."

"Oh, I'm gullible. Haven't you found that out yet?"

"Gullible?"

"It means trusting too quickly. I didn't think there was any English word you didn't understand."

"Well, I am sure you are right to think the Winther brothers are not trustworthy."

"No, no, you're getting it the wrong way round. Otto is what you say, but not you."

"Not me?"

I couldn't help looking at him because he was looking at me so hard. I felt the color rise in my cheeks. That seemed to please him, for he gave a sudden smile, and then we were dancing gaily, a little too fast for the music, but with great verve.

The champagne had been flowing while we were away. The old ladies around the fire were talking animatedly, their gray heads nodding, their eyes getting a dim shine, like tarnished silver. Otto's eyes were shining, too, and I knew as soon as he asked me to dance that he had been drinking too much.

"Mustn't let my brother monopolize you, Luise. Must have my share."

He wasn't too drunk to see me stiffen.

"Just for the sake of appearances. Isn't that what the English value most?"

Those large smooth hands were the ones that had caressed my body. I was squirming with disgust. Yet I had this awkward unwanted feeling of pity. He had, after all, slept in my arms, and I couldn't forget that.

"Too bad about our baby, Luise," he was saying now, his cheek pressed against mine as we danced. "That was the only thing that went wrong. I simply couldn't risk marrying a woman who couldn't have a child. So poor Luise. I was cruel to her."

"And calculating."

"That had to be. You didn't know the circumstances. The doctors used to tell my mother, when I was a child, that I suffered from uncontrollable emotions. It was to be hoped I would grow out of them."

"But you didn't."

He gave his loud merry laugh.

"Why should I? I like to feel things. Love, hate, anger, fear, excitement. Everything. It makes one alive. And if things get in my way"—he snapped his fingers—"they have to be moved."

"Like me."

"Sad to say, like you, *mine kaer*."

I dropped my arms, standing back from him.

"And like the *sognepraest?*"

He had picked up a bottle of champagne to refill his glass. He paused for the barest moment.

"I have never known who you meant when you kept referring to a *sognepraest*. It was part of your hallucination. Wishful thinking, the doctor called it."

"The man called himself Hansen, but I have since heard that his real name is Oller."

It was petty of me to want my bit of revenge. I could have waited until events took their inevitable course. Only Hans Oller, out in the dark woods, might escape, and Otto might go on deceiving women and moving people out of his way. That nice, innocent boy Niels, and his enchanting Liselotte, might be the next to be moved, cruelly and without compunction.

"Still sticking your pretty neck out, Luise! This, I suppose, is the famous English stubbornness." Otto was laughing again, and the thickness in his voice might have been due to drunkenness. "Hadn't you better remember that the Danes were once more than a match for the English?"

"You mean the Vikings."

He thrust out his massive chest.

"Am I less than my ancestors?"

A few months ago I would have laughed. and admired his virility and his pride. Now I thought he was just being rather silly and rather pitiable, a flawed person who had never quite grown up, charming when he was pleased, dangerously vicious when hurt or thwarted. I could well see how he had enjoyed stamping in the wake of his German heroes during the war—until they had ceased to be heroes, and had almost pulled him down with them in their fall.

Yet he had slept in my arms, and I in his, and although I now felt immeasurably older and wiser, he was still a little bit of me.

Damn, the champagne was making me maudlin.

"Otto, why don't you give yourself up?"

He stared at me, astonished.

"You know what I'm talking about. Your friend Oller followed me today. Or I followed him, I don't know which. But he must have come to see you. What did you do with him? Hide him in one of the dungeons?"

It was a wild guess. After all, I didn't even know that Oller had been able to contact Otto. But my remark had found some sort of a target, for Otto's eyes bulged, his face went a dark color, and he whispered, leaning toward me.

"Damn! You saw my jacket! Did you tell anyone else about it?"

Before I could answer, he added gratuitously, "I was fishing. But I caught only a small fish that I had to throw back." Then he began to laugh loudly, and walked away from me, across the black and white tiled floor of the hall, still laughing. His big blond head was flung back, his shoulders shaking. His step, I noticed, was perfectly steady.

A long cool gust of wind swept up the hall as he opened the heavy iron-studded door. A leaf rustled at my feet. The door thudded shut.

I was shaking so much that I could hardly speak when Erik found me. It couldn't have been more than a minute later, certainly not long enough for me to get so chilled.

"What are you doing out here, Luise?" He saw my face. "Has anything happened? I saw you talking to Otto."

"Yes, I was."

"What about? What has he told you to make you look like that?"

"How do I look? I'm only cold. And Otto didn't tell me anything in particular. Only that he had been fishing this afternoon."

"Fishing? Why did he tell you that?"

"I had noticed mud on his jacket. He was explaining how it had got there."

"So!" That short Danish expletive had never been so expressive.

I didn't want to stay here shivering. I didn't know how to go back to the party.

"There is nothing to do." I was asking for reassurance. "Is there?"

Erik pushed me briskly toward the door of the lighted noisy room.

"No, not for you. Go back in there. Someone will give you a drink. I haven't time just now. Forgive me."

So I went back and sat on the edge of the old ladies' circle around the fire. I felt old enough to be one of them.

"Are you tired already, Froken Amberley? How strange! When I was young I could dance until morning without the slightest fatigue."

I was sick of Emilie and her superiority. What an infuriating old creature she was! One day she would be found at the bottom of the turret stairs with her silly waggling neck broken.

"The poor young lady has scarcely had time to recover from her accident, Emilie. Surely you remember? Or is your memory failing, as well as your hearing?"

"There is nothing wrong with any of my functions, Sybilla. I could take another glass of champagne, if someone would be so good as to bring me one. I wonder where servants disappear to nowadays, just at the moment that they are wanted. Or is it," her voice dropped to a perfectly audible whisper, "that the best ones won't come to Maaneborg?"

My eyes were on the picture behind the nodding gray heads. It was the enormous battle scene of the dead invader, his victor standing over him, great shaggy blond head raised triumphantly against the frozen pink dawn, the rest of the enemy fleeing in a straggling rout, like blown leaves.

The old ladies were still making their polite bitchy remarks to one another, thoroughly enjoying themselves. I found I couldn't sit still after all. If I closed my eyes I could see nothing but the lake, and when I opened them it was still there, superimposed on the lights and the color and all the jolly people.

Otto said he had had to throw the small fish back . . .

But had it been alive or dead?

Tim would want to know. Tim would say, "What the devil were you doing sitting by the fire while these things were happening outside?"

But *I* don't want to know them, Tim. I know even less why I am being compelled, at this minute, to leave the house and go down to the lake, without even stopping to get a wrap, and hoping nobody will see me go. And it's cold outside, and dark. I can hardly find the familiar path . . .

In the summer there had been a swan's nest at the end of this path. In a clump of beige-colored reeds the big white bird had sat with immense dignity on her nest of ragged sticks. Now nest, swan and chicks had gone, and there was only the wind bending the reeds, and a dim shine of moonlight. The boat was a little farther out. One man was steadying it, while two others leaned over the side, trying to reach something in the water.

There was a great deal of grunting, and excited remarks in the strange throaty Danish language. The water splashed. A bird rose with a screech and soared away over the lake. My high heels sank into the soft earth. The hem of my dress was muddied, as Otto's jacket had been. And I was terribly cold. I would freeze to death if I had to stand here long.

But I wasn't going to have to do that, for a moment later there was a loud exclamation from one of the men, and a great swoosh of water as something was pulled out and dragged over the side of the boat.

I felt very sick, suddenly. I wanted to run away, but was literally without the will to move. The boat began to edge toward the shore, one man rowing while the other two supported their burden. I kept expecting to see Otto's head, the blond hair straggling and darkened with water.

"Luise, what are you doing here? Go back to the house at once."

That was Erik. He was one of the three men in the boat. I had never heard his voice so grim.

But how could I obey him, when I could neither move nor speak?

The boat shuddered against the bank.

Mud squelched. In a moment the three men had leaped out, leaving the long drenched shape lying in the bottom.

Erik said something to the men, and they both shook their heads and said, *"Nej, nej."*

Erik turned to me again. His face looked gray and eerie in the moonlight.

"Well, there's someone who won't be reading the marriage service over anyone again."

"Otto's fish," I managed to say. And then, "Is he dead?"

"Hours ago. If you won't go back to the house, I must take you." He had his arm around me and was leading me away. "If you go through the side door, you can get straight up to your room without being seen. Ring for Birgitte and get something hot to drink."

"You?" I could feel the dampness of his sleeve around me waist.

"I'll come in later."

"It's no use looking for Otto, because I warned him."

"You—what?"

"I told him a search was going on for the *sognepraest*."

"You're mad. You've given him a chance to get away."

"I know." I wanted to cry, and couldn't. "I had to, Erik. He was my husband for a little while. We slept in each other's arms. That makes a tie—for a woman, anyway. I can't argue about it now. It just is."

"And how do you think I feel, having to hunt down my brother?"

"Then give him a chance. Until morning."

"He's wanted for murder. Not only that of the two resistance leaders who were shot, but for that"—he pointed—"in the lake."

I nodded bleakly.

"Where would he hide, on Samso?"

"In the woods, probably. The island's too small for him to be able to hide for long."

"Then, please, Erik, don't look too hard just yet."

His wet arm was icy around my waist. And when he suddenly pulled me to face him, his lips on mine were just as cold. But only for a moment. Then they grew warm.

"I just kiss you for your tender heart," he said. "Can you get some sleep?"

"I scarcely think so."

"Try. So will I. When I have told everybody it's time the party is over."

"And the men searching the woods?"

"There are only two of them. And two down at the lake. They'll need to telephone the mainland for reinforcements."

I put my lips against his cold cheek.

"Thank you, Erik. Call me when you start in the morning."

"At daylight? You do like to punish yourself."

"I am part of this," I said, as I had said so long ago, so far away, to Tim in his safe office overlooking Trafalgar Square and the pigeons.

"You should have been with us during the war. We needed people like you. Or so they say. I was only a schoolboy."

"And I scarcely born."

"So we have to finish other people's war. Perhaps, then, you must come."

"Yes, I must."

He touched my hand. "I would like you to, I admit. I will need you, for my own sake."

And with that he pushed me indoors, and pointed the way to the back stairs.

My legs were wooden. I thought I would never get them to the top. And I could still feel the icy band around my waist where the damp lingered. My elegant dress must be ruined. It was very unimportant. There was only one important thing, and I didn't know why that mattered so much, either—that Otto should have his night of agony undisturbed.

Chapter Eighteen

⌐ I DIDN'T sleep, but at some time during the night I must have become semiconscious, for I suddenly felt appallingly cold, and I thought there was a figure standing over me. The Ice Maiden, I was trying to say, as I struggled back to consciousness, and found the eiderdown on the floor, and myself lying uncovered.

The Ice Maiden was death. Otto had told me about her at our first meeting beneath the yew trees in that melancholy garden, steeped forever in its dark enchantment, at Valldemossa.

Before I could get warm again there was a tap at the door, and Birgitte came in carrying a tray with coffee things, and saying that Herre Erik expected me downstairs as soon as possible.

It was just becoming light, with a few pink streaks in the sky behind heavy gray clouds. I could see the trees bending in a high wind. The surface of the lake was ruffled, and disturbed ripples stirred even the usually still water of the moat.

Wrap up well, I thought. Had Otto been out all night in this rising storm?

I swallowed half a cup of strong black coffee, finished dressing, tied a scarf around my head, and was ready.

Someone must have worked late and cleaned up after the party, for the downstairs rooms had returned to their somber grandeur. In the gloom of a stormy morning they looked funereal.

Erik was waiting for me in the great hall. He looked very plain, almost ugly, with the grim set of his mouth and the hollows of sleeplessness beneath his eyes.

"Luise, are you still sure you want to come?"

"Yes."

"It may be distressing."

"Why should I be spared?"

He took my arm roughly, and a small stir of warmth went through me.

"Haven't you been hurt enough?"

"It isn't me being hunted."

"It's too late to be sentimental."

"You're using the wrong word. Anyway, we said these things last night. Just let's go."

As we crossed the courtyard to the car, Niels' white Mercedes, the one in which I had nearly been killed, two men in heavy boots that made a jarring sound on the cobblestones came toward us.

They spoke to Erik in Danish. They were both shaking their heads. Erik answered them briefly, then opened the car door for me to get in. He shouted something back to the two men before we moved off.

"They've been searching the dungeons," he explained to me. "It was possible Otto might try to hide there, and escape when the search moved farther away. But there was no trace of him. And it would have been very uncomfortable, since the moat must have risen in the heavy storms we had last week. There is a foot of water down there, the men say."

"He would stay out in the air," I said with conviction. "He liked to be outdoors. In Majorca, we always had to have picnics and sunbathe and be near the sea. He said that was his Viking blood."

Erik gave a snort of disgust.

"Viking blood. Then he should have been more loyal to his country."

The car swept over the moat bridge and down the curving road into the beechwoods. The air was full of whirling leaves and the smell of the sea. A hare, its big ears up, sat a moment on a bank, then flashed away. Fat pigeons fluttered among the bare branches. A glancing shower struck the windscreen, then cleared almost at once, and the pink dawn showed behind the clouds again.

Erik was driving very surely, with some definite destination in view.

"Where are you going?"

"Has no one ever taken you to see the Viking graves? There's a lighthouse, and some old fortifications of Napoleon's. And a ruined castle. And millions of birds. Mallards, oyster catchers, herons, teal, plovers, peewits. Are you interested in birds? If you are, this is the place to come."

"And the Vikings?"

"There are ancient moorings from which they launched their long boats. And the graves that have all been opened by our inquisitive generation. It is a pity. But the burial stones are still there, rather eerie, like the shadow of old gods."

After a while he said, "It's a place that always fascinated my brother. Me, too, but Otto much more."

The cold fingers were around my heart again.

"He talked about Vikings last night. He was a little drunk. He said he wasn't less than his ancestors."

"Yes. He used to play a game of invading England. All his smaller friends had to be the English. Perhaps that make-believe went deeper than anyone ever thought. Perhaps that's why he went over to the Germans."

Otto, my charming, traitorous lover . . . I was filled with an overpowering dread as we emerged from the woods, and came into the full force of the wind, and a view of steel-gray sea beyond the dunes.

Erik told me to stay in the car, when he stopped it a little later.

I could see the lighthouse, and the ruined stones of the castle on the headland. On the seashore, straight ahead of us, were the strange tall stones of the Viking burial ground.

I didn't stay in the car. I stood outside it, the bitter wind in my face, and watched Erik running down the slope toward the graves. He turned to wave.

"Wait there. I won't be long."

He knew what he might find, and so did I. Through pain and sorrow, we both had begun to understand Otto.

This, after all, was why I had begged he should have his night of freedom.

I was in no doubt whatever about the outcome.

Erik disappeared from sight. The air was full of the wild shrieking of seabirds. They dipped over my head like huge flakes of snow. Their cries were a lament.

It seemed hours before Erik appeared again, walking slowly, his head bent. When he came near I saw that he was crying.

I put out my arms, and he came into them and we stood folded together, the wind beating about us.

"Dead?" I said at last.

"*Ja.*"

"How?"

"Revolver."

I shuddered. "Erik, he has got back a little of his lost honor. Can't we think that?"

"*Ja.*"

Presently he straightened himself and wiped his wet face.

"You are right, Luise. Now we must go." And then, "I am glad to have you with me."

Whatever things, both happy and grim, had been between

Otto and me, those few moments in the bitter wind on the seashore in each other's arms would always remain between Erik and me. We both knew that. There was no need to say it.

When I said, at the end of that long stormy day, that I would like to leave Maaneborg, everyone agreed that that was best.

"Will you go back to London?" Frue Dorothea asked. She had her Snow Queen look again, but only because of her private sorrow. Her voice was gentle and remote. Her expression only softened when she looked at Niels and Liselotte, who, I believe, had never stopped holding hands all day. They both looked very young and shocked and frightened, but soon enough Niels would hold up his head and take charge, as the new master of Maaneborg. Dinna had cried a great deal, and now when she heard I was going, her tears broke forth again.

"Oh, Luise! Everybody is leaving us. You, Papa, the baby you never had."

I stroked her tumbled hair. "Liselotte will have a baby instead." Liselotte blushed and smiled shyly, and I answered Frue Dorothea's question. "Yes, I'll go back to London."

"No," said Erik. "You will go to my house on Nyhavn, and wait there for me."

My silly heart leaped. What was this? Was I going to be impulsive and crazy all over again?

"I will telephone my housekeeper, and she will light fires and air sheets, and things like that. I will come in three or four days, at the most. You must only promise me one thing, that you won't wander into any tattoo shops, or strange cafés alone."

Bless him, he was trying to be lighthearted, when all the time the anxiety in his eyes was unbearable. He didn't even need to tell me what he was thinking, I understood him so well. Supposing, at some later time, the Winther disease struck him. After my experience with Otto, would I be able to stand that? Would I be able to love him? Would I be too unhappy if I never had a child?

"Is that what you would like to do, Luise?" Frue Dorothea was asking, in her courteous absentminded voice. "If it is, then you must do so. Though I would think you had suffered enough in this country to never want to see it again."

"But I love it!" I exclaimed. "I want to be here. I want—" Erik was grinning so broadly with pure delight that I forgot what I had been going to say.

I thought of the orange and pink and yellow houses along the quay, of the flight of bells from carillons, and the startled pigeons flying, of the first flakes of snow settling on the ancient rooftops, of the plane trees leafless, and the twisted cabbage-green spires of churches and city halls rising into the gray sky, like strange elongated leaves that had failed to shake down in the autumn gales.

I couldn't help it. That damned fairy tale was possessing me again.

And why shouldn't it? We might need it, Erik and I.